Titles by Dawn Banks

The Spreadsheet Situation

The Boyfriend Setup

THE BOYFRIEND SETUP

Dawn Banks

First published by

ELK AVENUE BOOKS

EST 2025

For Jennifer, the best Complete Asshole™ I know.

This book is also dedicated to Roy Kent's towel in season 1, episode 2 of *Ted Lasso.*

CHAPTER 1

Jaclyn

I'm not a plant person, but by the end of this evening, I expect I'll be able to identify at least ten houseplants by sight. Not because I'm at a greenhouse or anything, but because I've been staring slightly past my date at the plant wall behind him for what feels like ages, entertaining myself by reading the names off the cutesy mini chalkboards next to each bromeliad and succulent lining the space.

"So anyway, that's the short version of the differences between what the Vice President of Banking and the Vice President of Finances each do."

I blink. *That was the short version?*

I'm pretty sure this man has been droning on about the upper administration of the Sapling Grove Federal Savings

Bank for at least twenty minutes with barely a breath. I surreptitiously check the time on my watch.

Damn. It's only been three minutes.

I turn my attention back to the man sitting in front of me, trying to find something interesting in the litany of banking jargon. Unfortunately, Daniel Sutton seems to have no idea that my eyes glazed over when he started listing the various roles of the highest-paid employees at the bank.

The evening started off promising. Daniel was on time, which I know sounds like a low bar for a promising date, but you'd be surprised how many men can't manage this basic courtesy.

He suggested the restaurant, a relatively new bistro in an old office building that takes up most of a downtown block. I've been meaning to try it out, so I'm glad it's where we ended up tonight. It's a great place for a date, full of bright white marble counters, the lush green plant wall with the restaurant's name in neon lights (perfect for the occasional tourist's Instagram feed), and quirky mismatched dinnerware that I'm pretty sure the owners picked up at some of the local antique shops.

It's the kind of place I'd expect to find in a bigger city, not in downtown Sapling Grove where most of the restaurants haven't updated their decor since 1963. Not that I'm complaining about the familiarity of the downtown scene. There's something charming about the dated buildings and the meandering walking path by the river that cuts through the retail district. This place looks almost the same as it did when I was a kid. Except these days, too many store fronts in downtown have sat empty for years, so it's nice to see some attempt at growth. Especially in a town that took eighty-five years post-Prohibition to allow restaurants to sell alcohol.

Hell, even Daniel's presence in this town is a sign of growth. In the past few years, a slew of people my age have moved here. It's mostly white-collar professionals looking for more affordable mortgage prices than what they can get forty minutes away in Knoxville. In fact, the upper floors of this restaurant have been converted into high-end apartments specifically because of all the new doctors and lawyers who have moved to town. Better that than them snapping up all the local farmland and building subdivisions, I guess.

That thought gives me an idea for how I can make the best of Daniel's horrible attempt at conversation. He pauses long enough to take a sip of his drink, and I try to take control of the situation.

"Do you think the bank would have any interest in funding a project I'm involved in?"

The question seems to catch him off guard, like he wasn't expecting me to have anything to say. Weird, but whatever.

He recovers from the shock that I'd have anything to contribute and says, "We have a variety of loan options, depending on what type of collateral you'd be willing to put up."

"I was thinking something more like having the bank make a donation," I say. "I'm working with a group that's raising money for the new community center. The old one closed several years ago."

I remember how devastated I was when my mom told me they were tearing the building down. The community center was like a second home to me growing up, and I hated not being here when it closed. Not that I could have done much to stop it. I was away at college when the city decided to sell the property instead of increase taxes, and a local businessman bought it. Now there's a generic-looking strip mall in its place.

Most of the classes and services that the center used to offer shifted to the high school gym, but it's hard to schedule crafting classes and town hall meetings around high school sports events. Especially in a town as sports-obsessed as Sapling Grove.

When I moved back to the area to take a job at Cooke University, I started laying the groundwork for a community effort to bring the center back. I met with a couple of City Council members about the city's budget—to no avail. After that setback, I enlisted some of my mom's friends to help raise awareness about the project. It's taken a long time, but there's finally enough support among the people in town to move forward with finding a new location.

The only problem is the funding. We have enough raised for a down payment on a space, but we need steady cash flow to keep the center operational. Most of our donations have been from individuals, and it would be helpful to have a couple sponsors from the businesses in town. Since Daniel works at the bank, I'm hoping he might put in a good word with the administration on my behalf.

"I would have to run that by my higher-ups," he says. "That kind of request is above my pay grade."

"Of course, that makes sense—"

"Now as far as collateral, if you had something big you could put up, we could probably work with you on a loan."

I was going to tell him more about the project—give him some talking points for when he takes this to his superiors—but I guess we're moving on.

To my chagrin, the subject of collateral sets him off on another lengthy monologue about interest rates, and I let my gaze wander back to the plant wall as I check out from the conversation again, wondering whether I could keep a bromeliad alive in my office.

What's especially annoying is that I wasn't even sure I wanted to go on this date in the first place. I'm really only here because I'm trying to be a good daughter. For the past few months, my mother has taken on the quixotic task of trying to set me up with a variety of less-than-stellar men. I love my mother, but her sudden need for her eldest daughter to find a partner has been exasperating.

I certainly didn't grow up in a home that emphasized romantic relationships as a primary goal in life. Sure, until I was in high school, we were one of those textbook perfect families. Mom and Dad both worked but always seemed to have time to go to my debate club competitions and my sister Heather's art shows. We'd have family meals at home most nights. We'd cook elaborate breakfasts together on

Saturday mornings. We could have been the poster family for some parenting magazine.

Until suddenly we weren't such a perfect family.

After my miscreant of a father left, it was even more apparent that getting an education and finding meaningful work were the things that would bring us happiness. Mom threw herself into her work as a Realtor and hasn't dated anyone in the years since Dad blew up our lives.

But recently, Mom has gotten it in her head that I need to find love. I think it's because she's been spending more time lately with the Brandt Biddies (their name for themselves)—a trio of sisters Mom's age who are known around town for their devil-may-care attitude toward what people think of them. None of the Brandt Biddies is married, but they love playing matchmakers, and I think it's been rubbing off on Mom.

The problem is that Mom's idea of the kind of man I'm looking for is a bit...well. I know she's trying to be helpful, but her choices for potential partners for me don't always meet my criteria.

First was Derek, who spent most of our date talking about his extensive baseball card collection. That would have been fine—I love baseball—except that it seemed like he was trying to sell me the cards. I'm not actually sure if he knew we were on a date, to be honest, because he kept talking about how meeting my mom was such a great opportunity for him to network with other local business owners.

After that was Ben, my favorite of Mom's attempts. He

and I hit it off immediately, which surprised me after that first disastrous date Mom had set me up with. He was into the same TV shows as me, had read a book within the last month, and was generally kind and gentlemanly. Everything was great until we got back to his place and started making out. He was a good kisser, but somewhere between our lips first meeting and my bra coming unhooked, he started weeping. Not just crying, but full-on bawling. Once I got him calmed down, he explained he'd recently gone through a tough divorce and wasn't ready to sleep with anyone else yet. I'm not exactly the comforting type, but I let him have a good cry on my shoulder and told him to call me when he was ready. I haven't heard from him since. Pity, that one. He seemed like a catch.

Then there was Robert. On the night we were supposed to meet, I waited outside the restaurant for fifteen minutes. I was about to leave when a Tesla Cybertruck with an offensive vanity plate pulled up next to the sidewalk where I was waiting. As the window rolled down, a man in a red trucker cap leaned over the center console, introduced himself as Robert, and asked if I was Jaclyn Beckett. I gave him a fake name and said I'd never heard of any Jaclyns. Mom really lost her mind with that one.

So imagine my surprise when Daniel checked all my boxes. He's tall, at least six feet. Dark hair, chiseled jaw that's shaved clean. Piercing blue eyes. A smile that literally made me think I was hallucinating, because his resemblance to Henry Cavill is so uncanny that I thought he might *be* Henry Cavill for a second.

And his voice? So rich and deep as he said, "You must be Jaclyn," that my insides nearly melted with the heat that washed through me. When he reached out to shake my hand, it took a lot of effort not to imagine the way his grip would feel on my ass—his hands smooth and soft, his grasp firm but not too tight.

"Your mom didn't do you justice when she described you," he'd said.

Despite myself, my cheeks had colored at that. I never know how to respond to compliments, so I deflected and suggested we go into the restaurant.

Once we were seated, our server took our drink orders, and we exchanged pleasantries for a few minutes—chatting about the menu, discussing what we each planned to order. All the usual surface-level first date conversation starters.

Unfortunately, what seemed like a home run of an evening turned out to be a foul ball. The first sign of trouble came when I asked him how he met my mom.

"It's kind of a funny story," he'd said. "I was the loan officer for one of her real estate clients, and she told me she had a daughter about my age. Since I'm new to town, she gave me your number."

When he didn't continue, I leaned forward, indicating that I wanted him to go on, to get to the funny part, but he didn't say anything else. He looked back at me, as if waiting for me to laugh.

"Oh, that's the whole story?"

He nodded with sincerity. "Yes. Such a fun coincidence."

"So fun." Thankfully, I was able to keep most of the

sarcasm out of my voice.

"Helen told me you work at the university?" he'd asked after that.

"Yes, that's right. I teach sociology."

"That sounds interesting."

I smiled, pushing the "funny story" and its complete lack of anything other than statements of fact out of my mind for the moment.

"I love working with social dynamics and thinking about organizational structure. The relationships between humans can be so fascinating," I'd said.

His eyes lit up at that, and I thought he was going to ask me a question about the specifics of my work, but instead he said, "I love looking at organizational charts, too."

"Oh, that's not..." I didn't have time to finish my sentence because our server arrived with our drinks. When he left to give us a moment to finish looking over our menus, Daniel picked right back up with the organizational charts, and my unexpected interest in houseplants began.

He is still talking about loan rates when our server comes to take our order, and I'm grateful for the interruption.

My relief is short-lived because I don't have a chance to open my mouth before Daniel says, "She'll have the goat cheese and beet salad, and I'll have the steak, medium well. With a plain baked potato."

First of all, who orders for someone they just met? Not only that, but who eats a steak *medium well* with a plain baked potato? Gross.

Daniel is completely oblivious, though. He flashes me another of those heart-melting smiles, and I push aside the annoyance with a reminder that one little faux pas doesn't negate the very real possibility of a great night in bed with this man.

Because despite my hesitance to go out with the men my mother finds through god-knows-what-means, I like dating. It's just that I date with one very specific goal in mind, and it's not finding the love of my life.

And maybe this is where Mom's crusade against my singleness and my preferences really diverge. She seems to think it's time for me to settle down, but I mostly date when I need a good romp in the sheets. The second feelings get involved, I'm out.

My approach to dating has worked out well. No attachments means I can do as I please without feeling obligated to make weekend plans or go to brunch or whatever else it is that people in long-term committed relationships do.

Besides, the sex is usually adequate. I mean, I'm not really into snuggling after, which makes the fact that I keep matching with men whose only kink is cuddling a little awkward. But I don't have to see those men again, which is exactly how I like it.

Daniel is about to launch into what I can only assume is more excruciating detail about how things work at the bank, when our food comes. I immerse myself in savoring the earthiness of the golden beets and the tangy bite of the goat cheese in my salad. There's also the salty-sweet crunch of candied pecans that taste like a burst of brightness against the other strong flavors. The conversation may be dull as watching paint dry, but at least the food is excellent.

By the time I'm scraping up the last few bits of candied pecan, though, I can't take it anymore. Daniel has been waxing poetic on balance sheet nuances over our bougie entrées, but as good looking as he is, I am struggling to find anything beyond his chiseled features to excite me about this date.

I'm not even sure how I let Mom convince me to meet Daniel. You'd think I'd have learned my lesson by now. When your mother calls and says she's just met the most interesting man, you should say no to whatever else comes out of her mouth.

But I haven't learned my lesson at all, which is why I keep reminding myself that a night of meaningless sex with a man this gorgeous is worth the pain of the last hour. Unfortunately, my patience is wearing thin, and I'm afraid my streak of frustrating nights alone might not end tonight.

The biggest issue with dating in Sapling Grove, Tennessee, is that it's Sapling Grove, and there aren't that many potential partners worth my time. It's barely larger than a small town, and other than the university where I work, there aren't many places to meet the kinds of men I'm interested in dating.

Although I grew up in the area, I've never enjoyed the more rural forms of entertainment that most of my peers enjoy. I'm not a fan of football (a sacrilege!), Country music doesn't excite me, and I've never once gone hunting. It's not that I think I'm better than the people who enjoy those kinds of things. It's that they're not *my* kinds of things. Give me baseball, classic rock, and paperback thrillers any day. Bonus if I don't have be in the presence of anyone else while I enjoy them.

Even the university where I work doesn't offer much choice of partners. My friend Evie is engaged to the only person at Cooke I've ever remotely considered dating (long before Evie came around), but Andrew has always been more brotherly than boyfriendly where I'm concerned.

The rest of the men at Cooke are either married or otherwise unavailable—whether they're actually unavailable or if my standards are too high is a source of much debate among me and my friends. Plus, I still have to work with these people if things don't work out between us. I'll stick to keeping my dating life out of my workplace, thank you very much.

The dearth of availability—and the fact I haven't had even *inadequate* sex in months—is the real reason I agreed to meet Daniel this evening. But it's clear I should have listened to my gut on this one.

With a sigh, I turn my attention back to trying to follow Daniel's monologue, but he's deep in the weeds of actuarial analysis. My obvious boredom doesn't seem to phase him, and after a minute, I focus on what remains of my salad—a few stray pieces of lettuce that are too small to spear with my fork.

Realizing I've spent most of the last minute trying to stab a leaf that's actually part of the plate decoration, I finally admit defeat and set my fork aside. I have no idea how to save this conversation, but I desperately want to because even though Daniel looks like he would be amazing in bed, it always goes much better if my partner and I have at least a little chemistry.

I glance at my watch again and suppress another sigh.

Sweet Jesus, this is taking forever.

I'm about to excuse myself for the restroom—not that I actually need it, I just need a break from hearing about the differences between investment banking and retail banking—when our server reappears.

"Interested in dessert?" he asks, and I try to subtly shake my head.

I open my mouth to say, "No," as Daniel replies, "Sure! Could we get a slice of the chocolate cake?"

I smile tightly, and the server walks away.

"I think you'll really like the cake here," Daniel says, completely oblivious to the danger of me walking out of this restaurant. "It's incredibly moist."

The word reverberates through me, and I imagine him saying it in slow motion, his lips parting on a long "oi" sound then coming together with a vulgar-sounding wet smack.

"Moiiiiiiist."

A grossed-out shudder slides through me. "And that's strike three."

I push my chair away from the table and toss my napkin onto my plate.

Daniel looks confused. "What do you mean 'strike

three'?"

I take a fortifying breath. "Look, Daniel. You look like you would be incredible in bed, but this evening hasn't gone well. First of all, you ordered for me. Twice. Secondly, you completely shut me down when I tried to ask you a question about a project that means a lot to me. And to top it all off, I cannot abide a man who uses the m-word to describe cake."

He opens and closes his mouth a few times. "I...thought we were hitting it off?"

I rub a hand down my face. "No, not really."

He gapes at me as I collect my purse. Then he sputters, "But I thought we could go upstairs to my apartment and... enjoy the cake together."

I cock my head to the side. "You live in this building?"

Daniel straightens and says, "Yes" in a clipped tone.

"Of course you do," I mutter under my breath. If he lives in one of those pricey apartments, I doubt he would have gone for helping with the community center project. The one demographic we've had push back from is the residents of those apartments. Awkward conversation dodged, I suppose.

I sigh. "Daniel, It was very nice to meet you. The salad was delicious, but the conversation was not. No sex is worth what I just experienced."

I walk away. I don't even look back to see if Daniel is protesting my leaving.

As I step onto the sidewalk outside the restaurant, I pull out my phone and send a message to the person I should have spent my evening with in the first place.

ME: Another one bites the dust.

RHYS BLACKWELL: It must be bad if you're quoting Queen.

ME: I think I need to scrub the last hour from my brain.

RHYS: Meet at your place in 20?

ME: You got it.

RHYS: I'll bring beer.

CHAPTER 2

Rhys

One of these days, I'll stop torturing myself by dropping everything whenever Jaclyn texts me after a bad date. But today is not that day.

I don't know when it started, exactly, but in the four years that we've been friends, I've been her first call any time she's gone out with another Tom, Dick, or dickhead and the date has gone south. Not that debriefing bad dates is the only time we see each other, but I imagine that if she ever got serious with any of the clowns she usually goes out with, our friendship would be over. Because who wants a broody Englishman hanging out with his girlfriend all the time?

At least tonight I don't have to worry about being kicked out of Jaclyn's life, because from the tone of her texts, tonight's date was no better than any of the ones she's been on lately. Luckily—or unluckily—Jaclyn rarely likes the men she goes out with, and I have ample opportunity to spend time with my best friend.

The windows of her condominium are dark when I arrive, so I park but stay in the car, waiting to enter her home until she's here. A few minutes later, her car appears, and she parks in the garage. Only after the garage door closes do I get out and make my way to the front door. I knock lightly on the door as I unlock it.

"You should have let yourself in and waited inside," is all the greeting I get from her.

"You know I don't like to do that." It's an argument we've had before.

"But that's why I gave you a key. So you wouldn't have to wait for me."

"It's not right for me to sit in your living room like a prowler."

She laughs, and it is the most beautiful sound. Like a mellow wind chime playing in the breeze.

"You're not a prowler if I've given you permission to be here." She playfully rolls her eyes. "Besides, don't you think it's more prowler-like to sit in the driveway and wait for me to get here?"

She doesn't wait for an answer, just gestures for me to follow her. "Let's go to the porch."

We each grab a beer from the pack I've brought—a dark ale from a local brewery—and make our way too the back porch. She takes the porch swing, leaning against the armrest with her feet planted on the seat. I sit across from her on the wicker chair and stretch my long legs out in front of me. We've sat like this so many times, it's become our usual setup for chats on the porch.

"Rhys, it was awful," Jaclyn says, skipping any pretense of small talk and charging straight to the heavy stuff. "He had the audacity to order for me not once but twice! Twice!"

I don't say anything, just shake my head and take a sip of my beer.

"And then he called the cake 'moist!'" She shivers, like saying the word makes her skin crawl.

"What an arse." I chuckle.

"I knew you'd understand," she says, smiling. "He was hot, too."

She frowns at that, shaking her head like she's truly disappointed. I am instantly jealous of the banker her mum set her up with, even though I shouldn't be. I don't have any claim to Jaclyn's heart, no matter if I wish I did.

Jaclyn has no idea how excruciating it is for me to hear about the men she dates because she has no idea that I've been in love with her since the day we met. I didn't mean to fall in love with her. I'm not really someone who believes in love at first sight. But from the moment our mutual friend Aiden Carter conspired to throw us together at a volunteer event, I have craved Jaclyn's attention like a drowning man craves oxygen.

It was supposed to be a casual day of helping Aiden with the intake paperwork for some pro bono work he was doing, setting up wills and Powers of Attorney for economically disadvantaged people in the area at a big outdoor event in the Sapling Grove High School parking lot. Not a life-changing experience for me—at least not romantically.

But I hadn't expected Jaclyn Beckett.

Or rather, I hadn't expected Aiden to be right about her. He begged me for weeks to help out with the event, not only because the previous year had been so busy that he and his friend who usually helped could barely keep up with the number of clients. It was also because he wanted to introduce me to his friend. To Jaclyn.

From the first moment he mentioned her, it was clear he thought this was some kind of matchmaking scheme. He wasn't good at hiding it, either. Always dropping hints that she was single. Once he even threatened to give her my number after I complained that there didn't seem to be any women our age actually living in Sapling Grove.

"They're here," he'd said. "You just aren't looking in the right places."

"You know I'm not looking for a relationship right now," I told him. It was stressful enough trying to establish permanent residence in the States without the pressure of trying to date.

Eventually, Aiden wore me down—about the volunteering, not the dating.

The day of the event, I met Aiden early to help set up the tent, but five minutes into unloading everything, he realized he'd left a file box at the office. He left me in charge, and I busied myself with organizing the forms and weighing everything down with the quirky paperweights Aiden had brought for that purpose. One of them was a bobblehead of a wasp dressed in a baseball uniform. The base holding the wasp had a small plaque that said, "2005 Blue Ridge Minor League Baseball Champions."

I was making progress setting everything up until I heard a throat clear behind me. I turned and nearly dropped a box of forms all over the asphalt. Standing in the gap between Aiden's tent and the food truck that was setting up across the parking lot was the most beautiful woman I'd ever laid eyes on.

She had hair the color of dark coffee—not quite brown and not quite black—that cascaded in perfect waves around her face and stopped right above her shoulders. I wasn't close enough to discern the color of her eyes, but I wanted to get that close.

She stood with her arms crossed, giving me a skeptical look.

"Can I help you?" I asked.

"You're in my tent." She shifted her feet into a more powerful stance, making herself a little taller.

I know I was new to volunteering at this event, but I had no doubt that Aiden knew exactly which tent was his.

"I don't think so," I said, shifting the box in my hands and moving it under the table.

"Just because you don't think this is my tent doesn't mean it's yours." The indignation in her voice grated on me, making me doubt my initial reaction to the sight of her. "In fact, I'm certain you wouldn't know if it is or isn't my tent because I've never seen you before."

The nerve of this woman.

"I know whose tent this is." I narrowed my eyes at her and almost told her to piss off.

And then she quirked her eyebrow at me, and I got the sense that she was enjoying the exchange. That she was playing with me a little. Something about the way she held herself, in a stance of confidence and perceptiveness, sent a frisson of awareness through me. Like I'd met not only my equal but my match.

"Well, then. Whose tent do you think it is?" Her lips slid into a smug grin.

Instead of answering, I asked, "Who did you say you were?"

"I didn't. And I could ask you the same question." There was a liveliness to the way she was talking now.

"Rhys Blackwell. I'm a friend of Aiden's," I said, reaching out my hand.

"That makes two of us. Jaclyn Beckett." She shook my hand, and I tried to ignore the zing of heat at the contact.

I couldn't stop myself from smiling, though. Aiden was right about one thing. Jaclyn was exactly the kind of woman I'd be interested in. "I've heard about you."

She narrowed her eyes at me. "What have you heard?"

I was saved from answering by Aiden's voice from across the car park.

"Oh good! You've met!"

We turned in tandem to see Aiden approaching with a coffee tray and a box of donuts. It wasn't lost on me that there was no missing file box. Almost like he'd planned to have us meet without him present.

I hate to give Aiden credit, but without his sneaky introduction, Jaclyn and I might never have met and become friends. We spent the entire day together, getting to know each other, making jokes, and feeding that initial pang of attraction that I hoped she felt as much as I did.

At the end of the day, I was going to ask for her number—my rule about not dating during my Green Card process be damned—but her date for the evening showed up. Jaclyn has gone out with so many men since then that I don't even remember what the man that night looked like.

After that, we met a few more times at other social events that Aiden organized, and eventually we started hanging out just the two of us. I never acted on that initial impulse to ask her out as more than a friend, not after witnessing Jaclyn's dating habits. I didn't want to be just another guy she went out with once.

"I was really looking forward to some decent sex tonight, and then he had to ruin it," she says, jolting my thoughts back to the present. She sighs, and I tamp down the urge to tell her I'd take her to bed right now if she'd let me.

Over the past four years, I've mostly done a good job of pretending I'm satisfied with only being friends with Jaclyn, but lately, the lie is starting to wear thin. Initially, it was easy to tell myself that I never made a move because dating would only complicate things with my immigration status.

Now, though? I'm almost at the end of the process, and I

can't keep using that as an excuse. The only problem is, Jaclyn has never given any indication that she sees me as anything more than a friend.

She takes a long drink of her beer, sighing again as the bottle leaves her lips.

"What were you up to this evening before I crashed your plans?"

"Just some cleaning." It's not a complete lie. I was cleaning. But I was also making a dating profile, something I haven't done since moving to Sapling Grove five years ago. Making one didn't seem wise in the first year I lived here. I was still new to town and dealing with the paperwork of setting up permanent residence in the States. And then I met Jaclyn. It never felt right to try dating someone else when I was burning a candle for her.

"Glad I could spice up your evening," she says with a smirk.

I respond with half a laugh but don't say anything inane like "That's not the only way you could spice up my evening," even though I think it. Because why not have intrusive thoughts while your best friend who you wish would kiss you tells you about her latest dating disaster?

But honestly? I'm tired of holding out hope that one of these days Jaclyn is going to realize that something good might happen if we let ourselves be more than we currently are. The lie I've been telling myself—and her—is that I am still too new to this town to want a relationship with anyone. But five years in a town is on the edge of not being new anymore.

"Actually, I was working on my dating profile." I look away from her and mumble it so low, I'm not sure she hears me, because she doesn't respond at first. But when I dare to look at her again, she's staring at me with a gleeful expression.

"Rhys! That's so great for you! I'm proud of you, friend."

She tips her drink toward me in a "cheers" gesture, and I can't help but clink my beer bottle against hers.

My mind keeps snagging on the word she used. "Friend."

It's a good reminder that no matter what those deep down feelings of mine say, friendship is all I can hope for with Jaclyn. All the more reason to make sure my dating profile is in top shape so I can get over her.

"Let's see it. I want to make sure you sound like the amazing person you are and not like a weird creep."

I pull out my phone and open the app. When I reach to hand her my phone, she shakes her head and points to the spot next to her on the swing.

"No, this is a group activity. Get your butt over here."

I grumble a little—mostly to mask the thrill that stutters through me at the thought of being close to her. I'm careful not to touch her as I sit down, but she scoots closer to me anyway. Our hands brush as I give her the phone, and I ignore the zing of pleasure at the contact.

"Alright, let's see what you've got, Blackwell."

She scrolls through the profile like it's an intriguing dataset from a research study, her eyebrows scrunched like she's deep in thought. When she suddenly pauses and looks at me with a wicked grin, my heart rate kicks up.

"What?"

"Your profile needs some help."

"It's not that bad."

She laughs. "Not that bad? Rhys, you sweet summer child."

I cross my arms across my chest. "You said it should show that I'm a good person. That's literally what I wrote."

"Exactly the problem. You think women are going to take your word for it that you're a good person?"

"No," I concede.

"Precisely why we need to show them that you're a kind-hearted man with a serious sweet tooth."

"Why does that feel like code for something sexual?"

Jaclyn barks a laugh. "No, dummy. Because you've never met a dessert you didn't love."

"Whatever." I roll my eyes. So what if I like a wee bit of dessert at the end of a good meal?

"What do you want in a partner?"

"You..." I catch myself. "I mean, why do you need to know?"

"Because you can't just say stuff about yourself. You have to show what you're looking for from them, too."

She laughs again, then types something on my phone. I try to look over her shoulder to see what it says, but she turns the screen away from me. The number of times she deletes and retypes is beginning to make me sweat, when she suddenly straightens and hands me the phone.

"What do you think of this?" She hooks her index finger over her lips and rests her chin on her thumb, like she's nervous about what I'll say.

"British expatriate living in rural Tennessee. I'm a physical therapist who enjoys quiet evenings at home with a good book, preferably nonfiction. Favorite authors include Brené Brown, John Green, and Maya Angelou. My ideal partner is smart, funny, and doesn't mind a man who always wants the last bite of dessert."

I nudge her with my elbow. "Are you sure that's not a euphemism?"

The look she gives me is equal parts evil and sexy, and I push away the urge to kiss the smirk right off her face.

The truth is, what she's written is a thousand times better than what I had, but it also reignites that ache I get when I think of how things might have been different if I'd had the courage to ask Jaclyn out when we first met. Because the woman she's described as my ideal woman? It's so much like her that I want to throw the phone across the porch and declare my undying love to her. In fact, I'm about to do it, to forget the dating profile entirely and tell her, when she interrupts my thoughts.

"I'm glad to see you getting out there." Her smile is warm.

I give her a half-hearted smile in return and take another sip of my beer to hide my disappointment at her sentiment. She must sense that I don't want any more discussion of my dating life—or lack thereof—because she doesn't say anything else for a long time.

After a while of us gently swaying on the porch swing and listening to the sounds of cicadas screaming in the trees at the back of Jaclyn's property, she turns to me and says, "Can I tell you about another weird thing from today?"

I nod and tip my beer in a "go on" gesture.

"Ron came to my office today to tell me about a new project he's recommended me for."

I raise an eyebrow. Jaclyn's relationship with her boss is one filled with frustrations and resentment. Mostly on her side of things.

"You'll never guess what the project was."

I rub my beard as I think. "Head of curriculum development."

She snorts. "Think weirder."

"Chief of the Grass-Height Inspection Committee?" I ask with a quirk of my lips.

The university went through a period a couple years ago where the president was obsessed with making sure all the grass on campus was exactly two inches high at all times. Their facilities employees were run ragged trying to mow everything to keep up with his specifications.

"Not that weird, although somehow I would have been less surprised if that was it. He asked me to join the yearbook committee."

"That seems...strange."

"I know, right? It was so out of left field that I didn't know how to react. I didn't know we still had a yearbook, and I have no idea why Ron thinks I would be a good fit for a committee related to it."

I narrow my eyes at her. "Did you tell him no?"

Jaclyn doesn't say anything, which is all the answer I

need. The stern look I give her makes her squirm. Ron Owens is the dean of Social Sciences, and Jaclyn is his associate dean, which as far as I can tell means she ends up doing all the shit he thinks he's too good for.

I let it drop, though, because we've had this conversation before. She's convinced that if she stands up to him, he won't recommend her for promotion when he retires. But from my perspective, it shouldn't matter if he recommends her. It's not his decision who takes his place when he's gone. Bringing up that old argument now will only result in us both in sour moods.

"I know the Ron situation is complicated," I say as I stand, ready to head home for the night. Our beers are empty, and I don't want to overstay my welcome. "I wish there was something I could do to help."

"Thanks. I appreciate it."

She stands, too, and when she takes a step toward me, for one wild moment, I think she's going to wrap her arms around me and kiss me goodnight. But instead she reaches past me to adjust the cushion on the porch swing, which must have gone askew when I stood.

I clear my throat, suddenly anxious to get out of here. "Have a good night. Talk soon."

"You, too!"

I jog down the porch steps and go around the outside of her condo back to my car. When I arrive at home, I log in to the dating app again and hit "publish" on the profile.

CHAPTER 3

Jaclyn

"I don't understand what went wrong. Daniel seemed like exactly the kind of man you'd be interested in. Are you sure you didn't say something to put him off?"

I cringe as my mother's voice blares through the speaker on my phone. I've been dreading this conversation since I left Daniel sitting at the table with the infamous piece of cake. But when she called and asked how the date went, I couldn't lie to her.

It's something I've never been good at—lying to Mom. Even as a teenager, I rarely got away with anything because she'd ask me if I was telling the truth, and I would be physically unable to say yes. My face would get splotchy, and my ability to make eye contact would evaporate, and before I knew it, my car keys would disappear into the squeaky drawer in the hallway console table for a week. She always put them in that drawer, knowing that it was impossible to open it without waking the dead with the whiny scraping sound it made, no matter how gently you tried to ease the drawer out.

I may hate lying to her, but it doesn't mean I enjoy getting the third degree about my dating life. In my adult life, I've curated an image of being aloof and a bit of an iconoclast, but deep down, I'm still a rule-follower.

I pinch the bridge of my nose, then run my index finger and thumb across my eyebrows in an attempt to release the tension headache that's building.

"No, Mom. I am certain that I *did* say something to put him off, but not before he was an asshole to me."

"Language, Jaclyn!" she chides.

I stop myself from letting out a frustrated groan. It's amazing how quickly conversations with my mother have me devolving into the same patterns of combativeness from my teenage years.

"Well, I'm sorry it didn't work out, dear. I really thought you'd hit it off. No matter, though. You'll never guess who I ran into at the grocery store."

It could literally be anyone. Sapling Grove only has one grocery store, and unless you're willing to drive forty minutes there and back to Knoxville, everyone shops at Gary's Food Mart.

"I have no idea. Who did you run into?" I ask, trying to keep the sarcasm out of my voice.

"Landon Cunningham! You remember Landon, right?"

How could I forget him? We only dated for two years in high school.

"Mom. No."

"You don't remember him?"

"That's not what I mean, and you know it."

"I'm just saying. Landon was always the nicest boy. He's just moved back to the area. Has some fancy new job at Montgomery Therapy."

"Good for him."

"Anyway, we got to chatting, and guess what? He's coming to Andy's wedding!"

"Shi…I mean, great. I'm sure I'll catch up with him then." I'm grateful we're on a regular call so Mom can't see the face I'm making. Running into my ex at the wedding of two of my best friends doesn't sound like a fun time to me.

"Yes, of course. And who knows? Maybe that old flame will spark something more permanent this time."

"Mom, we've talked about this. I'm perfectly fine not to be in a long-term relationship."

"Yes, yes. I know that's what you say. But I want you to be better than 'perfectly fine.' I want you to be happy."

I almost laugh, but I know that would hurt her feelings. Romantic happiness isn't in the cards for me. Falling in love is one of those emotions that people have because of sappy made-for-tv movies and unrealistic romance novels. It's not the sort of thing that Complete Asshole™ like me has any interest in ever doing.

"Mom, I have to go. I'll talk to you later."

"Ok, honey. Talk soon."

As I hang up the phone, I shake my head at my mother's attempts at coupling me off. I know she means well. But marriage and kids have never been something I've been interested in, and she knows that. I never bought into the "one true love" bullshit that a lot of the girls I grew up with did. But I remind myself that my going on the dates she sets up is making Mom happy. Even if I'm not going to find my soul mate or whatever.

I let out a long breath as I approach the bar where I'm meeting my friends. It's across the street from the park downtown, in a block with an ice cream shop and a pizza place. It's one of the few areas of downtown with any activity tonight. Most of the other shops on this end of downtown are either businesses that close early during the week or empty, forlorn spaces.

The bar is anything but forlorn. It's a cool evening, so the windows aren't open onto the sidewalk patio, but a few people sit in the wrought iron chairs anyway. The inside is filled with thrifted mismatched furniture and a boardgame shelf near the entrance, giving the space a cozy, welcoming atmosphere.

Over the past year, my friends and I have met up here nearly once a week. Last summer, they hosted a movie series in the park that we took full advantage of. It's also become our go-to meeting place for important conversations. Like last year when Evie and Andrew nearly broke up because he thought she was moving six hours away.

I spot my friends sitting at our usual table and wind my way through the crowd to join them. After a quick greeting and placing our orders, Kylie turns to me and asks, "Well? How did it go?"

"About as well as you'd expect if you were going to date a wet blanket."

"That bad?"

I fill them in on the worst parts of the date. Evie and Kylie listen attentively, gasping and furrowing their brows at all the right places as I lay out my tale of another woefully bad date. The look of horror on both their faces when I describe the cake fiasco is how I know we were meant to be friends.

It's relatively new, this friendship dynamic with Evie and Kylie. I've always been more of a friendship floater. A lone wolf, if you will. But about two years ago, Kylie talked me into going out with her and Evie one evening after work, and the three of us hit it off. Evie had been going through a rough patch with her anxiety disorder, and Kylie was trying to help her feel more adjusted to life away from her gigantic family. Little did I know that once you win Evie's love, she basically sticks to you like glue for the rest of your life. But in an endearing way.

"Why does your mom keep setting you up with these guys when it's clear she has no idea what you're looking for from a relationship?" Evie asks when I finish telling them about my dramatic exit.

"I wish I knew. With as many dates as she's set me up on, I'm starting to feel like I'm on the most boring reality dating show ever created. But let's talk about something else." My friends look like they want to push the issue, but I shoot them both a look that says that's the end of the discussion for the night. "I want to hear about the wedding plans."

It's a calculated statement to get Evie to take over the conversation, and it works. She launches into a litany of details about her upcoming nuptials, and I lean back and let her excitement fill the space. She and Andrew are perfect for each other, and after a year and a half of dealing with a particularly evil English professor, plus the big flood in the library last summer, the woman deserves to float on the clouds a little.

"Have you decided who the ring bearer will be?" Kylie asks when Evie pauses long enough to take a sip of her drink.

"We came up with a perfect solution! We're going to have both a ring bearer and a flower girl! That way both Kimberly and Darlene will have a grandkid involved in the ceremony, and my dad will be able to keep the peace between his sisters."

"Good solution," Kylie says.

"Oh, I have to show you the outfits we picked out for them!"

Evie pulls out her phone and scrolls to a picture of a little boy in a tuxedo and a little girl in a frilly blue dress. It's not my style, but even I have to admit they're cute.

All this talk about the wedding has my mind wandering back to the conversation I had with my mom. I'm not surprised Landon will be there. He and Andrew both ran cross country when we were in high school, and with the way Evie has been inviting everyone under the sun to this wedding, I've no doubt anyone she and Andrew have ever interacted with is on the guest list.

But the Landon thing won't leave my mind alone, and I have a thought that is either brilliant or terrible.

"Is it too late to add Rhys as my plus one?" I ask abruptly, cutting off whatever Evie was saying.

I've never seen someone's mood shift so quickly as Evie's does. She's gone from looking like she's just seen the most adorable kittens in the world to an expression that could cause a horse to keel over out of fear.

"Oh no. No, no, no, no, no. That won't work. I've already set the seating chart, and you said you weren't going to bring anyone."

Evie invited the entire Cooke faculty and staff to the wedding, and based on what I saw on her kitchen table the last time I was at her house, most of them have rsvp'd "yes." Not only that, this wedding was already practically a high school reunion for Andrew and me. Add in the fact that everyone we work with will be there, too, and the only people I won't know at this shindig is Evie's gaggle of cousins.

"Just bump one of your cousins to a different table."

The look of horror on Evie's face is almost comical.

"I can't *bump* one of my cousins! If I'm going to move one of them, it has to be for a good reason and they have to go to an appropriate table. It's not like I can move Robbie to

Cindy's table. Can you *imagine* the outrage?"

Kylie and I stare at her, completely in the dark about whatever Watson family drama Evie is worrying about.

"I have to call my mother!" Evie announces suddenly and stands up. I watch out the window as she goes to the patio and brings her phone to her ear. There are still a few people on the patio, and Evie keeps to the end away from where they are enjoying their evening libations. Through the glass I see her gesticulate wildly as she explains the situation to her mom.

"Why the sudden need to bring Rhys to the wedding?" Kylie's voice draws my attention back to our table. She fixes me with a mother-hen stare, and I almost roll my eyes.

Kylie is the oldest of the three of us, and I swear she thinks that means she's in charge of the group. She has a tendency toward bossiness that has always grated on me a little. If I had a choice, I'd rather hang out with Evie, but Evie always brings Kylie with her. Which is fine. She and Kylie make all the plans, and I'm just along for the ride.

"No reason," I say, taking a sip of my drink.

"That was believable," Kylie says sarcastically.

"Fine. If you must know, my mom's whole 'when are you going to meet someone and get married' thing is getting under my skin. She outright told me she wants to set me up with my high school ex, which is a no-go. And even if she's unsuccessful with that, I'm worried she'll set her sights on one of Evie's cousins."

"But if you're there with a friend, you think she would back off?"

"I mean, she knows Rhys and I aren't romantically involved, so I wouldn't put it past her to try anyway. But at least it would look like I'm there with a date, which should keep any potential setups from agreeing to her schemes."

Kylie nods. "Makes sense."

Evie reappears, looking slightly flustered but calmer than she was when she got up from the table.

"Mom and I figured out how to make the table arrangements work so that you and Rhys have a place together. We'll have to do some creative ushering to keep Robbie and Cindy away from each other, but my brother Simon is good at that. What did I miss?"

"Jaclyn doesn't want to date one of your cousins," Kylie says with a smirk.

Evie's puzzled expression makes me laugh, and it clears away most of the uneasy feeling I've had since my phone call with Mom. We bring Evie up to speed, and by the end of the night, that knot of frustration with my mom has dissipated.

Once I'm home, I pull out my phone and send Rhys a text.

ME: I need a favor.

I am weirdly nervous to ask Rhys to go to this wedding with me. I blame it on the fact that I should have asked him weeks ago when I got the invitation. I didn't want him to feel obligated to go to a wedding with me. Something about the idea of being there together felt too much like what a couple would do, and we aren't even close to being a couple. And since the wedding is less than a month away, asking him now seems like an afterthought.

I shouldn't be nervous, of course. Rhys is one of the most laid back people I know. Not in a surfer dude kind of way, but more like he's game to do whatever I ask of him. It's one of the things that made our friendship solidify so quickly after we met. I remind myself of that fact, and my jitters over the wedding invitation subside a little.

RHYS: Sure, what's up?

ME: I need you to be my date to Evie and Andrew's wedding.

It takes a long time for him to respond. After several minutes, there aren't even three dots showing he's typing. It doesn't help my nervousness about asking him, but I toss my phone on the bed in attempt to convince myself of my impartiality toward his response.

In the middle of brushing my teeth, a notification finally chimes.

RHYS: Yeah, I can do that.

ME: Took you long enough to agree. I hope this experience won't be too unpleasant.

I send a winking emoji and am surprised at how quickly his response comes through.

RHYS: Not unpleasant at all.

CHAPTER 4

Rhys

I wouldn't call myself someone who overanalyzes things, but I spend the next few days doing exactly that. *I need you to be my date to Evie and Andrew's wedding.*

I read the text conversation over and over, my heart skipping every time I see the word "date." I know Jaclyn doesn't mean that this is a *date* date, but the word trips me up every time I look at my message thread with her.

I hope this experience won't be too unpleasant.

If she only knew. Any unpleasantness will have nothing to do with suffering through the wedding and everything to do with the fact that we're going as friends and nothing else.

I shake my head at myself, trying—and failing—to clear the thought from my mind. Instead, I attempt to focus on reading through my notes from the last time Mr. Anderson was in.

"Good mornin', son," Mr. Anderson says as I walk into the reception area. He's a retired contractor with a full head of gray hair and laugh lines around his deep brown eyes. He's honestly one of my favorite patients.

"Mr. Anderson." I nod once. "How's the knee?"

"I can almost bend it again, see?" He puts his weight on his cane and lifts his foot barely above the ground. The motion he makes only vaguely resembles a bend, but it's an improvement.

"Looking good. Let's see if we can get it go a little further today, shall we?"

"Indeedy. Gotta get back into good enough shape to clean my gutters this fall."

I give the older man a stern look. "No. No ladders."

"Always spoiling my fun, Dr. Blackwell." He says it with a good-hearted laugh, and I realize he's "yankin' my chain" as he likes to say.

"That's what I'm here for," I say curtly, which only makes him laugh harder. I hold the door for him as we enter the therapy gym.

We spend the next twenty minutes going through various stretches designed to help Mr. Anderson's knee return to full functionality.

I like the work of being a physical therapist. Each patient's care requires a specificity tailored to their needs that makes the job interesting and challenging. Even in a place as small as Sapling Grove, there's a variety to the work that suits me. I wasn't sure that would be the case when I took the job. In fact, if it weren't for Aiden, I never would have considered starting my career in such a small town.

Aiden and I met at university in Knoxville. We were both there on athletic scholarships for football—I refuse to call the sport of my childhood soccer—and we hit it off at first year orientation. Since traveling back and forth to London was too expensive during the semester, Aiden invited me to Sapling Grove for the shorter school holidays. I fell in love with the place on those trips. It was like being in one of my Nan's cozy mystery novels—a small town where everyone knows everyone else and you feel like you're part of the community even when you're a visitor—but without the murder. There was a friendly, slow pace to life in this town, and after my upbringing in London, it was nice to be in a place that didn't feel so hurried.

After university, I stayed in the States while I was getting my physical therapy degree. Aiden and I lost touch while we were both in graduate school, but I couldn't get the little town in the mountains of Tennessee out of my head. When I reconnected with Aiden at a sports camp our university team was running one summer, I told him how much I missed his hometown, and he told me about the job at Montgomery Therapy. With his newly minted license to practice law, he put me in touch with Larry Montgomery and helped arrange things for the clinic to sponsor me in the Green Card process.

The work also requires intense concentration, which means dwelling on the upcoming not-date with Jaclyn isn't possible. That is, until Mr. Anderson asks me a question that I wasn't expecting while we're doing terminal knee extensions.

"So I hear you're taking Jackie Beckett to Andy Brandt's wedding?"

I nearly drop Mr. Anderson on the floor at the shock of the question. Also, I've never heard anyone call her Jackie before. I bet she hates it.

"Is there no privacy in this town?" I mutter.

Mr. Anderson belly laughs. "Can't say there is, son. Especially not when the Brandt Biddies are involved."

I don't know what to say to that, but it doesn't seem to matter. Mr. Anderson keeps on talking.

"I remember when she was just yea high." He holds his hand flat about two feet above the ground. "She and Heather were like little sprites, always gettin' into trouble around town. I still can't believe their daddy up and..."

He stops abruptly, like he's said something he shouldn't. I don't know much about Jaclyn's dad. Only that something happened years ago, and he disappeared from Jaclyn's life. Jaclyn doesn't talk about it much.

Heather, on the other hand, is often a topic of discussion. Mostly because Jaclyn wishes she would move back to Sapling Grove. She flits in and out of town like a whirlwind every six months or so, usually because she's found some new job or adventure and needs a place to land in between things. She reminds me of my brother Rupert, before he met his husband, Colin. Always on the go, never putting down roots. Jaclyn wouldn't admit it, but I think she misses her sister in the same way I often miss Rupert.

"She's a catch, our Jackie. You're a lucky fella." Mr. Anderson's voice is wistful, like it's *his* daughter we're discussing. I guess in a way, Jaclyn is the town's daughter. She seems to be woven into this town in a way that feels foreign to me. Everywhere we go, people know who she is and who her mum is. Almost like she's Sapling Grove royalty. It's funny, because she's not the kind of person who likes all the attention to be on her.

Growing up in London it was easier to be anonymous. I doubt there's anyone back there who would talk about me in the same affectionate way Mr. Anderson is talking about Jaclyn.

I don't correct his assumption about our relationship status. It's not that I want the rumor to get around that we're more than we are, but explaining myself to a patient isn't really my style. Honestly, this conversation has been more revealing about my personal life than I usually care to be, and I haven't even been the one doing the talking.

"Lordy mercy. You really ran me through the ringer today, Dr. Blackwell." Mr. Anderson wipes a bead of sweat from his brow with a cloth handkerchief he's pulled from his back trouser pocket.

I walk Mr. Anderson out to the lobby and hand his paperwork to the receptionist. He and Mr. Anderson chat briefly and set his next appointment, while I make my way back to the therapists' shared office to write my notes before my next patient arrives. I say "office" but it's really more like a narrow closet that's been converted to a workspace.

I stop short at the door because someone else is already in the tiny room. Sophie Hyder has her laptop and a stack of what looks like children's drawings spread all over the desk. There are two desk chairs, but with Sophie's things, there's no room for me to sit down. I knock lightly on the door frame, and she looks up, startled.

"Oh, sorry! I didn't mean to take over the whole thing!" She shuffles some papers and moves something that looks like a television antennae attached to a spatula handle to make space for me. Sophie is an Occupational Therapist, which basically means she helps people function in their daily lives. She sometimes jokes that she has a Masters degree in how to tie shoes because she's taught so many kids how to tie them.

I squeeze past Sophie to the second chair, careful not to bump into her as I slide through the tight gap between the wall and the back of her chair. As I sit, she turns and smiles at me.

"Sorry again. I'm not used to having so much room to spread out."

I laugh because I know she's only half joking. Sophie mainly works in the local schools, and she's always talking about how she usually has to work with kids in hallways and classroom corners because most of the schools don't have enough space for a dedicated therapy room. Today must be one of her clinic days, where she works with kids who need OT for things unrelated to functioning in school.

"It's fine. I wish they'd knock this out and build us two proper offices, though." I gesture toward the wall behind us. On the other side of the wall is a private patient room that is twice as big as it needs to be.

"Yeah, but then we wouldn't get to have our fun chats about how tight things are in here."

"That's true." I don't know whether to take her statement as innuendo. There's a playful sparkle in her eye that could be because she's a pediatric OT or could be because she's flirting. With the way my heart has been bound up in one woman's hand for so long, Sophie could probably blatantly tell me she was flirting and I still wouldn't pick up on it.

Thinking about dating makes me shudder, but I catch myself so that she doesn't interpret it as a reaction to her. I've matched with a few women on that dating app since Jaclyn made me update my profile, but I don't know whether I'm supposed to swipe left or right or what. So I've done nothing.

"I heard a rumor that Larry was looking at moving the clinic to that property over on Elm Street that just went up for sale," Sophie continues, thankfully redirecting my thoughts away from dating.

"Which property?"

Sophie shrugs. "Some old house as you come into downtown. It's a cute place, but I can't imagine there's space for a therapy gym unless you knocked out most of the walls."

I wonder if it's the house on the corner of Elm and

Sycamore. If it is, then I'm definitely familiar with it because Jaclyn has commented on how much she loves it almost every time we drive by it. But Sophie is right; there's no way it has the right kind of layout for the type of work we do.

"Who knows with Larry?" I turn to my stack of papers, thinking that's the end of the conversation. But a few seconds later, Sophie sighs, like she has something more to say.

"It wouldn't be so bad, moving to a new office, you know?"

I make a noncommittal sound, and she continues.

"We'd probably get at least a little say in how to set the place up." She looks at me like she wants me to agree with her, but I have almost no stake in where Larry chooses to move or not move the office. As long as he continues to file my Green Card paperwork, I'm happy to be where I am. Even if Larry Montgomery is a grade-A asshole who thinks he's the king of Sapling Grove. If it weren't for Larry, this would be a perfect job. It kept me in the U.S., and most of the people—other therapists as well as patients—are delightful to work with.

When I don't respond to Sophie other than to tilt my head in agreement, she takes the hint that I'm not in the mood for small talk. We each turn back to our documentation and work side by side for a few blissfully silent minutes until another person appears at the doorway to our tiny "office." I plan to ignore the person and continue with my work, but alas. Today seems to be the day for office gossip.

"Did you hear that Larry might move the practice to that place over on Elm Street?" the newcomer, Tabitha Brandt, asks. Tabitha is another physical therapist and the biggest gossip at Montgomery Therapy. She usually has the inside scoop on everything, and she likes to let everyone know that she's in-the-know. She's older than most of us, in her mid-fifties or early sixties, I would guess. But she has a youthfulness in her demeanor. She's also somehow related to Jaclyn's friend Andrew, but then, everyone here seems to be at least distantly related.

"We were just talking about that!" Sophie responds. I set my pen on the desk, slightly annoyed that I can't focus on my work.

"I heard something else, too." Tabitha drops her voice to a whisper. "I heard he might not have a choice but to move the clinic because he and Joan are getting divorced."

I grunt. It's none of my business what Larry gets up to outside of work.

"Seriously?" Sophie is clearly shocked by the news, but she's not worked here long enough to have witnessed the strange tension between Larry and Joan at the annual company picnic.

Tabitha nods sagely. "Oh yes, it's very serious. I think it will actually happen this time."

I chuckle at that, and both women shoot me a look that makes me think they forgot I was here.

"Sophie, what you don't know is that Larry and Joan have been 'going through a divorce' off and on for the past four years." I say, hoping to put an end to this conversation.

Tabitha glares at me, but Sophie genuinely thanks me for giving her the context for the current rumors.

"Well, if Rhys is going to fill you in on all the details, I guess I'm not needed anymore," Tabitha says with a huff. She walks away before either of us has a chance to say anything else. When she's gone, Sophie and I look at each other for a moment, then break out in laughter.

"I think you hurt her feelings," she says.

"She'll get over it."

A sweet expression crosses her features before she turns back to her stack of papers, and I'm struck by her attractiveness. She's not as gorgeous as a certain friend of mine, but there's a loveliness to her features that I haven't fully noticed before. I've always thought of her as pretty in that interchangeable way that a lot of women in this line of work are.

Maybe it's because of the way the light is catching her hair, or maybe it's because every time I look at the dating app my stomach knots up. I don't know. But for a moment, I consider asking her out.

I have a feeling she would say yes, and we'd probably have a fine time going to dinner somewhere, maybe seeing a movie. If I were to guess, she and Jaclyn have very different tastes in movies. Jaclyn has never met an action film she didn't love, but Sophie strikes me as the romantic comedy type, which is honestly more my speed. I grew up watching them with my Nan, who loved them almost as much as she loved cozy mysteries. But watching the latest car chase movie with Jaclyn is always entertaining, even if it's not what I would choose. Sometimes I discretely watch her delight in the absurdity of a person stopping a torpedo with his bare hands or hooking a helicopter with a rope mid-flight just so I can see the glow of joy on her face.

I shake my head at myself. I can't even think about asking out another woman without Jaclyn showing up in my thoughts. It doesn't bode well for the increasing list of women I've been ignoring on that app. I remind myself that sitting around waiting for Jaclyn to change the way she views dating isn't good for me.

I dismiss the idea of asking Sophie out. Not only is there no spark of mutual understanding between us like there is with Jaclyn, it's also that dating a colleague would get too complicated. But I resolve to figure out how swiping works when I get home this evening. It's the right thing to do. I'm sure of it in my head. I just need to convince my heart.

CHAPTER 5

Jaclyn

"**I**'m pleased to introduce for the first time Andrew and Evie Watson-Brandt. Everyone raise your glasses to the happy couple!"

I let out a loud whoop along with the rest of the crowd under the reception tent as my friends enter the space. After months of enduring Evie's massive number of wedding spreadsheets, I'm glad to finally be at this wedding. For as intense as Evie has been about the wedding plans, the woman knows how to throw a party.

Evie and Andrew somehow managed to convince the Cooke facilities services folks to transform the center of campus into a wedding venue, complete with a makeshift dance floor and twinkle lights. There's a bar between two of the giant oak trees where a couple of bartenders are serving up a variety of drinks, including a signature Watson-Brandt cocktail that's basically a variation on the boozy milkshakes Evie sometimes makes when Kylie and I come over. The table centerpieces are vases of bright blue irises from Ruth Brandt's garden, and there are matching blue ribbons tying off gauzy drapes at the entrance to the tent. With the fading summer light and the mildly warm air, the campus feels like a dreamy forest instead of an academic institution.

It's not just the campus that's transformed. Everyone is dressed impeccably. I hardly recognize some of my colleagues. Even Rhys is almost unrecognizable. I usually see him in a Montgomery Therapy polo and athletic pants because his job requires him to be able to move easily. But tonight, there is no trace of sportswear.

He's wearing a tailored jet black suit jacket over a black shirt and black tie. On most men, the black on black on black would seem an odd choice for a wedding. But on Rhys, it works. Instead of making him look like he's in mourning, the suit conveys the swagger of a high-profile athlete at a red carpet event. His sleekness is only enhanced by his neatly trimmed beard and deep set eyes. I would be lying if I said his whole look wasn't giving me flutters. Not that I'm attracted to him, of course.

Rhys went to the bar a while ago to get fresh drinks for the two of us, but Andrew's grandmother has cornered him and seems to be flirting quite shamelessly with him. And who could blame her? That suit truly may be the greatest invention of all time.

I pull my eyes away from Rhys and survey the crowd.

There's a contingent of faculty dancing wildly to the rendition of "Electric Boogie" that the Cooke jazz band is playing, and I nearly choke on my drink when I realize who's among the group. I never thought I'd see Mike Pierce, the Dean of the library and Evie's boss, doing the Electric Slide.

My amusement is interrupted by the arrival of two of my favorite people, Phoebe and Tabitha Brandt. They're Andrew's aunts, and along with his mom, Ruth, they're affectionately known around town as the Brandt Biddies.

"I see you're here with that dishy Englishman." Phoebe wiggles her eyebrows conspiratorially as they approach, and I laugh.

"Yes, he's my plus-one. I needed someone to dance with." I don't mention that I also need someone to keep Mom from pushing any more loan officers or ex-boyfriends in my direction. I love them, but Tabitha and Phoebe are both horrible gossips, and I don't need my protection plan getting back to Mom.

"As long as you tell him to save a dance for each of us," Tabitha says with an exaggerated wink. "Maybe I'll fake an injury, and he'll have to give me physical therapy!"

"Nonsense! You're too dainty to be convincing," Phoebe says. "And besides, you work with him. You can't fawn over him the same way I can. *I'll* fake an injury, and you can watch while Rhys massages my—"

"No one is faking any injuries," I interject. The Brandt sisters laugh.

"He's too young for us, anyway," Phoebe says when their

laughter dies down.

"That's right. He needs someone his own age who could keep up with him," Tabitha adds, giving me a wink.

I roll my eyes at them in good humor, but I know better than to deny there's anything between Rhys and me. They'll only tease me more.

Our conversation is cut short as Kylie takes the stage to give a toast to Evie and Andrew.

"Once her speech is over, Tab and I are singing a duet," Phoebe says, and the two women scuttle toward where the musicians are taking a break. Which means I'm standing by myself at the end of the tent, leaning against a tree and resuming my people watching when someone else appears in front of me.

He's about my age. Blond hair. Light blue eyes. A dimple when he smiles at me.

I straighten and hope the sudden movement doesn't nick the fabric of my outfit. I know I'm here with Rhys, but he won't mind if we leave separately. But when the newcomer clears his throat and says my name, I do a double take.

"Landon?"

Intellectually, I should have expected to see him. Mom told me he was coming, after all. But I guess when you don't want to see someone, you hope they forget to show up to the biggest wedding this town has seen in decades. Alas, I am not so lucky.

"How have you been?" Landon asks, as though he has the right.

It's not only that I haven't seen Landon Cunningham in over a decade that has me wanting to hide in the bushes. It's that the way things ended between us still chafes even after all these years.

"I've been well." I intentionally do not ask the same of him.

"That's good to hear." He pauses for a moment, and I hope it means he's about to leave. But then he says, "Listen, I was hoping I would run into y—"

"Enjoying the wedding?" I ask, cutting him off. I want to keep this conversation at the small talk level, and whatever it is that Landon has to say to me would take us into territory I don't want to visit at my friends' wedding.

He shrugs. "It's nice."

It doesn't feel like a compliment. I narrow my eyes at him, about to tell him to take his negative attitude somewhere else when I hear Kylie ask for everyone's attention. I take the opportunity to step away from the tree entirely and put a little distance between Landon and me.

"Thank you all for coming tonight," Kylie says. "I'm so excited for Evie and Andrew and their new life together."

She pauses while the crowd cheers and claps. When they finish, she continues, "I have to admit, when Evie first told me that she and Andrew had started seeing each other, I was skeptical. I'm very protective of Evie. She's like a sister to me. But seeing these two together, I know I don't have to worry about Evie. Andrew adores her. I can see it in the way he looks at her and the way he treats her. I'm so glad I was wrong about him."

I take this as my cue to shout, "And if he ever hurts her, Kylie and I will come for him!" A few people chuckle, and then Kylie rolls her eyes and finishes her toast. As she steps down from the stage, I turn and see that Landon is still here, and he's taken up my spot leaning against the tree.

Dammit. I hoped he'd disappear.

"Is there something I can help you with?" I ask in a deliberately annoyed tone.

He opens his mouth to say something, but we're interrupted by the arrival of my mother.

"Landon, it's so good to see you again! How's your Momma since I saw you at the store?"

Landon gives my mom a sheepish grin as she pulls him into a hug. The vibe of this wedding just took a turn into emergency root canal territory.

"Mom's great, Mrs. B. I was catching up with Jaclyn."

"Oh, that's wonderful!" Despite my clear request to keep Landon out of her boyfriend schemes, I know what's about to come out of Mom's mouth, but I don't have time to stop her. Instead I brace myself as she says, "Are you seeing anyone? You know Jaclyn's not had any steady boyfriends since the two of you broke up."

As much as I want to make my mom happy, I can't let this conversation with Landon go any further. Not if she's going to push me toward getting back together with this asshole.

"Actually, that's not true."

"Honey?" My mother gives me a questioning look, and Landon takes a step backward as though he's trying to gracefully bow out of this conversation. Unfortunately for him—and me—his path is blocked by the tree, so there's no way to escape without going around my mom, and she's not going anywhere at the moment.

"I am dating someone. I just...haven't told you yet." I inwardly cringe at the lie.

"Haven't told me yet? Well, why the heck not?"

I stop myself from saying something I'll regret. Something like "Because when it comes to my dating life you're completely insufferable." No, I've already said enough regretful things in the past two minutes.

"I haven't had a good chance to tell you." It's a weak excuse. I know it. Mom knows it. Hell, even Landon looks like he knows it.

But Mom doesn't call me on it. Instead, she asks, "Well, when do I get to meet the lucky fella?"

"You know him already."

Shit. Dammit.

That was not what I meant to say. I meant to tell her that he travels a lot for work and that I don't know when he'll be here next. But instead, when she asked me, my eyes wandered across the crowd and snagged on the way Rhys is wearing the hell out of that suit. It seemed right that it would be him.

Mom follows my gaze to where Rhys is still talking to Andrew's grandmother. When she looks back at me, the delight in her eyes makes me want to throw up. I know I shouldn't lie to my mother, but now I'm in too deep.

I glance toward Rhys again, and we make eye contact.

He says something to Andrew's grandmother, then stands and walks toward us.

As Rhys approaches, I don't think. I reach for him, pulling him toward me and wrapping my arms around him. I go up on my toes and crash my lips into his in an awkward kiss.

I mean it to be a quick peck on the lips. A greeting, like you'd give a boyfriend who has been on the other side of the room all night, and you're in public. But Rhys stiffens in shock for a moment, and then he's kissing me back, his arms snaking around me and pulling me closer. I forget where I am and who I'm with and lean into his embrace with more fervor than is strictly necessary.

His lips taste sweet and a little tart, like the bourbon lemonade I'm guessing he's been drinking. It's smooth against my tongue, and I want more of it.

His tongue teases my lower lip, sending sparks and fizz through my bloodstream.

I want to bite down on his lip and then kiss away the sting.

I want his mouth to trail down my neck and for him to nibble at my collar bone.

I want—

I can't even finish the thought because a throat clears beside us, and Rhys's mouth leaves mine. He rests his forehead against mine, and the intimacy of it makes me shiver.

Damn. That was a kiss.

"How's it going over here?" Rhys's voice is more gruff

than usual, the way I imagine he'd sound in my bedroom.

Oh god, no. I should not imagine Rhys in a bedroom. And especially not my bedroom. I shiver at the thought, and it's not clear to me if I'm repulsed or turned on.

The sound of another, more insistent throat clear wipes the mental image of Rhys in my bedroom out of my mind.

We're still holding each other, and Rhys's eyes search mine. I can't tell what he's looking for, and worse, I can't tell what signals I'm sending him. But I'm pretty sure they're something like the signal for "Please take me to bed right now and tell me I'm a good girl."

Color rises in my cheeks as I turn to see Landon looking at us like he's walked in on his parents having sex. Seeing Landon dumps a giant bucket of cold water on the direction my thoughts were taking.

"Oh Jaclyn! Rhys! I'm so happy for you!" If Landon's presence was a bucket of cold water, my mom's reaction is a dousing in liquid nitrogen.

Rhys gives me a questioning look but doesn't say anything.

"I'll have to have you over for dinner this week so you can tell me all about how you realized you had feelings for each other."

Rhys tenses slightly beside me, but blessedly doesn't contradict my mother's rambling.

"I'll call you tomorrow, Jaclyn. I have to go tell Ruth and the girls that my baby's finally found love."

My mother dashes toward Andrew's mom and aunts, and I watch in horror as the four women chatter excitedly.

No doubt they're already planning Rhys's and my wedding.

At some point during Mom's animated outburst, Landon seems to have slipped away. I can't say I'm sorry to see him go. Whatever it was he wanted to talk about is the last thing on my mind right now because I owe Rhys an explanation.

"So...my mom thinks we're dating."

"I gathered."

"I'm sorry. I don't know what came over me. Landon was here, and my mom came over, and I thought she was going to try to set me up again, and..."

"It's alright."

"It is?" I glance at him skeptically.

"I know your mum has been pushing you to date more. If telling her we're dating gets her off your back for a little while, that's alright with me."

"I'm sorry I kissed you like that." The heat of embarrassment surges through me.

"Don't worry about it."

I stare at him gobsmacked. He is taking the fact that I kissed him without warning with a surprising amount of cool, even for Rhys.

He shifts his weight, and that's when I realize that Rhys's arms are still wrapped around my waist. I look up at him and whisper, "You can let go now."

He shakes his head. "Think I'll keep up the appearance for a little longer. Don't want your mum coming back and giving you a hard time again tonight."

"Oh, right. Of course." I blush for the second time in as many minutes. Strange, because I almost never blush.

We shift so that we're standing side by side, but Rhys leaves his arm wrapped around my back with his hand resting on the top of my hip. His hand is warm through the fabric of my bridesmaid outfit. I hate dresses, so when Evie said we could pick our own outfits as long as the colors matched the wedding colors, I opted for a flowing silk wrap blouse with a low vee neck and satiny black stretchy pants. It's the perfect outfit for a warm May evening, but it also means that the barrier between Rhys's hand and my ass is *very* thin.

Goosebumps spread across my skin, starting with the spot where Rhys's hand lingers. It doesn't help that he's slowly rubbing his thumb over the top of my hip. I involuntarily shiver, and he pulls me closer.

"Are you cold?" he asks. His voice in my ear makes me shiver again, and I'm right back to that mental image of him in my bedroom.

Before I know what's happening, Rhys is removing that sexy black suit jacket and draping it over my arms.

I don't mean to breathe in so deeply as I wrap the jacket a little more tightly around myself. I'm suddenly flooded with the smell of his cologne, a wave of cedar and lemon washing over me.

"Thanks," I manage to croak out.

"No problem. Don't want you freezing out here."

I turn and look Rhys in the eye. "I don't only mean the jacket. I meant for going along with the kiss, too."

He gives me a short nod. "Right. Of course. Any time."

I give him a puzzled look.

"I mean. Not any time. I was glad to. No, that's not right." Rhys seems to flounder for the right word.

I don't think I've ever seen him like this before. He's usually so matter-of-fact and doesn't overthink what he's saying.

"Damn. What I mean is, I'm happy to help you with your mum."

"I really do appreciate it." I smile as I turn back to watch the rest of the wedding-goers dancing. I catch sight of Evie and Andrew in the middle of the dance floor and wave to the happy couple. Evie waves back and gives me a thumbs-up. No doubt my love struck friend saw our kiss and is convinced it means we're falling in love. As if.

CHAPTER 6

Jaclyn

The aggressive buzz of my phone startles me awake. I reach for it and jab at the button to silence the notification, then swipe my hand down my face as I let out a groan. Memories of everything that happened last night slam into me, leaving me feeling emotionally hungover.

I might also be regular hungover. There's a throbbing at my temples, and my mouth is dry and disgusting.

Without looking at my phone, I stumble out of bed and make my way to the bathroom to find some aspirin. I gulp down an entire glass of water with the pills. I lean my hands on the counter and hang my head as images from the night flood my brain.

Rhys's arm draped across my shoulders.

His hand on my thigh as we sat with the rest of the wedding party and ate our cake.

His fingers lacing through mine as we walked through the crowd to chat with other guests.

That goddamn kiss.

I try to shove that memory deep down where I'm certain I won't be able to bring it back up and play it over and over again like a movie clip. But it doesn't change the fact that we were basically inseparable for the rest of the night after I made the worst decision possible. I assume that Rhys kept his hands on me because he knew Mom was still watching us, which is fine. Because getting her to stop meddling in my dating life was the point.

Still, if I hadn't let Mom get under my skin, I wouldn't have tried to prove to her that I'm capable of finding happiness without her interference. And I wouldn't have kissed my best friend and spent the rest of the night completely out of sorts.

I'm clearly still unsettled by it, as evidenced by the fact that every time I close my eyes, the sense memory the firm grip of his hand on my ass plays across my skin. But this is Rhys. My best friend. I'm not supposed to have thoughts about how his tongue felt skating along mine, let alone imagine what *else* his tongue might be good at.

Maybe I should have stuck things out that night with Daniel—eaten the cake I didn't want and gone with him to his overpriced apartment for a roll in the sheets. It's been so long since I've been laid that the kiss must have stirred something up in me, that's all. No more fantasizing about my friend.

I'm jolted out of my musings by another loud buzz from my phone. With a sigh, I shuffle back to my bed and lean against the headboard as I unlock the phone. My messaging app has a bunch of missed messages on the group chat with Evie and Kylie.

EVIE: @Jaclyn You and Rhys. Kissing. I need details.

KYLIE: Wait, what did I miss?

EVIE: Jaclyn and Rhys with their tongues down each others' throats

KYLIE: Interesting...Yes, I do believe you owe us details.

With a groan, I curse my friends for asking me about this at such an ungodly hour of the morning. Especially Evie. Shouldn't she and Andrew be somewhere cut off from the world while they bang each other into oblivion?

But I know that I put on quite the show last night, and I feel like I owe her an explanation. Besides, I'd rather her hear it from me than from the old ladies gossip network that Mom and the Brandt Biddies have going.

ME: About that...

I hit send, then debate how much to tell my friends. I don't want it getting back to my mom that I outright lied to her about the nature of Rhys's and my relationship. But I also need to figure out how to keep this from going any further than last night, and Evie and Kylie are both creative thinkers.

EVIE: Don't leave me hanging!

ME: Sorry, there's a lot to explain.

ME: So you know how my mom has been trying to set

me up?

I don't wait for a response.

ME: Last night my ex from high school showed up, and Mom had that look. The one where I can tell she's about to suggest a date. So I panicked and told her that Rhys and I were together.

KYLIE: Yikes. This can only end badly.

EVIE: YOU'RE FAKE DATING RHYS?????!!!!!! OMGGGGGGGG I bet you'll fall in love!!!!

ME: No one is falling in love. I need you to help me get out of this mess.

It shouldn't surprise me that seconds after I send the message, my phone vibrates with a video call request. I grumble as I accept the call, and Evie's face appears on the screen. I don't care if my friends see my tangled hair or notice that I'm still in my pajamas. From the looks of it, Evie is, too. I try not to think about the fact that she got married last night and all the sex she and Andrew have probably been having. Because thinking about your friends having sex is weird.

Moments later, Kylie joins the call, and I brace myself for the inquisition I'm about to endure.

"It's not a mess. It's an opportunity," Evie says without greeting either of us. "Think about it. You and Rhys already spend most of your time together, and he is so easy on the eyes."

Evie is briefly interrupted by a shout of "Hey!" from the background, and she turns the phone toward Andrew, who is, thankfully, clothed.

"I love you, babe, but even you can admit that Rhys Blackwell has a swagger that anyone would be attracted to," she says over her shoulder.

Andrew reluctantly admits that his wife is correct, and Evie swings the phone back to herself.

"As I was saying, this is an opportunity. Your mom wants you to be happy. You and Rhys get along so well already. I say skip the faking it part and go straight to dating him!"

"That is not happening."

"Why not?" Evie tilts her head to the side, and her question is so genuine that I struggle to come up with a satisfying answer.

"Because...because we don't like each other that way."

"I'm not sure it matters how you feel about each other." This is from Kylie, who has been suspiciously quiet this whole call.

"What do you mean?"

"I mean that your mom's attempts to set you up have been ramping up the past few months, and it's clearly pissed you off enough that you're ready to do something about it."

I start to protest, but Kylie gives me a look that silences the words before they cross my lips. I sigh, relenting. She's right, and I hate her a little for it.

"Fine. What do you have in mind?"

"Go on a few 'dates' with Rhys in places where your mom will see you and then quietly 'break up' in a few months. Or tell her that you and he decided it wasn't the right thing." She uses air quotes around "dates" and "break up."

"That's doable, I guess. Especially because we already hang out a lot."

"Exactly! You just have to make sure that your mom believes you're dating. So you might have to kiss him again." Evie says this with a look so syrupy that it almost makes me gag.

"What if I tell my mom that we're dating and leave it at that?"

"No, that won't work. Because your mom is going to want to see the proof. And if you're not convincing, she'll find another loan officer or surgeon with no social skills." Kylie is ever the pragmatist.

"I'm with Kylie. You're going to have to be all in on this until you can figure out a way to end it so that your mom won't immediately try to set you up with someone else. Or until..."

"No." I cut Evie off before she finishes her thought. I know what she was going to say, and she's dead wrong. There's no way that Rhys and I are going to fall in love, even if we keep up this charade.

Evie sticks her tongue out at me, but she doesn't push the lovey-dovey stuff for the rest of the call. Instead we devise ways to make sure my mom will see Rhys and me together in couple-y ways. Since it's only my mom we have to convince, I try to keep us to normal activities like dinner at her house or holding hands if we see her around town.

But my friends have other ideas, most of which seem to

be designed to razz me, because the plans they suggest are increasingly ridiculous. When Kylie suggests learning to fly a plane so we can skywrite our love for each other over Mom's house, I *know* they're trying to get the best of me.

"Yes, because an ostentatious, environmentally harmful confession of love is so my style." I settle my mouth into a flat line, but those two clowns laugh.

"Jay, we know you'll never do half this shit, but you have to admit, it would be pretty funny if you had to kiss him in public again." I bristle at the nickname she always uses for me. She's always shortening people's names, whether they like it or not.

I know she's trying to make me laugh, but the thought of kissing Rhys in public again doesn't sound so funny to me. In fact, it sounds...like something I do not want to consider, even for a fraction of a second. Because Rhys and I are friends and always have been and always will be. Nothing more than that.

We wrap up the call without my having any more intrusive thoughts about kissing my best friend, and Kylie and I both wish the newlyweds safe travels as they leave for their honeymoon tour of the Lake District. Andrew said something about *Pride and Prejudice* bringing them together last summer, but I always thought it was some kind of spreadsheet situation that helped them find each other.

After the call ends, I pace the bedroom, unsure what to do next. Ok, maybe I am sure, but the thing that I have to do sends shivers of nervous energy through me.

It's not only that Rhys and I kissed and have to deal with

the fallout of knowing what each other's lips feel like. It's also that we're going to have to come up with some kind of story about how we've been secretly dating that my mother will believe. Not the easiest thing, since we've both insisted for years that we weren't dating. Because we weren't.

But Helen Beckett can smell a lie a mile away. In fact, I don't know how I managed to convince her last night that my brazen tongue tangle with Rhys was anything other than me bluffing my way out of an awkward conversation. With dinner at her house on the horizon, Rhys and I had better be on the same page before we're around her again because she will absolutely run us through a thorough interrogation.

I consider texting him to get our story straight, but as I stare at the blinking cursor in the message box, I forget how to form sentences. Because as much as I don't want Mom pushing any more men in my direction, I'm not sure how to talk to Rhys after everything that went down at the wedding.

In a masterful act of avoidance, I toss my phone on the bed and take a shower instead of facing the post-kiss reality that awaits me. After the shower, I further delay the inevitable by cooking myself an elaborate brunch—quiche with some leftover veggies and an obscene amount of cheese. I make it from scratch the way Mom taught me when I was in middle school, even the pie crust, because if my hands are busy, I can't text Rhys.

As I sit down to eat, I open my laptop and click on the browser icon. It takes me a minute to sift through the thirty saved tabs to find the one I want. What better way to distract myself than throwing all my energy into a project?

After that horrible date with the loan officer, I decided to do some digging about the bank's charitable giving. I knew I had seen them listed as donors for other events and organizations around town, and I couldn't believe someone supposedly as well-connected as Daniel wouldn't know about their philanthropic endeavors.

I was right. Sapling Grove Federal Savings Bank has an entire department for Community Outreach and Support that runs a charitable foundation, but Mr. "What Kind of Collateral Do You Have" failed to mention it. The other thing Daniel failed to mention is that they're currently accepting proposals for something called "Give Back," an investment competition they're hosting to give away a huge donation they recently received. The grand prize would be enough to fund the first year of the community center's expenses.

With the chaos leading up to the wedding, I haven't had time to dig in to the application requirements for the Give Back event until now. I scan through the form, making note of what I'll need to collect for the application process. It's a pretty standard list—a description of the project, an itemized budget, a list of goals and benchmarks. The one thing that I'm snagging on, though, is that they also want to know what other investments have already been secured. And that's where my problem lies.

Even though there's wide community support for opening a new center, we haven't been able to raise enough money to sustain the project. Every time we've talked to potential investors, they ask whether Larry Montgomery is on board. But Larry has refused to take any meetings with anyone from our group. If we could get his support, the rest of the town would follow suit, and we might even convince the City Council to put the community center back in the town's budget.

But those are problems for another day, and I focus on the issue at hand. I decide the only thing I can do is be perfectly honest on that question and hope for the best. I open a new document and write a rough outline of my answers to the application questions. I'm making good progress—only two long narrative questions left—when my phone buzzes, startling me enough that I flinch and jostle the mug next to me. Coffee sloshes over the side and pools near my laptop. I mutter a curse under my breath and grab a paper towel from the kitchen counter to dab up the spilled coffee.

My phone buzzes again, an insistent reminder that I haven't looked at the incoming message. I run the paper towel along the table one more time, not so much because I think there's still coffee there, but because I have a feeling I know who that message is from, and the longer it takes me to clean up, the longer I can delay dealing with the fallout of last night.

I glance at the notification, and my suspicion is confirmed.

RHYS: Can we talk?

It's funny, the way changing a word or two changes the meaning of a sentence. If he'd said, "We should talk" or, worse, "We need to talk," then I could justify the feeling of unease that sinks into my stomach as I read his message. He's put the ball in my court, which should be a relief. I like to be in control. To know what the next three steps are before anyone else has even figured out the first one.

But this situation? The one where I kissed my best friend? It's not normal. It's messy and emotional, and I don't do messy and emotional. Because that is the farthest thing from being in control.

I push past my hesitation and send a quick response. Rhys replies almost immediately.

ME: Where and when?

RHYS: I'll come to you.

ME: Ok, see you in a few.

The ten minutes it takes him to drive from his place to mine feel like both the longest and shortest minutes of my life. I try to distract myself by cleaning up the remnants of my quiche-making, but the anticipation is screwing with my head so much that I almost put the dirty dishes in the refrigerator instead of the dishwasher. I shake my head at myself and get everything into the correct appliance. I'm closing the dishwasher—after double checking that I've put the correct detergent pod into the dispenser—when I hear a knock on the front door. A moment later, I hear the click of the lock and the slight creak of the door.

My heart weirdly hammers as Rhys's heavy footsteps echo down the hallway. As he rounds the corner into the combined dining and living room, one thing becomes perfectly clear. I am not ready to face the man I kissed last night.

CHAPTER 7

Rhys

If there's a heaven, it feels like soft lips and a graze of breasts against my chest. Like the fullness of hips in my hands and a sigh of bliss against my mouth. It feels like everything that kissing Jaclyn awakened in me last night.

Except kissing her isn't supposed to happen. We're friends, dammit. And that's all we'll ever be, despite...

It's not worth thinking about what comes after "despite." I'll only torture myself if I let my mind wander down that path. Just like every other time I've woken up with the thought of Jaclyn in my arms.

This morning is different from the others, though. Because now I have a physical memory of her body against mine, not merely the shadows of frustrated dreams and unrequited lust. It seems wrong to handle the aftermath of last night the way I usually do when I wake up like this, so I force myself out of bed and into a cold shower.

The shower calms down the physiological side effects of dreaming about Jaclyn, but it can't wash away the recollection of her kiss.

I don't have time to dwell on the memory because when I get out of the shower, my phone is vibrating on my bedside table, like it does every Sunday morning at eight o'clock. I tap the accept button and put the call on speaker so I can dress while I talk.

"Morning, sunshine!" The slightly mocking tone of my brother's voice is tinny through the speaker.

"Rupert, you know I hate it when you call me sunshine," I say as I take my clothes out of the closet.

"All the more reason to do it, sunshine."

My responding growl of annoyance is met with a bark of laughter.

"Can we just get on with it today?" I ask as I put on my trousers.

"Someone's testy this morning. Cat piss in your breakfast?"

I roll my eyes even though he can't see me. "You know very well that I don't have a cat."

"You rolled your eyes, didn't you?" Rupert asks with a playfully scolding tone. "C'mon, Rhys, what's eating you up today? You're more grouchy than usual."

He's not wrong. Rupert is the exact opposite of me in both looks and temperament. He's all light and breezy, from his light blond hair to his easy laugh; whereas I've always been the darker, more serious brother. His easy-going nature and penchant for playfulness makes him a great primary school teacher. Despite our personality differences, we've always been close. Living away from him is the one thing I regret about moving to the States. Our weekly phone calls are great, but there are times I wish I could grab a pint with my brother at the end of the day.

"It's nothing," I lie, but Rupert immediately calls me on my bullshit.

"Like hell it is. Out with it."

"Fine." No use trying to keep it from him. The other thing about Rupert is that he's relentless. Even if I hang up on him now, he'd call me incessantly until I finally gave up. "Jaclyn kissed me."

"What? No way! That's amazing!" There's genuine joy in his voice, and I wish I felt the same way about it.

"No, it's not. It wasn't because we're together or anything."

I can hear his confusion when he says, "What do you mean? Why'd she kiss you then? Did someone dare her?"

I don't know how to answer him because I don't know exactly what caused her impromptu kiss. All I know is that when her mouth met mine, my brain short-circuited for a fraction of a second. Because, *holy fuck*, it was finally happening. The thing I've longed for since the first moment I met this woman.

It was as amazing as I knew it would be, which isn't surprising because Jaclyn never does anything by half measures. The way she whimpered when my tongue slid against her lips. The flush in her cheeks when we stepped apart. The sparkle of desire in her eyes. To be honest, it was all I could do not to pick her up in a fireman's carry and take her back to my place to bed her after that. Judging by the vibes she was giving off, she might have been alright with it.

"Rhys?" My brother's voice wrenches me back to the present.

"No one dared her. Her mum has been pestering her about dating, and I think she was tired of it."

"So she revenge kissed you?"

"Something like that."

After a pause in which I'm sure he's rubbing his hand against his cheek in the way he always does when he's thinking, he says, "Honestly, that tracks."

Rupert and his husband, Colin, visited Sapling Grove last year, and Jaclyn offered to serve as their local tour guide because she enjoyed their company so much the night they met. It's a good thing, having my brother and my best friend get along so well.

"She told her mum that we're dating. As a way to keep Helen from pushing more men in her direction." I pull on my shirt and take the phone off speaker, bringing it to my ear.

"And you're alright with that?"

I run my hand through my damp hair and blow out a breath. "Yes. No. I don't know."

"Very decisive, Rhysie," Rupert says with a chuckle. I hate that nickname even more than when he calls me "sunshine."

"Fuck off," I tell him, but he just laughs.

When his laughter dies down, he asks in a serious tone, "Are you going to keep up the appearance of dating her?"

"I'm not sure what choice I have. It's not like I'm going to throw Jaclyn under the bus to her mum."

"Yeah, but what about you, mate? Are you really alright with only pretending to be in a romantic relationship with the woman you're actually in love with?"

My phone chooses that moment to send a series of rapid notifications.

"Hold that thought," I say, pulling the phone away from my ear. There are fifteen notification bubbles on the screen from that damn dating app. I'm turning that thing off as soon as I get off the phone with Rupert.

"Fucking hell," I mutter under my breath before returning to the call with my brother.

"Everything alright?"

I don't tell him about the dating app. Instead, I stare blankly at the wall, wondering what I did to deserve my current mess of a love life.

"Rhys?" Rupert interrupts my thoughts.

"Sorry, what were you saying?"

"Just be careful. I don't like to see my baby brother get hurt."

A sudden knot of emotion obstructs my throat at Rupert's sincerity. I clear it and mutter something about needing to get on with my day.

"Call me if you need to talk," Rupert says.

"Say hello to Colin for me," I respond, hoping the change in subject will distract him.

"Seriously, Rhys. Call me."

"Goodbye, Rupert."

After we end the call, I sit on the bed, unable—or unwilling—to do the things I'd planned for the day. My mind keeps puzzling over the question Rupert asked.

Am I alright with continuing to lie to Jaclyn's mum?

When the silence doesn't provide any answers, I hang my head. Because one thing is clear. Before this gets too out of hand, I need to talk to Jaclyn and set the record straight about how I feel.

With my heart pounding in my ears, I text her to see if we can meet up and talk. She doesn't reply immediately, but the app shows that she's read my message.

After what feels like ages, her response lights up my phone. It's simple and a little curt.

JACLYN: Where and when?

ME: I'll come to you.

I want to say more. To tell her that I'll always come to her, no matter where she is or what she needs, but I know that would make me sound like a lovesick fool. Which, alright, maybe I am one. But I need to act like a normal person for this conversation.

On the drive to Jaclyn's place, I practice what I'm going to say. I'm still practicing when I get to her home, muttering under my breath even as I knock on the door when I let myself in.

"Jaclyn, I need to tell you something. When you kissed

me last night, it was a dream come true. I've had feelings for you since we met."

No, too sappy.

"Jaclyn, I think we should date. Each other, that is. For real."

Oh god, not that.

"Jaclyn."

"Yes?"

I stop short as I round the corner from her hallway to the great room, realizing that she's not upstairs getting ready for the day like I expected her to be. Instead, she's standing in the kitchen, the morning light peeking through the curtains and surrounding her in an angelic glow.

My face grows hot and then cold as I play back what I said, trying to figure out if she could have possibly heard my awkward practice declaration.

"Glad to see you finally used the key for its intended purpose," she says, with a laugh. It's not her usual wry laugh, although it's clear she's trying to make it sound that way. There's a nervous tension behind it, like she's hiding her true feelings behind her humor. She doesn't say anything about my murmured confession of desire, which I take to mean that she didn't hear it.

She takes a step toward me, but I put up a hand in a stop motion.

"Can you just...stay over there?"

"Alright?" Her statement feels like a question, but I don't elaborate on why I want to keep her at a distance. It's better for my sanity if she doesn't know that the temptation to fold her into my arms and pick up where we left off last night is making me question whether I should have called instead of doing this in person.

"So, um, what did you want to talk about?" She crosses her arms across her stomach, more closed off than I've ever seen her. Shit. This is already not going well.

"I..." *I don't want to talk. I want to kiss you again.*

I shake my head, clearing the thoughts of her lips and hands and that little moan that I doubt she even remembers letting out when my tongue met hers. Involuntarily, I close my eyes, savoring the memory, even though I shouldn't.

"Rhys, are you okay?" Concern lines her voice.

I hang my head and take a deep breath.

"I'm fine. A little hungover from last night." The lie is not far from the truth. I was drunk on Jaclyn's kiss for the rest of the reception.

Jaclyn lets out a little nervous sounding laugh. "Me, too."

Neither of us says anything else, and the silence is excruciating. It's the first time that's ever happened between us. The quiet moments have never been awkward when it's only Jaclyn and me, but today it's like we don't know how to be around each other anymore.

I blame myself. Yes, she technically kissed me first, but I was the one who took it too far. The surprising thing was that she let me. Even more shocking was that she didn't put up a fight about keeping up the appearance of intimacy for the rest of the reception. She doesn't like to be touched, but even as we walked to the car at the end of the night, she didn't let go of my hand. And that's the thing I fell asleep thinking about last night, the thing that haunted my dreams.

Jaclyn, taking my hand, drawing me close to her, letting me kiss her again.

She didn't, of course. Kiss me again, that is. But, god, how I wanted her to.

"Why did you kiss me?" I let out a long breath after the words are out, like relieving a pressure valve.

I know part of the answer already. She told me as much last night, and besides, it's been most of what we've talked about over the past few months. Her mum's incessant blind date setups have been wearing her down, and she was at her tipping point. But what I don't understand is why she chose me.

"You know why," she says.

"That's not what I mean."

She closes her eyes and lets out her own long breath. When her eyes open, she says, "I panicked. Mom was trying to set me up with Landon, and I couldn't take it."

"I know that. Why did you kiss *me*?"

"It made sense," she says, shrugging. "We've been close for years. Everyone asks all the time if we're together even though that would be absurd."

She laughs as she says it, and it stings, knowing the thought of actually dating me is a joke to her. When I don't join in her laughter, she stops abruptly.

"Look, Rhys, it's no big deal. I saw you across the lawn and said it without thinking. I'm sorry. I know it puts you in an awkward position, having to pretend to feel that way about me."

If she only knew how wrong she was.

"No big deal." I attempt a smile, but I'm sure it looks like a grimace because she gives me an odd look like she's not sure what to say next.

When she does finally speak, she seems less confident than a moment ago.

"So...that kiss was, um..." She lets her words trail off, and I'm left guessing what comes next.

That kiss was great? A revelation? A mistake?

"Anyway..." She's as flustered by this as I am, clearly. Which is good, I think. It means that whatever changed between us—and something most definitely did change—it wasn't only on my end of things. The only problem is, I don't know if what she says next will be along the lines of "I'm so glad we finally kissed" or "I don't think we can be friends anymore."

"It didn't mean anything," I say, cutting her off, too scared to face what she was actually going to say. I am a fucking liar, but I don't want to lose Jaclyn's friendship over this.

Jaclyn's eyes widen at my statement, and I wonder for the briefest moment if I've said the wrong thing.

"Of course it didn't mean anything!" Her voice is overly cheery, which is unsettling. Cheery isn't a word I'd use to describe Jaclyn. "But, uh, here's the thing. I think we should keep it up."

Now it's my turn for widened eyes because those are words I never thought I'd hear.

"The pretend dating, that is, not the kissing," she adds.

"Yes." I say it too quickly, too eagerly.

"Yes? Wow, ok. I thought it would take more convincing. I had a whole speech prepared."

I rub my hand through my hair to the back of my head. "Oh, uh, that is...I want to help you out...with your mum."

I can't interpret the look she's giving me. It's somewhere between bewilderment and desire, which doesn't make sense because she said the kiss meant nothing.

"Right, of course. Helping with Mom and her weird obsession with seeing me romantically entangled."

"So what did you have in mind?"

"Well, I talked to Kylie and Evie this morning, and they think acting like we're dating is the perfect solution. We already spend a ton of time together, after all."

"Kylie and Evie think we should do this? Both of them?"

"Well, Evie more than Kylie. She has this idea that you and I might..." She stops suddenly. "Never mind about that. The point is, Mom has been relentless in setting me up, and I need a reprieve."

I let out a slow breath, taking a moment to think through what pretending to date Jaclyn would actually entail. "What do you have in mind?"

Jaclyn lays out her plan. We'll go to a few functions around town together. Places where her mum or her mum's vast network of spies—Jaclyn's words, not mine—are likely to be. Honestly, it doesn't sound much different from what we've been doing as friends.

"Of course, we'll need to do more than be seen together. We might have to...um...kiss again. In public. Nothing more than light pecks on the cheek or the lips." Jaclyn's face blooms into a rosy color I've never seen on her before, and I look away before I can imprint the image on my mind.

"That's alright." I sound surprisingly calm, considering that the thought of kissing Jaclyn again sends my heart rate rocketing. Neither of us says anything, and after an awkward beat, I change the subject. "Do we have an end game?"

"An end game?"

"Like a date when we end the charade. When we..." I don't know why it's so hard to say it. Maybe because there's a part of me that hopes...I shut down that line of thinking before I turn sappy.

"You mean when we 'break up'?" She uses her fingers to make air quotes.

"Yes, exactly. A deadline."

Jaclyn scrunches her lips together, pensive. "A month? That seems like enough time to convince her that this is real, and then I can pretend to be too heartbroken to consider dating for a while."

"A month." I nod. A month of permission to kiss Jaclyn in public? I can handle it. I think.

"Great. I'll add a reminder to my phone so that we can start planning our 'dates.'"

I chuckle at that. Jaclyn lives and dies by what's in her phone's calendar. She always says that if it's not in her phone, it doesn't exist.

She clearly doesn't appreciate my amusement, because she tips her head toward me with her eyebrows raised.

"You, too. I don't want to set up all these dates and then find out you have soccer practice or something when we're supposed to be holding hands."

"You know I don't have training right now," I say, but I open my calendar all the same. In the spring I play football with an adult rec league, but our tournament was a few weeks ago, which Jaclyn knows since she was at the final match.

"I don't know your entire schedule," she says in mock defensiveness.

It's a welcome return to our usual dynamic—the way we were before we kissed and made things strange between us.

I scan my calendar even though I know I don't have many plans for the next month. I still haven't reached out to any of those women on the app, despite finally figuring out which way to swipe. It's just as well, if I'm going to pretend to date Jaclyn. This town is too small for me to go out with someone else while I'm allegedly dating her.

One entry on the calendar jumps out at me—the Montgomery Therapy company picnic in a few weeks.

"Would you be willing to go to a work event with me?"

"That's a good idea. Andrew's aunt Tabitha will probably be there, right? Plus the more people in town who believe us, the better."

The reality that we're going to have to lie to a lot more people than only her mum hits me, and I mutter a curse under my breath.

"Is that...a problem?" Jaclyn asks, a worried expression crossing her face.

I force myself to shake my head. "No problem."

It is actually a big fucking problem.

Because I was ready to move on. Because I had found a way to get over her. Because I have no idea what pretending to date Jaclyn is going to do to me. I smile despite my discomfort and hope I'm not making a mistake.

CHAPTER 8

Jaclyn

The last time I remember being this nervous to join my mom at dinner, Heather and I had broken into the school to edit my report card before it came home to Mom. I had come home in tears one afternoon after seeing my latest science test grade. I was convinced that the grade would tank my GPA, making my dream of getting a full-ride scholarship to any college but Cooke University nothing but a pipe dream. Heather, ever the adventurer, hatched the plan to "fix" my grade. I may be older, but Heather was the one always getting us into trouble and out of it.

She was sure we could get into the school, change the grade in Mrs. Bradley's gradebook, and get out without anyone ever knowing. She was right about the actual breaking in and grade-doctoring, but she hadn't accounted for my total fear of being punished. When we sat down to dinner with Mom the next night, I burst into guilty tears.

To this day, I hate lying to Mom, although I'm less likely to cry about it now. Even so, the tingle of nerves threatens to cause a repeat of my high school mistakes as Rhys and I arrive at Mom's house.

"Are you alright?" he asks before we get out of the car. He must sense my anxiousness.

"Yeah, I just don't like lying to Mom."

"Don't think of it as lying. We're just having dinner with your mum like we've done dozens of times before."

But it's not like we've done before. Not really. Because before, whenever he's come over to dinner at Mom's house, it's been as a friend, not as a pretend boyfriend. The last time I had a boyfriend over here was in high school. The rules about how to behave when you're a high schooler bringing your boyfriend over for family dinner are totally different from the rules for doing the same as an adult. But I don't know what those rules are.

Even worse? Rhys is my *fake* boyfriend.

How am I supposed to convince my mother that we're in an actual relationship?

I take a deep breath and turn to Rhys right before he knocks on the front door.

"She's going to expect us to touch each other."

He pauses with his hand raised and slowly turns to look at me, eyebrows raised. I can tell he thinks I meant something much more salacious than I do.

"Not like that. Holding hands. Light touches. Hugs."

I try really hard not to shudder on that last word. Because hugging Rhys wouldn't be so bad, especially not if he smells as good tonight as he did at the wedding (he does). But hugging might be my least favorite form of intimate contact. He knows that, though, so he doesn't look offended at my involuntary reaction.

"Jaclyn." His voice is low, intimate, and he steps closer to me. For the space of a heartbeat, I think he's about to kiss me. When he doesn't, I'm surprised by the flash of disappointment that zips through me. "Just act like you normally act when we're here. I'll take care of the rest."

I am not prepared for the flicker of desire his authoritative tone ignites in me. I step in front of him and grab the door handle, knocking on the door frame as I enter the house. Beside me, I hear Rhys mutter, "No sense of privacy," and it's enough to make me laugh and loosen the emotional cocktail of nerves and heat that's swimming in the pit of my stomach.

"Mom?" I call as we step across the threshold.

"In the kitchen," she shouts.

The scent of basil and garlic wafts from the direction of her voice, and I can't help the grin that breaks out on my face. Helen Beckett has two super powers: selling houses and making the best spaghetti and meatballs this side of the Atlantic. It's my favorite dish, and I'm instantly transported back to days when she, Dad, Heather, and I would gather in the kitchen, assembly-line style, and add ingredients to the giant metal mixing bowl she always uses for making meatballs.

"It smells delicious in here," Rhys says as we round the corner from the living room to the kitchen. I almost jump as he gently slides his hand around my waist, but he gives my hip a light squeeze of assurance. I let out a breath, sending nervous energy out of my body.

"Is there anything I can do to help?" he continues.

Mom smiles and points toward the cabinet above the dishwasher. "Get the big bowls out of there, and I'll plate us each a starter portion."

Mom's "starter portions" are more like an entire box of spaghetti for each person. But I'm not complaining. I've never turned down a generous helping of her cooking.

Once we have our bowls, we make our way to the dining room. Mom sits in her usual spot at the head of the table, and I make for the chair I always occupied growing up. Rhys takes the seat next to me, which makes sense to keep up the ruse that we're "dating."

"Smells amazing, as always, Mom," I say, managing to sound like myself despite the awkwardness I'm feeling.

"Dig in, sweetheart. Rhys, you can pass the salad around."

Rhys complies, and we fill our salad plates with heaping piles of dark green kale tossed with Caesar dressing.

After that, I relax as we eat and talk and laugh, all thoughts of lying and pretending pushed to the side. Rhys was right. It's like any other dinner with Mom. I catch her up on the latest in the Ron saga—always a favorite topic of hers—and Mom fills us in on Heather's most recent phone call. She has a new job at a PR firm in Nashville.

"She says it's her dream job," Mom tells us, and she sounds like she believes Heather. I'm less convinced. Heather called her last three jobs her dream jobs, too. But it's good to hear what's going on with my sister. She and I don't talk much, although that's because our lives are busy in opposite directions, not because of any ill will between us.

Almost everything about the evening feels normal. Except that every now and then, Rhys sets his hand on the back of my chair or brushes his fingers against mine. It's so normal, in fact, that I'm unprepared for the curveball Mom throws as we clear the dinner dishes before dessert.

"So, Rhys, how are things going at your job? Larry treating you well?"

Rhys's hand pauses as he brings a spoonful of Mom's famous pineapple upside down cake toward his mouth. The question sounds innocuous, but I'm immediately on high alert. I warned Rhys about the possibility that he'd have to endure the most prying game of twenty questions he'd ever experience, but between Mom making my favorite meal and plying me with an excellent Cabernet Sauvingon, I didn't expect her to come out swinging. I should have, though. She's never been afraid of the tough conversations.

Rhys takes the question at face value, or at least appears to. Honestly, I can't tell if he's fazed by it. This man is so even keeled sometimes that he's hard to read, even for someone like me who's been close to him for years.

"Work's been good, yes. Larry's been a good boss."

It's not the kind of answer she wants, but she doesn't let it show. Rhys should know that Mom hates Larry Montgomery, and she's digging for dirt. She works hard to keep her hatred of him from becoming public knowledge. But Rhys has been around her enough that he has to have picked up on what kind of currency Helen Beckett wants. Gossip.

Mom has always used these little interrogations as a means of finding out juicy gossip from the people Heather and I have dated. Because the thing about living in a small town in Appalachia is that no matter who you date, somehow your mom knows their dad or their cousin or some other random relation. And when you're as well connected as my mom is, it's doubly important that you're careful who you date. Because Helen Beckett knows the dirty little secrets of every house in this town, thanks to her job. Like where the literal bodies are buried.

Not that Larry has literal bodies buried in his backyard. I think. Actually, I wouldn't be surprised if he does.

But what I do know is that Mom wants Rhys to unleash whatever bits of information he has on Larry, so when he gives the polite response, I'm worried that the evening is ruined. It shouldn't matter, but for some strange reason that I don't want to examine, it does.

I have nothing to worry about, though, because he follows up with, "But between you and me, lately his focus has been less on the office and more on inventorying his assets."

"Oh, do tell?" Mom leans in and rests her chin on the

backs of her fingers. Shockingly, Rhys mimics her movement, and I'm left blinking at the two of them as I listen to Rhys dish out succulent morsels of scandal.

"Well, you didn't hear it from me, but word at the office is that he and Joan are getting a divorce—for real this time—and he's having to split the company. They've been keeping everything quiet, but I suspect the news will be out soon enough."

My eyes widen in shock at the salaciousness of Rhys's tone and the sly smile he gives my mother, who is tittering at what has to be the biggest piece of local intelligence to hit Sapling Grove in years. Because even though everyone in town knows that Joan and Larry secretly hate each other, no one ever thought they'd actually divorce.

"I knew it! I knew when he came by the office and started asking about properties zoned for health care that something must be up with him and Joan."

That's the other thing about Mom and Larry's antipathy. I think it's all one-sided. She still works as his Realtor any time he has some piece of property he wants to buy, even though she can't stand the man. Sometimes I truly do not understand my mother.

"Are any of those properties ones that would be good for the community center?" I don't know what prompts me to ask. Mom and I haven't talked much about my hopes of opening the center. Not since she suggested reaching out to the one person I'd rather not have anything to do with.

Mom and Rhys both turn to me. The look of glee fades from Mom's face, and in its place is an expression that's hard to read. I mentally kick myself for shifting the mood so abruptly, but Rhys takes my hand below the table and gives it a reassuring squeeze.

"If you want to come by the office tomorrow and look at options, I'd be happy to help. You know the place on Elm Street just came on the market."

"Are you serious? That place would be perfect." The knot of anxiety unwinds in my chest, and I smile at my mom. It's the first time this evening I've felt like myself.

"Which place on Elm Street?" Rhys asks. I'm not sure why, but there's a little worry line between his eyes.

"The one on the corner that we always talk about." I've always loved that house, and for the kinds of services and classes the center will offer, it would be perfect. It's a gorgeous American Craftsman style house, one of the bigger ones in Sapling Grove.

"Oh, right." Rhys's expression is inscrutable, and I make a mental note to ask him later if something's wrong about that house.

"How is the fundraising going?" Mom asks, oblivious to whatever is plaguing Rhys's thoughts.

"Fundraising is going alright. I have a couple leads on some exciting possibilities, actually. I submitted an application to participate in that funding competition that the Sapling Grove Federal Savings Bank is hosting." I don't tell her that I learned about the event because of that awful date she set me up on with the loan officer.

"That's great, honey!" She beams at me as I pick up my glass to take a sip of my drink. "You let me know if you want me to make the call about that other option we talked about, too.”

The glass stops midway to my mouth, and I give my mom a tight smile.

Rhys notices my expression and raises his eyebrow in a question. “Other option?”

“It’s nothing,” I say, setting the glass down a little too hard.

“Oh fooey. It’s not nothing,” Mom says with a wave of her hand. “He’s offered to help, and I think you’d be crazy not to take him up on it.”

“Mom, could we not?” I can’t believe she brought him up. She knows how I feel about anything to do with the lowlife ostensibly known as my father.

“Honey, he only wants to help.”

“If Dad wanted to help, he should have stayed.” There’s a bite to my voice as anger flares through me.

Mom takes a deep breath while pinching the bridge of her nose, which I know is a sign that her patience is being tested. Instead of letting me have it, though, she pastes a smile on her face and turns to Rhys.

“I hope dinner was to your satisfaction.”

Rhys looks between Mom and me with a worried expression. I don’t think he’s ever seen the Beckett women get into a real fight before. But he’s a class-act and takes Mom’s cue to change the conversation.

“Absolutely delicious. Thank you for the invitation.”

Rhys’s extreme politeness breaks the tension between Mom and me, and the rest of the evening is full of pleasant, if surface-level, conversation. By the time we've finished dessert, I've mostly forgiven Mom for bringing up Dad and his pity money.

Outside, Rhys places his hand on my lower back as we walk to the car. He opens the car door for me before going to the driver's side and getting in. As we back down the driveway, neither of us says anything.

But in the quiet, the bizarre events of the evening play back through my mind. Everything about tonight was strange—from the small touches between Rhys and me to the way Mom brought up Dad in front of a guest. Although, from her perspective, I suppose he was there as more than a guest. I laugh to myself at the memory of Rhys and my mom swapping tidbits of juicy gossip.

"What was that, back there?" I ask, breaking the silence between us. At Rhys's puzzled look, I continue, "Your little gossip session. Since when do you dish like a little old lady?"

Rhys's laugh fills the car and reverberates through me, knocking the last of my tension over my dad away, at least for the moment.

"I know how to 'dish like a little old lady,' as you call it, because my Nan had a weekly book club of women in their seventies that met in our parlor growing up, and Rupert and I were responsible for keeping their teacups filled." He smiles at the memory.

It's a side of him I don't see often, because he rarely talks about his life before he came to the U.S. It makes me want to ask him more about his childhood, about why he left, but he usually shuts down the conversation when we venture that direction. I'm about to ask him to tell me more, when he changes the subject.

"Can I ask about the money thing?"

"I'd rather you didn't." My response is terse, that tension from earlier back in full force. It doesn't seem to bother Rhys, though. He grunts his "Fair enough; I'll leave it alone" grunt, and neither of us says anything more until we've parked in front of my condo.

I reach to unbuckle my seat belt, but Rhys puts his hand on my arm. For reasons I do not wish to acknowledge, my heart stutters at his touch, and I flash back briefly to the wedding and the kiss that started this ruse.

"If you ever want to talk about it..."

I blink at him, all memory of what we were discussing gone the moment his hand wrapped gently around my arm.

"About the money from your father?"

"Oh. Yes. Of course," I manage to say.

He gives my arm an affectionate squeeze before letting go. He doesn't push me to say anything more, and it's that silent support that prompts me to let out a long breath and say, "He cheated on her. That's why they split up."

I expect him to say something, but he gives me the space to drive the conversation.

"It's why I don't talk to him. Why I don't want his money. Because that money comes with strings."

"What strings?"

"Letting him back into my life. I don't want that."

"That's understandable. Thank you for telling me."

My heart warms at his response. Rhys isn't pushy or

nosy when it comes to things like this. He listens and only offers solutions when specifically asked for them. It's part of what makes our friendship so strong. Unlike Evie and Kylie, who always want to solve my problems for me, Rhys lets me vent without judging me for my asshole tendencies.

I put my hand on the door handle to get out of the car but stop for a second and turn back to Rhys. There's a glimmer of something in his expression that makes me wonder if he's thinking the same thing I am. That we should kiss again before I get out of his car. I shake the sensation off, my mind clearly addled by the events of the night.

I wish him a good night, then make my way to the door. Inside, I let my shoulders sag as I take a deep breath. And if for a second I feel a twinge of regret that he didn't follow me in—well, that's only because tonight was stressful. At least that's what I tell myself as I change into my pajamas and climb into bed alone.

CHAPTER 9

Rhys

Over the next week, Jaclyn and I find as many opportunities as we can to be seen around Sapling Grove. She keeps saying it's so that we can spread the word as far as possible that "Helen Beckett's daughter is officially off the market." We've mainly done the same kinds of things we do as friends—go to local breweries for tastings, visit the independent bookstore downtown, sit on her back porch and debrief our "dates."

The difference is that our hands keep finding each other. There's a physicality to our time together that wasn't there before. Even when we sit on her porch, our usual setup has changed. Now, instead of her on the swing and me on the chair across from her, we both sit on the swing. We didn't discuss it or plan it. It just happened.

We met up at her place the night after dinner with her mum, and it seemed natural that we would sit together. I think she was still reeling from the strangeness of that night. We didn't touch, but the possibility was there.

I've been trying to temper my excitement every time Jaclyn's fingers brush mine or she lets me slip my arm around her waist. Because as much as I want to enjoy this new aspect to our relationship, I know it's temporary. Not only that, but time feels like it's sped up since we decided to pretend we're dating. It won't be long before we "break up" and have to stop doing all these things that are coming naturally for me.

I push aside thoughts of what happens after the proverbial clock strikes midnight and focus instead on preparing for our latest attempt at convincing the town that we are a couple.

We're meeting at a pizza restaurant that recently opened downtown next to the ice cream shop. The place is tiny. There's hardly enough room for the six tables inside, but there's a garage-style door that opens on a small patio with a few more tables. The scent of fresh baked pizza wafts from the open door, and my stomach grumbles at the enticing smell.

Because the place is so small, it doesn't take me long to surmise that Jaclyn hasn't arrived yet, so I linger on the sidewalk while I wait for her. After a few minutes, my phone buzzes with a message.

JACLYN: Running late! Order what you want. I'll eat whatever.

I join the line to the counter and peruse the menu, settling on a sweet and spicy pepperoni pizza that I know Jaclyn will love, plus an order of breadsticks with a variety of dipping sauces. As I finish ordering, a couple vacates one of the tables on the patio, and I waste no time claiming the open spot.

While I wait for her, my mind wanders back to dinner with her mum. It was our first real test of this scheme, and while I was concerned that we wouldn't be convincing, I was more worried about how Jaclyn would handle things than I was about myself. Not because of any flaw in her but because I didn't have to pretend I wanted to put my hands on her.

The only thing that threatened to ruin that night was when her mum brought up her father. Jaclyn's relationship with her father is one area of her life that she's never shared with me, and while I don't feel I have the right to be upset about it, it still stings knowing there are parts of her that she's not comfortable discussing with me. It's the kind of thing a real romantic partner would know about, which is a good reminder that as much as I'm enjoying the physical parts of what we're doing, at our core, we're still just friends.

I don't dwell on my disappointment for long because Jaclyn arrives soon after I take my seat. The sight of her walking toward me in the glow of the evening light takes my breath away. She's dressed in brown trousers with a sharp crease down the legs and a dark green top that hugs her chest in a way that makes my mouth go dry. The neckline is wide enough that I can see my favorite little freckle at the top curve of her chest. She looks so neatly dressed that I want to muss her up a little, run my finger over that freckle and see if it makes her shiver.

Intellectually, I know her outfit choice is because she wants the people who see us to think we're on a date, but there's a part of me that hopes she had me in mind when she picked something in my favorite color.

"What are you looking at?" she asks as she sits next to me. Our table is in the corner of the fenced area with the two chairs positioned so they look out over the river that flows through downtown Sapling Grove. It's a bit more intimate a set up than I'd have picked for a friendly night out. But for a date—even a pretend one—it's perfect.

"You look incredible." Her cheeks color at my honest statement, and the urge to lean across the arm of my chair and kiss her is too hard to resist. I reach for her hand and bring it to my lips. I maintain eye contact as I brush my lips against her knuckles, then give her a little wink to let her know it's part of the fake dating.

She visibly swallows, then clears her throat and looks away from me for a second. I worry I've gone too far and am about to apologize when she turns back toward me. She slides closer and plants a small kiss on my cheek.

"Good call," she whispers before scooting her chair a little away from mine. She inclines her head toward a woman walking toward us. "That's Mom's hair dresser. Exactly the kind of person we want seeing us be all...you know."

"Right. Of course." The memory that this is temporary dampens my mood slightly.

"How was work today?" she asks, as though everything is normal.

"Busy. I had back-to-back evaluations. This woman came in with..." I trail off as I notice Jaclyn's eyes going wide at something behind me. "Everything alright?"

"No, everything is not alright," she says.

I half turn to see what's happening behind me, but before I can fully pivot, Jaclyn hisses, "No, don't turn around! He'll notice us."

"Who will notice us?" I drop my voice to match hers.

"Daniel Sutton." At my blank expression, she adds, "The cake guy."

Understanding dawns, and I'm about to ask how I can help when Jaclyn picks up her chair and moves closer to me.

"Kiss me," she says, and before I fully know what's happening, her hands are on me, and she's planting her mouth against mine. It's awkward, not only because I wasn't expecting to be kissed, but also because I'm leaning uncomfortably over the chair. But after a moment, the frantic movements of the initial kiss die down, and we find a rhythm that is...not unpleasant. In fact, it's so far from unpleasant that I let out a sound not strictly appropriate for a public place.

"Jaclyn?" A voice near us brings the kiss to an abrupt halt. But neither of us turn to look at the owner of the voice for a moment. Instead, Jaclyn's eyes search mine, a question marking her expression. But she doesn't ask me anything.

She turns to the man standing on the other side of the fencing and pastes a false smile on her face.

"Daniel, how nice to see you again." From her inflection, it doesn't sound nice to see him at all. I haven't spent a tremendous amount of time with Jaclyn's mother, but I've heard her use this exact tone with people she doesn't care for. For my own safety, I suppress the urge to point out the similarities between mother and daughter.

"You, as well," Daniel says with the same sarcastic politeness.

"Meeting someone for pizza?" Jaclyn asks, looking around.

"No, I don't like pizza. Too much cheese."

Jaclyn raises an eyebrow at that, and I don't blame her. There are few pleasures in life as good as a fresh, hot slice of pizza.

Daniel doesn't seem to notice our reactions and instead points to me. "Aren't you going to introduce us?"

"Sure, why not?" She points to Daniel. "Rhys, this is Daniel Sutton. He's a loan officer my mom knows."

Daniel reaches a hand toward me to shake, and I reluctantly take it as Jaclyn gestures toward me.

"This is Rhys. My..." She hesitates, and I can see the uncertainty on her face about what to call me. After too long a pause, she clears her throat and says, "Date. He's my date. For tonight. And other nights. We date each other now."

Daniel looks between the two of us, an eyebrow raised in question. I take Jaclyn's hand, making sure that Daniel sees the gesture.

"It's a new relationship," I say. "But one that's been a long time coming."

Jaclyn's gaze slides to mine, and I don't have to hide the sincerity of my words. As far as she's concerned, it's all part of the act. She squeezes my hand twice, slowly. Somehow I know it's her way of saying "thank you" for saving the conversation without blowing our cover.

Daniel either doesn't notice or doesn't care about the private moment Jaclyn and I are having and barrels on with the small talk. "And what do you do for work? Rich, is it?"

"It's Rhys. I'm a physical therapist."

"Ah. Excellent line of work. I have a friend who's a physical therapist. Couldn't hack it in med school, so he dropped out and did PT instead."

I smile tightly at the insinuation that my profession, which also requires a doctoral degree, is a fall-back. "Good for him."

A tense silence engulfs our little corner of the patio. I have no desire to advance the conversation, and judging from the pinched look on Jaclyn's face, she doesn't either. Daniel seems like he's trying to get her attention for some kind of side conversation, but she's not taking the bait. Luckily, someone in an apron with the pizza place's logo on it is walking toward our table with our food. Jaclyn notices the server's approach and uses the opportunity to cut our interaction with Daniel short.

"Well, it was so great to run into you again, Daniel, but I think our food is on its way."

He frowns and looks like he wants to make one last

attempt at pulling Jaclyn aside, but she fixes him with a stare that could eviscerate a man. I have never been more in awe of this woman than I am in this moment.

"Right. Well, bon appetite." Daniel mispronounces the French, and I can't decide if it's purposeful or not.

As our server places our food on the table, Daniel slinks off down the street. Once he's out of earshot, Jaclyn looks at me, and I cock an eyebrow.

"That was the guy your mum thought you should date?" I ask as I take a slice of pizza. I bite into it, and make a sound of satisfaction. The crust is that perfect texture between crispy and chewy, and the toppings have a decadence that only comes from using high quality ingredients.

"I have no idea what she was thinking. Well, except that he looks like Clark Kent." She sighs, and I have the sudden urge to run down the street and punch the man in the face. But with my luck that would probably make him look more ruggedly handsome.

Jaclyn narrows her eyes at me.

"What?"

Her lips twist into a playful smile. "Rhys, are you jealous?"

"What? No. What would I have to be jealous of?" I cross my arms and lean back in my chair.

"Oh my god. You're jealous." Her grin widens. "You're doing that thing you do when you lie."

"I don't do a 'thing' when I lie."

"Yes, you do. You cross your arms and scrunch your

face. There, exactly like that." She reaches toward me and gently presses against my eyebrows to smooth them out. My heart rate picks up, and I involuntarily close my eyes as her fingertips brush my cheek in a whisper of a touch. I want to grab her hand and make her stop, but I also want to feel her hands on my face like this forever.

I shift in my chair, and the movement snaps us out of this strange bubble of intimacy. I open my eyes as she pulls her hand back. She moves her chair away from mine a bit, and I clear my throat, desperately hoping that my face won't betray how arousing her touch was.

Jaclyn takes a big bite of pizza, and I wonder if she's trying to cover her own reaction to the intimacy of her hands on my face.

"Pizza's good," she says after she finishes the bite.

"Yeah."

We lapse into an awkward silence, both of us immersing ourselves in enjoying our food. I wish I knew what she was thinking. If the direction of her thoughts mirrors mine. It's doubtful that they do, of course. Because the only real thought I've had for the past several minutes is imagining what she would say if I asked her to come back to my place when dinner is over. But when we finally decide to get a takeaway container for what remains of the food, I don't ask the question.

I assume we're going to go our separate ways for the evening, but as we pass the ice cream shop next door, Jaclyn grabs my hand and pulls me to a stop.

"Let's get ice cream," she says with a sparkle in her eyes.

She knows I can't resist a good dessert, and the ice cream shop is one of my favorite places in Sapling Grove.

"Yeah?" I try to keep my response aloof-sounding, but the corner of my mouth ticks up in a slight smile, betraying my pleasure at the thought of extending our evening and indulging in something sweet after the savory pizza.

"Yes." She squeezes my hand twice, the same way she did earlier. My heart skips a beat at the realization that she's created a physical code word for us. That a double hand squeeze is our little secret way of communicating.

The only problem is, I don't know for sure if it's part of the act or if it means that something between us is shifting. I don't dare ask her to clarify.

Pushing the whirring of my mind aside, I squeeze back, and we join the line to the ice cream counter with our hands still clasped.

The ice cream shop has been here for at least as long as I've lived in Sapling Grove. It's locally-owned, and they make their ice cream on-site. Their menu rotates weekly, so there's always something new and delicious to try. Tonight they have one of my favorite flavors—peanut butter S'mores. It's toasted marshmallow ice cream with swirls of peanut butter and chocolate and topped with bits of graham cracker.

Jaclyn orders a scoop of strawberry with black pepper, which I find an odd combination, but she swears the pepper takes the strawberry to a level of excellence otherwise unattainable.

With our ice cream in hand, we step back out onto the

sidewalk. The sun is setting, and the lamps in the park across the street are lit. For a moment, I'm transported back to the night of Andrew and Evie's wedding—the soft glow of the fading sunlight, the look of joy on Jaclyn's face.

"Want to wander through the park while we eat our ice cream?" she asks, bringing me back to the present.

"I would like that."

We cross the street and deposit the takeaway box in her car then head for the walking path that winds through the park to the covered bridge that sits above the river. Neither of us says anything for a long time, but it's not awkward like during dinner. This is a comfortable silence, the kind we usually fall into. The quiet of enjoying each others' company without feeling the pressure to talk.

We walk like that for a while. We finish our ice cream, and I take our empty bowls and toss them in a trashcan by one of the lamps that lines the path. When I turn around, Jaclyn is standing in the beam of light, and I notice a little smudge of ice cream at the corner of her mouth. Without thinking, I reach to wipe the spot with my thumb. She gasps in surprise but doesn't move back.

"Sorry, there's a little something..." My thumb grazes her lip, and my breathing shallows. She closes her eyes, and I realize her chest is moving in time with mine. The thud of my heart grows faster.

The next thing I know, I'm leaning closer to her. Our lips brush against each other, and she hums out my name. It's enough to make my brain catch up with the movement of my body, and I take a rapid step back.

"Sorry. I..."

Her eyes open, and there's confusion in them. Is she upset with me because I tried to kiss her? Or because I stopped?

I could lie. I could say I thought I saw her mum walking toward us. But I don't want to lie to Jaclyn about this. I take the coward's route and back further away from her.

"I should go." I start toward the parking area where I left my car, but Jaclyn's voice stops me before I've taken two steps.

"Rhys, wait. I need to say something."

I take a fortifying breath, prepared for the worst.

"I'm sorry I kissed you without your consent at dinner. I shouldn't have done that."

"It's alright. I..." I cut myself off. What was I about to say? *I liked it*. No. I mean, yes, but I don't need to tell her that.

She flushes, and dammit, it makes her even more attractive. She shakes her head. "It's not alright. Consent is important to me, and I violated your trust and—"

I take her hands in mine, and she looks up at me.

"It's alright," I say again. "In case you didn't notice, I figured out what was happening fairly quickly."

"That's good." She says it softly.

"I'm sorry about just now, too. I don't know what came over me." It's the truth, even if it's not the whole truth.

"No, it's ok. I, um, I figured you thought you saw my mom or something."

Is she listening to my thoughts?

"Honestly, we probably should, um, practice a little." She laughs nervously.

"Practice?" It doesn't even sound like a real word, more like a squeak and a breath.

"You know, in case we really do run into my mom and the opportunity, um, presents itself."

I take a step toward her. "Are you saying you want me to kiss you again? Right now?"

I can only hope that I'm following her logic correctly. But I don't have to hope for long, because she looks up into my eyes and dips her chin in a "yes" gesture. It's not good enough for me, though.

"I need to hear you say it. Because you're right. Consent is important."

"Ye—"

I cut off the end of her word with my mouth, the vibration of the "s" captured by my lips and zipping through my body.

CHAPTER 10

Jaclyn

I didn't mean to ask Rhys to kiss me tonight. I especially didn't mean to ask him to kiss me twice. But I'm having a hard time regretting it as my "yes" echoes through the small space between us and his lips find mine. Because something I didn't know about Rhys Blackwell until recently is that this man is a damn good kisser.

Even when I've surprised him, the awkwardness has faded quickly, and there's been nothing but pure, sensual skill on display.

But this time? When he knew it was coming?

Ho-ly fuck.

If I didn't know any better, I'd think he was into me. Because the way he's kissing me, like it's his sole purpose in life? I've never been kissed like this before.

The kiss starts out soft and sweet—worshipful, even. A graze of lips against lips. Gentle, tender strokes of his tongue, enough to send sparks through my body.

When I shift closer to him and my breasts brush his chest, his responding hum of pleasure makes my stomach swoop. His mouth leaves mine, and he kisses the spot right below my right ear, causing a sound to escape me that I don't think I've ever made before. I thought the kiss at the wedding was a world-tilting experience, but it has nothing on this.

Oh god, I wish this wasn't fake. The thought takes me out of the moment, and I step back, breath shallow as I gaze up at my best friend.

He looks bewildered, like he's coming out of a dream.

"I think that will be convincing," I breathe out.

"Convincing?" He says it like a question, and I wonder if maybe the kiss broke his brain.

"You know, if we have to kiss in front of my mom?"

He blinks as though he's just waking up.

"Yep. Yes. Right," he says finally.

"Unless you think we need more?" My voice is more sultry than I intend it to be, but as arousing as that kiss was, vocal modulation is the last thing on my mind.

"More?"

"Practice, that is." At his blank look, I backpedal. "Not that you need any more practice. Because that was...great. Excellent, even."

"But you want to do...more?"

"No!" My denial is too forceful, too obviously the

opposite of what I want. Except, he doesn't hitch his lips into a teasing smile, letting me know he's on to my bullshit. He stares at me, and I have no idea how to interpret the expression on his face. He's closed off in a way I've never seen before. Like he doesn't want me to know what he's thinking.

He clears his throat and looks at his watch. "Shit, it's later than I thought."

I check the time, too. It's only nine o'clock. I narrow my eyes at him. "Do you need to get home?"

"Yes. Home. To take care of the thing. That I have to do."

"Rhys, you're acting weird."

He lets out a long breath, while I stare him, puzzled. "Sorry, I, uh..."

An embarrassing thought occurs to me. One that would explain his strange reaction to me asking for more. "Was the kiss not good?"

"I...need to go." He turns and walks quickly away from me, leaving me staring after him with my mouth agape.

I stand there frozen to the spot for several minutes before I make my way home, my thoughts a whir of confusion and embarrassment. In the seconds before I stepped back, I could have sworn he was as wrapped up in the rhythm of the kiss as I was. But the way he blanched at my suggestion of continuing our "practice" stings, and I spend the rest of my evening second guessing what I thought was a sign of chemistry between us.

The ache of rejection follows me for the next several days. It creeps in when I least expect it. In the morning as I'm brushing my teeth. At lunch with my friends. During a meeting with my boss when I should be listening to him expound upon the latest enrollment projections for the sociology program.

It's still there the morning of Rhys's company picnic, an event I agreed to attend when I thought this fake dating thing was going to be a breeze. Turns out, realizing you want to make out with your best friend who is not interested puts a damper on things.

As a firm believer in canceled plans, I've tried thinking of a convincing excuse to skip, but the problem is that Tabitha Brandt, Andrew's aunt and one of Mom's best friends, works for Montgomery Therapy. If I ditch, there will be questions about why Rhys's "girlfriend" wasn't at the picnic. I don't need that information getting back to my mother.

Rhys arrives at my place promptly at the time he said he would pick me up, but I'm not ready to leave yet. Usually, he comes in and waits for me when that kind of thing happens, but today, he texts me and lets me know he's waiting in the car. It doesn't take a genius to figure out that the weird way we left things the other night is affecting our friendship. Honestly, I'm glad to have a few extra minutes to get my mind sorted before facing him.

I delay as long as I can, straightening things on the entry table that aren't really crooked before sighing and grabbing my keys and wallet. On the front porch, I distract myself by checking the mail, even though I know the mail is almost never delivered before three o'clock on Saturdays. Unfortunately, I can't think of any other ways to delay the inevitable—deciding to water the front yard when Rhys is waiting on me seems like a stretch.

When I get to the passenger side of his car, I fight the temptation to run back to the house and lock the door behind me.

I pull open the door of his sleek electric SUV and step up into the seat. He tilts his head in greeting but doesn't say anything. In any other situation, this would seem normal, but there's a tension to his movements that I usually only see when he meets new people.

We ride to the picnic in silence, and I hate it. I want to clear the air between us, but I don't know what I could possibly say. Admitting that I'd be down for a friends-with-benefits situation doesn't seem like the best move right now. Because I not sure what Rhys wants.

My opportunity to have it out with him before we have to face his coworkers has come and gone. We park, and the next thing I know we're standing in a food line with a surprising number of average-height women with brown hair.

It's always weird going to a function in a small town and realizing you don't know nearly as many people as you expected to. As I look around the group of gathered therapists, I'm shocked at how few faces seem familiar. But that doesn't mean they won't recognize Helen Beckett's daughter. Which means that regardless of the weirdness between Rhys and me, we have a show to put on.

With a steadying breath, I raise my head confidently and slide my hand into Rhys's free hand. He stiffens slightly at the contact, but doesn't drop my hand as we make our way with our plates of food to a shaded spot where a few people have set up lawn chairs. We take two of the empty seats, and I awkwardly balance my plate on my lap.

"Rhys! How are you?" We both turn at the question to see a woman standing behind us. She's shorter than me with a build that screams athletic—a runner maybe. Her hair is that rich brownish auburn like you see in shampoo commercials, at once natural-looking and completely unachievable without professional intervention.

In a word, she's gorgeous, and I tell myself the sharp stabbing feeling in my gut is because I'm hungry and not because I'm jealous that Rhys is smiling at her in a way that seems brighter than his usual gruff demeanor.

It makes me wonder if this is the kind of woman he would actually date if it weren't for my antics at the wedding. They would make a very cute couple. Unlike me, she's significantly shorter than him. With me, he only has to bend his head slightly to kiss me. With her, it would be a full-on head tilt and she'd still have to stand on the tips of her toes like one of those pint-sized heroines in the books Evie is always reading.

I shake that thought off, because *why am I thinking about kissing him again?*

"Sophie, this is Jaclyn," Rhys says. "My girlfriend."

I am not prepared for the feeling of warmth that overtakes me at those words. Because Rhys and I are friends, and I shouldn't have warm feelings about the way his smooth, deep voice sounds saying my name and the word "girlfriend" in the same breath. Especially not after he outright rejected the idea of kissing me ever again.

"It's nice to meet you," Sophie says, shaking my hand. She turns to Rhys. "I'm so sorry to pull you away, but would you mind helping me get my lawn chairs from my car? They're heavier than I expected."

Rhys looks at me as if to ask if it's alright with me, and I don't know what else to do but give my assent.

"Back in a few," he says to me, and I watch as he and Sophie walk toward the parking area.

It takes more effort than I care to admit to keep myself from following them and eavesdropping on their conversation. Not that I don't trust Rhys. It's just that I'm insatiably curious about whether he would rather be here with Sophie than pretending we're something we're not.

Not wanting to seem like a creep, I force my gaze away from the cluster of cars where they've disappeared. Instead, I turn to the man sitting across the circle of chairs from me and smile at him as warmly as I can manage.

"Name's Bob, by the way," he says. "Rhys is one of our favorite PTs at Montgomery."

I move my head in a vague polite gesture.

"And I'm Anne." The woman in the chair next to him stands up to shake my hand.

"So, how did you and Rhys meet?" Bob asks as I take a

bite of the smoked chicken leg from my pile of food.

I do the awkward thing where I try to chew as quickly as possible so that I can answer the question, and Bob laughs good-naturedly.

"Take your time!" he says.

"Through a mutual friend. We've been close for years," I say once I finish chewing.

"Always good to be friends with your significant other. The best kind of relationship, if you ask me." Bob is beaming at me.

I don't really know what to say to that, so I give him a half smile.

"How long have you been dating?" Anne asks.

"Oh, um." *Shit*.

As much as we've been out together these past few weeks, we haven't had to explain ourselves to anyone. Not after dinner with Mom, anyway. Even then, Mom didn't question us much, and I let myself forget that we needed a believable backstory. The simple question leaves me floundering. Fortunately, Rhys reappears as I'm about to make up a complete lie.

"Doesn't feel like long enough," he says as he sits in the chair next to me and takes my hand. He lifts my hand to his mouth and softly kisses my knuckles. I cannot help the flash of warmth in my cheeks at his gesture. He's a natural at this, pretending like he's besotted with me.

"Did you get your coworker's things settled?" I ask Rhys quietly. I don't examine why I emphasize that she's his coworker.

"All good." His voice is even, but something in his eyes doesn't seem like he's actually all good. It reignites my curiosity about his conversation with Sophie, and I surreptitiously try to find her in the crowd.

I'm not as sneaky as I'd hoped, though, because Rhys twines his fingers in mine and gives them a squeeze, drawing my attention back to him. He leans toward me, resting his forehead against mine, and I can only hope he can't hear the thundering of my heart in my chest.

"What's the matter?" he asks. I am vaguely aware that Bob and Anne are watching us, probably trying to hear what we're saying.

"Nothing," I lie. Whether I'm lying to him or to myself, I'm not sure.

"You don't need to worry about what this looks like. You're doing great."

"Thanks." The corners of my mouth tilt into a small smile, and I pull back slightly. But Rhys gives a slight tug on my hand, stopping me.

The kiss takes me by surprise. It doesn't last long, and his lips barely brush mine, but it's enough to leave me breathless and even more confused about where we stand. I'm too late to suppress the shiver that ripples through me, and Rhys clocks it, mischief sparkling in his eyes.

Oh god. He knows what I'm thinking.

Anne places a hand across her chest and gives us a wistful look. "Ah, young love," she says with a sigh.

I turn my attention back to the other people in our little circle, suddenly embarrassed by the overt display Rhys and

I have been putting on. Luckily, no one besides Anne is paying attention, so I smile at her and take up my fork to try some of the various salads on my plate.

We eat and chat, our conversations covering everything from the weather to yesterday's Sapling Grove Stingers game. Sapling Grove may be small, but we boast one of the most successful Minor League Baseball teams in the Blue Ridge Mountain League. It's your basic small talk gamut, and I'm perfectly content to keep everything surface level with Rhys's coworkers. Because the truth is, I don't need to get to know these people. Not when Rhys and I are only "dating" for a few more weeks.

A little while later, Larry Montgomery calls everyone to attention, and we all gather in the picnic shelter where the food is set up. I note that his wife Joan is standing off to the side giving him a pinched look.

"Thank you all for being here this afternoon. It's good to be together on a such beautiful day."

Most of the crowd nods their agreement, and a few people clap their hands.

"Every year at our annual picnic, we recognize our newest employees as a way of making them feel like part of this family."

I resist the urge to make a snide comment about the idea of a workplace as "family."

"I'd like to ask Landon Cunningham and Sophie Hyder to come on up here."

I jump at the mention of Landon's name. I forgot Mom told me that he was working here, and honestly, I'm not sure how I didn't see him before now. But he's here, in all his tall, blond, and chiseled glory. Standing next to Larry, they look almost like they *could* be family. They have the same shiny smile and sheen of superiority. I make a mental note to ask Mom if the Montgomerys and the Cunninghams are related—not uncommon in a place like Sapling Grove.

Sophie makes her way through the crowd to join the dude-bro twins, and when she turns around her eyes scan the crowd, landing on Rhys and me. We've been standing close, our hands entwined. But when Sophie's gaze catches his, he shifts his weight, dropping my hand and folding his arms across his chest.

My suspicions from earlier are back—that Rhys wishes he was here with someone else. Specifically with Sophie.

Larry blathers on about how glad he is to have two fine young people working for him and how much he hopes they feel like part of the family. He says "family" a disturbing number of times, actually. To the point that I start imagining him saying it in a Vin Diesel voice, which causes me to snicker at an inappropriate moment.

Rhys cuts me a look, but I snake my arm around his waist and whisper, "I don't have friends. I have family," in a terrible impression of Dominic Torretto. The effect is instantaneous. Rhys shakes with silent laughter, which makes me laugh. It doesn't help that every time Larry uses the word, Joan looks like she's taken a bite of something sour.

We do our best not to disturb the people around us, but every time the word comes up in Larry's speech, one of us sets the other off again. The worst moment is when Rhys pinches me to keep me from giggling, and I let out a little yelp. Larry looks right at us.

"Something you want to share, Doctor Blackwell?" The way he says "doctor," with the edge of a sneer, sobers me up. It also makes me want to ask him what his problem is, but Rhys and I have already caused enough trouble.

Rhys clears his throat, trying to regain his composure. "No, sir. My girlfriend thought there was a bee."

Larry narrows his eyes at Rhys but doesn't press him.

A flush of warmth slides through me at Rhys's use of the word "girlfriend" again, but it's quickly tempered by the reactions of the rest of the crowd. The murmur of people gossiping moves through the group, and the number of people we have to deceive in this dating scheme increases exponentially.

I notice Landon's suspicious glance between Rhys and me. Since he was witness to the first lie about our relationship, I'm not surprised he's skeptical.

Thankfully, the chatter about Rhys and me doesn't last long, because Larry calls everyone back to attention as someone wheels a cart with a giant cake to the middle of the shelter.

"Dessert is served," Larry says in a tone that suggests this is some kind of fancy affair and he didn't buy the biggest cake Gary's Food Mart has to offer.

Rhys, ever a dessert connoisseur, squeezes my hand before he zips to the front of the line, leaving me to stand awkwardly among his coworkers. For a second, it seems like he's abandoned me, but I quickly realize what his plan is. He snags two pieces of cake for us, then catches my eye and tilts his head like he wants me to follow him. I'm beyond ready to leave the party, so I'm relieved that instead of leading me back to the chairs where we ate our meal, Rhys turns toward the parking area. He waits for me to catch up, and when I reach him, I link arms with him in case anyone is watching.

"I hope it's alright with you if we skip the rest of the picnic," he says as we make our way through the crowd.

"More than alright. It's harder than I thought, answering questions about our 'relationship.'"

Rhys lets out a long breath. "Agreed. I'm sorry. We should have prepared better."

"It's not your fault. I made things weird the other night."

"No. It wasn't weird for me." He practically cuts me off, and I stop suddenly and blink at him in surprise. He nearly drops the cake at my abrupt stop but manages to hold on to both plates.

"Oh." It's all I can say. Does that mean he enjoyed it? But if he enjoyed it, why did he leave so suddenly?

I open my mouth to ask him at the same moment he says, "Jaclyn, I have something I need to—"

"You're not staying for the fireworks?" Larry's voice startles us. We're not far from where he's standing with a small group of other therapists, and he must have seen us moving toward the parking area.

"No, we have somewhere we need to be," Rhys says. This is the first I'm hearing about other plans for the day, but I'm smart enough not to say that in front of the man who signs Rhys's paycheck. "Thanks for the lovely afternoon."

I consider taking the opportunity to ask Larry about supporting the community center project, but since I interrupted his "family" speech, it's probably not the best time.

"Thanks for coming. Have a nice evening!" Larry calls back.

We say goodbye and continue our escape to the car. Once we're on the road, I expect Rhys to finish what he was saying before Larry interrupted us, but instead he glances over at me and smirks.

"I bet this cake is incredibly moi—"

"Rhys Blackwell, don't you dare." I shove his arm lightly—not enough to disrupt his driving—and he laughs. Just like that, we're back to ourselves, all the awkwardness of pretend relationships and practice kisses forgotten.

When we get back to my house, it's like old times. Without having to tell each other what the plan is, we walk through the house, stopping only to grab a couple of forks, then take up our places on the porch swing and enjoy our dessert and each other's company.

CHAPTER 11

Rhys

"I almost told her, Rupert. I almost told Jaclyn that I want this to be more than an act." I lean my head back against the top of my reading chair and let out a deep sigh.

"Why didn't you? Sounds to me like she's as into it as you are."

"Larry interrupted us, and then the moment was gone. I couldn't say anything after that."

"That's a bullshit excuse, and you know it." The video feed on our call may be slightly grainy, but I can still make out the skeptical expression on his face. When I don't respond, he says, "Ah, I see. You're afraid."

The sound I make is somewhere between a growl and a grunt, because he's right, damn him.

"Listen, Rhysie, I can't tell you what to do, but I can tell you that waiting around hoping she'll figure it out on her own isn't going to pay off."

"You're right," I reluctantly admit.

"'Course I am. That's what older brothers are for." He grins at me, and I make a rude hand gesture at him, which only makes him laugh.

"Enough about my sorry love life. What about you? How's Colin?"

His face breaks into a wistful smile, and a pang of jealousy stabs me in the chest. I should have known it was a mistake to ask him about his relationship. I'm glad my brother is happy, but it's another reminder that I've been miserable in love for a long time.

"Colin is great. Want to say hello to him?"

"Yeah, sure."

The video bounces a bit as Rupert makes his way through their flat, I assume to the sun room where Colin usually spends Sunday afternoons writing. Colin is a mystery writer. He's written a couple of popular series and has a sizable fan base.

"Col, Rhys is on the line," he says as he rounds the corner from their kitchen.

"Hullo Rhys!"

Rupert hands him the phone, and Colin's pale skin and bright red hair appear on my screen.

"Rhys is finally going to tell Jaclyn how he feels about her," my asshole of a brother says as he comes into the frame next to Colin.

Colin's eyes widen as he smiles. "Really? That's brilliant! Good for you!"

"No. That's not what I said at all."

"Maybe not, but I think it's what you should do. Especially now that she's kissed you so many times."

"She kissed you again? That's wonderful!" Despite his career writing gruesome murder stories, Colin is one of the most jovial people I've ever met.

"Like I told Rupert, it was practice. In case we have to kiss in front of her mum."

Colin blinks in confusion. "Why would you need to kiss in front of her mum?"

"Because..." I trail off, realizing that I don't have a good answer for him. I've been doing my best not to think about our "practice" kiss, because dwelling on that night will only lead to frustration, both of the mental and physical varieties.

"Because when you're pretending to be with someone you have to oversell it," Rupert says, pulling me back to the present. He may think he's being helpful, but he's not.

"Ru, don't tease him."

"Anyway, how's the book going, Colin?" Maybe my attempt at changing the subject will distract my annoyingly perceptive brother.

Colin's expression shifts from chastising my brother to one of delight. "Really well, actually. I'm up to sixty-thousand words."

"That's wonderful. Is this the one where Richard and Alex finally declare their feelings for each other?" Colin's current series is about two detective inspectors who solve crimes and have an extremely slow burn romance. If I didn't know any better, I would think he's based some of their longing on my situation with Jaclyn.

"You'll have to read it to find out. You know I never reveal major plot points before publication."

"Fair enough."

We chat for a while longer, and thankfully the conversation never comes back around to what I'm going to do about my feelings for Jaclyn. After we bid each other goodbye, I find myself wondering if Rupert and Colin are right that I should tell her how I feel.

It's true that most of the times we've kissed, it's been her initiating. Could that mean she feels the same way I do? I have no idea. I wish it were easy to tell what she's thinking, but she's always so guarded when it comes to her emotions.

I decide to take my brother's advice, and over the next few days I look for opportunities to start that conversation with Jaclyn. Ideally, we'd have another moment like the one at the picnic. One where she brings up the subject, and I can tell her that I want more than the occasional make out session in service of the lie we're telling her mother and this town. Unfortunately, the universe seems set on conspiring against us having that conversation.

I'm so busy at work the next several days that instead of calling or texting Jaclyn when I get home, I collapse on the sofa, exhaustion seeping through my body. There's been a rash of broken legs in Sapling Grove this month, probably because summer means an increase in daring and ill-advised activities, like jumping from the tops of waterfalls or make-shift zip lining. Between that and the regular knee surgeries and youth sports injuries, I'm up to my eyeballs in teaching people how to walk again.

I'm working with a patient on exactly that problem when Larry appears in the therapy gym one afternoon. Amelia is sixteen and broke her leg on a bad bounce off a trampoline. She's making good progress, and I hope to discharge her from therapy soon.

"Blackwell, stop by my office when you're finished with Miss Harrogate," he says with no preamble. I would be worried, but direct and to the point is Larry's style.

"Will do," I say, then turn back to Amelia. "A few more exercises, and we'll be out of here for the day."

"Sounds good, Dr. B!"

I wrap up the session with Amelia several minutes later and make my way to meet with Larry. His office is at the end of the hall past the tiny space that the rest of the therapists share. Unlike the pathetic excuse for an office that we use, Larry's office is spacious and airy with windows on the back wall. A trophy case full of sports memorabilia lines the wall to the right of his desk, and along the opposite wall are framed pictures of Larry with coaches and players from the local high schools and the Minor League team.

I rap my knuckles lightly on the open door, and Larry looks up from whatever he's been doing on his computer. He gestures to the chair opposite him, and I take my seat. It's not often I meet with the owner of the company, so I'm not sure what to expect from this conversation. As far as I know, there haven't been any issues with any of my patients.

"How did you enjoy the company picnic, Blackwell?"

The question sounds like small talk, but something in his tone makes the small hairs on the back of my neck prickle. Not in fear, but in warning that I'm not going to like what he has to say to me.

"Excellent, as always."

"Good, good." He tilts his head in a pensive look, like he's deliberating what tactic to take with his next statement. After a moment, he sighs and says, "I'll cut right to what I need from you. As you've probably heard, Joan and I are getting a divorce."

I nod, and for a moment, I wonder if my earlier apprehension was unfounded. If this is merely Larry unloading some of his burdens. That thought is cut short by the next thing he says.

"It's been a long time coming, and it's going to mean some big changes around here."

The phrase "big changes" immediately puts me on high alert. Is he telling me he's going to let people go?

"Look, I wouldn't normally do this, but when I saw you brought Jaclyn Beckett to the picnic, I thought of a way to minimize some of the damage that this divorce will bring."

I blink at him in confusion.

"Joan is getting the building in the divorce. Actually, it's already hers. Her family owns the property, and we've had a rent-free agreement with them for years. It means I'm in the market for a new space."

"I don't understand how Jaclyn and I fit into this."

Larry gives me a look like he can't believe I'm not keeping up, but I am truly flummoxed by what he's said.

"Influence, Blackwell. Influence."

At my bewildered expression, Larry continues, "I have my eye on a certain piece of property, but Helen Beckett keeps giving me the runaround when I ask her about it. She's been my Realtor for years, and we've never had an issue. But something must be special about this property, because there keep being 'reasons' we can't view it."

It feels like I've swallowed a stone. I'm certain I know exactly which property he's talking about, and it won't take any investigation to know why Helen has been cagey about him viewing it.

"There's this house on the corner of Elm Street. I don't care so much about the house, but the location would be prime for our practice. Right on the edge of downtown. A stone's throw from the high school. I could knock the old house down and build a proper facility."

"Wouldn't it be less expensive to keep the original structure?"

Larry waves a dismissive hand. "Once my divorce is finalized, that won't be a problem. Joan and I had a very agreeable pre-nup. Think about it, Blackwell. State of the art therapy gym. Maybe even a second gym so we could have more patients in at once. Real offices for the therapists to use."

His words feel calculated specifically to my complaints

about working here.

"What, exactly, are you asking me to do?"

He rubs his hands together like he's about to dig into a prime rib dinner. "Find out what's special about that house. Helen won't talk to me about it anymore, and I need to know why. Next time you're at dinner with your future mother-in-law, find a way to bring it up."

I force my face to remain impassive. Because I know exactly the reason Helen Beckett won't let Larry near that house, but he doesn't need to know that. I'm not about to get myself in the middle of a fight between my best friend and my boss.

"I don't know about that. I try to stay out of Helen's business."

He narrows his eyes at me. "This is company business, son. It's in your best interest."

I don't like the tone of his voice or the false look of the smile on his face.

"Best interest or not, find someone else," I say as I stand. I'm not going to sit here and let Larry manipulate me.

"There is no one else. Tabitha Brandt is surprisingly tight lipped about it, even though I know she's friends with Helen."

"I have a patient to see," I say. I move toward the door, ready for this conversation to be over.

"Let me know what you find out," Larry shouts after me.

I roll my eyes as I walk to the reception area to collect my next patient—another teen with a broken leg, this one from a car accident. I go through the motions of treatment with him and my last two patients for the day. I'm distracted with thoughts of telling Jaclyn how I feel combined with how to deal with Larry trying to get me to spy on Helen. But I need to figure out how to balance those two things, because tonight Jaclyn and I have another date, and all her friends will be there.

CHAPTER 12

Jaclyn

I expect the ax throwing place to be mostly full of big burly men with ZZ Top-esque beards drinking Natty Light while they complain about the government or women or, I don't know, lawn mower repair. But I couldn't have been more wrong.

Instead of stepping into what I assumed would be a dirty, backwoods bar environment, this place is clean and cozy. The bar along the back wall is topped with a natural-edge counter that gleams in the soft lighting from the Edison-style bulbs hanging from the ceiling. The booths and tables look like they're made from similar wood slabs, giving the place a rustic, barn-like feel. It's certainly not upscale, but it's neither dingy nor neglected.

I was skeptical of checking this place out. It's on the state highway, outside the city limits, in an area with little else besides cow pastures and a Dollar General. Definitely not the kind of place I would normally choose to get together with my friends. But I have it on good authority that Landon has been spotted hanging out here. He mentioned the place to my mother the last time they ran into each other at Gary's Food Mart. After the way he seemed to scrutinize us at the Montgomery Therapy picnic, I suggested Rhys and I go on a "date" where we were likely to see Landon. That way we could quell any potential rumors about our relationship status that might upset the plan to keep my mother off my back about dating.

It's not only the decor that's giving those cozy vibes. The people in this place aren't who I expected, either. Instead of being packed with groups of walking toxic masculinity, there's a wide slice of the Sapling Grove demographic pie here. In fact, I recognize a few people from my volunteer work and wave hello to them as Rhys and I make our way to our ax throwing lane.

One person is notably not here, though. I scan the crowd looking for Landon, but there's no sign of him. I'm slightly disappointed because I was looking forward to showing off how couple-y Rhys and I can be. It's why we agreed to meet at his place and drive together instead of showing up separately.

My disappointment doesn't last long, because across the room, someone shouts my name, and I turn to see Kylie, Evie, and Andrew walking toward us. Inviting my friends was an attempt to take some of the pressure off Rhys and myself. Make it seem less like a "date" with the way the lines between what's real and what's pretend with Rhys have been blurring for me. I need a little bit of normalcy tonight.

Evie is the first to get to us, and she immediately hugs us both. I allow it, because I know it's her way of expressing excitement.

"How was the Lake District?" I ask. She and Andrew returned from their trip a few days ago.

"Absolutely divine!" She beams at me, then turns to Rhys and asks with a wistful sigh, "How did you leave England?"

"Turned left at Greenland," he says in a serious tone, but there's a cheeky quirk of his lips.

Evie's laugh fills the room, and a few heads turn toward our group.

"The real answer is that I came to the States for university and fell in love." For a second, his eyes flick toward me, but it's so brief that I wonder if I imagined it.

"I get that. Sapling Grove does have its charms," Evie says. Like Rhys, Evie is a transplant to Sapling Grove.

"Glad to know I'm one of its charms," Andrew says, draping his arm across his wife's shoulders.

Evie playfully rolls her eyes but doesn't argue with him.

"And how are things with you two?" Evie's eyebrows lift conspiratorially. I know what she's trying to insinuate, but I refuse to take her bait.

"Everything's peachy."

She gives me a skeptical look, but Kylie intervenes. For once, I don't mind her taking control of the situation.

"I'm ready to throw some axes. I'll go find our

instructor." She walks toward the service counter and returns moments later with the instructor who is carrying a clipboard.

The instructor passes us the clipboard, which holds a stack of waivers that we have to sign, then she goes over the safety rules and the basics of throwing. She demonstrates the best techniques and then gives each of us a turn throwing at the target. She giggles a little when Rhys asks her to show him the hand motion again. When she takes his hand and guides his arm in the proper motion, a surge of jealousy runs through me. I have no idea where that came from, but something about seeing her hands on him makes my blood boil.

When she drops his hand, I position myself between them and put my hand possessively on Rhys's shoulder. He slides an arm around my waist and gives me a squeeze. I turn at the sound of whispers behind me and shoot a glare at Kylie and Evie, who are trying to look innocent. I can guess what they were saying to each other, though. Probably something about how my actions were more like an actual girlfriend's than a fake one's.

The instructor finishes her spiel about safety protocols and moves away from us. I don't mistake the frown she flashes toward Rhys and me as she bids us goodbye.

Once she's out of earshot, I step away from Rhys.

"Sorry, I thought I saw Landon," I lie.

"No problem."

The fact that he accepts the lie without question has me even more confused. We walked past all the other groups here tonight. Landon is clearly not here.

Did he not mind the way I was touching him?

I give myself an internal shake to clear the unwanted thought as I take a seat at one of the high top tables near our lane.

"Sorry I'm late!"

Our group turns as one toward the voice, which belongs to Sebastian Thacker, the new English professor at Cooke. He grins widely at us as he approaches. He's wearing a ridiculously thick cardigan for this time of year, and his reading glasses are hanging at a jaunty angle from his right ear. He reaches to shake everyone's hands as he joins the group, and there are ink stains on his fingers. If I were to guess, I'd say he was grading papers in the car.

"Who invited you?" Kylie asks with a glare when he gets to her. The goofy smile slides from Sebastian's face at her iciness.

"I did," Andrew says and shoots Kylie a pointed look.

"We thought it would be nice to get to know him a little," Evie adds.

Kylie clenches her jaw but doesn't say anything else.

"Thanks for the warm welcome," Sebastian says with a wry tilt of his lips.

"We're glad you came, Sebastian. It means we've got even numbers, so we can split into groups for throwing." Evie is ever the peacemaker.

"How about we divide into groups of three?" I jump in. From the look on Kylie's face, being paired off with Sebastian would probably end in someone losing a limb.

Most likely Sebastian.

"Sounds great! Men versus women?" Andrew asks, and the group agrees.

"How about a round of drinks on me?" Sebastian asks. When his question is met with enthusiasm, he walks toward the bar. Kylie stares after him with a mixture of annoyance and something else that almost looks like regret.

"What do you suppose that's about?" Rhys whispers. In the shuffle of Sebastian's arrival, he's moved closer to me again. It's something that's started happening more and more the longer we've been pretending to date. Like magnets that can't seem to stay apart.

"No idea. There's some sort of bad blood between them, but I don't know why. They only met a few months ago when he started working with us."

"I filled out the score card so that we can keep track of points," Evie says, putting an end to our side conversation. "Rhys, you're up first."

He stands and gives my arm a squeeze before making his way to the throwing lane. He picks up one of the axes from the table by the lane and weighs it in his hand like he's testing its heft. There's something sexy about the way he does it, a flex in his hand muscles that should not be as enticing as it is. I bite my lip as I watch him move into the throwing stance then lift the ax over his head in one smooth motion. His throw sticks in one of the outer rings of the target.

"Like what you see?"

I let out a squeak of surprise at the voice beside me.

"Jesus, Andrew." I elbow my friend in the ribs. He grins at me.

Rhys lines up another shot, and I tear my eyes away from him and face Andrew.

"I can admire a well-assembled man."

"I think we both know you were doing more than admiring. You were practically salivating, Jack."

"You are as annoying as your wife. You know that, right?"

Andrew's laugh lights up his face, and the woman in question looks over from where she and Kylie have been chatting. Andrew gives her a wink, and she blows a kiss back at him.

"Ugh. You two are so gross."

"Yeah, I know. I wouldn't have it any other way." He says it with a sentimental sigh.

A twinge of something—surely not jealousy for what he and Evie have—pricks at my chest, and I look away from my friends who are so clearly in love. My eyes drift toward Rhys again, and I take the opportunity to continue admiring Rhys's athleticism. He's not one of those big, beefy arm muscles kind of men. Instead, there's a leanness to him. Strong but not ostentatious. Even though he hasn't played in anything more than a recreational league in years, he still has the build of a highly-trained soccer player.

"So what's really going on with you two?" Andrew asks, pulling me from my thoughts.

"Nothing." I deny it too quickly. Andrew raises an eyebrow, but I keep talking. "We're just trying to keep my mom from pushing me to date anyone else for a while."

It feels like a lie. I don't know when things shifted from lying to my mom to lying to myself, but I'm not about to tell Andrew that.

"Jack, you don't have to lie to me."

I glare at Andrew, because *how the hell did he read my thoughts?*

"It's all over your face every time you look at him."

"I don't know what you're talking about."

Andrew chuckles. "Sure you don't. Look, I know you've been hurt before, but I don't think Rhys is that guy. The way he looks at you? Landon never looked at you like that."

I bristle at the mention of my ex, but if anyone could draw a comparison between what Landon and I had and what's currently happening with Rhys, it's Andrew. He's known me longer than any of the rest of our friend group.

"It's not like that at all. Besides, we gave ourselves a deadline for when this whole thing is supposed to end. We've only got a few more 'dates' before we stage an epic break up, probably in front of my mom. I'll be too distraught to date anyone else for a while, and then Rhys and I will lay low until Mom gets the idea that I don't want or need her help with my dating life."

Andrew raises an eyebrow at my little speech. "You really think that's going to work, Jack? Seriously?"

I don't respond to Andrew because Rhys has finished his throwing round and is making his way to our table. Instead, I swallow back the weak assertion that was on the tip of my tongue. Andrew notices my disquiet and gives me a knowing look.

Curse him and our lifelong friendship.

Kylie is up next on Evie's scorecard, and she moves into the throwing lane as Sebastian returns with a pitcher of beer and six frosty glasses. Probably for the best that we keep those two separate when one of them is holding a weapon.

As Sebastian sets a glass in front of me, Rhys slides into the seat next to mine and drapes his arm along the back of my chair. I tense at the gesture, the conversation with Andrew swirling in my brain.

So much for treating tonight like a casual night out with friends.

Rhys must sense my unease because he removes his arm and reaches for the glass of beer that Sebastian has set in front of him.

"Thanks for inviting me out tonight," Sebastian says to Andrew. He takes the last seat at our table.

"No problem. Sorry about Kylie's frosty reception."

Sebastian laughs wryly. "It's alright. She's always been a tough nut to crack."

I raise an eyebrow at his use of the word "always." As though he's known her longer than the six months since he started at Cooke. I don't question him, though, because Andrew asks how he's adjusting to life in Sapling Grove before I have the chance.

"I love it here, and not only because Cooke had a full time job available. I'm so glad I could leave the adjunct life behind, but this town is also great. Exactly what I was looking for."

"I completely understand," Rhys says. "Moving to Sapling Grove was one of the best decisions I ever made."

His eyes find mine, and warmth blooms in my chest. It spreads to my cheeks and zaps the breath from my lungs. I clear my throat and break eye contact.

I tell myself it's all part of pretending. That the heat in his eyes was for show. Because Sebastian doesn't know that we're faking it, and the fewer people in on the secret, the less likely my mother will find out the truth.

Thankfully, Evie comes up to our table to announce that it's Andrew's turn to throw, giving me an excuse to turn my gaze away from Rhys.

Andrew does reasonably well, but Evie is the real surprise of the night. All of her axes stick in the target, tying the women's score with the men's. Sebastian also does well, and the men pull ahead.

"Alright, Jaclyn, we're down six points, so we need you to score at least seven," Evie says as I take my place at the throwing line.

I take a couple practice throws to get the feel of the ax in my hands and see how hard I need to fling it so that it will stick. The first throw bounces, but the second one stays in the target. I roll my shoulders back and take my first real throw. It lands in the outer circle and stays in place.

"That's one!" Evie calls.

My next throw bounces, but I have three more axes to throw. The third one lands solidly in the second ring, meaning I've scored another three points. When the fourth ax sticks in the outer circle in almost the same spot the first one did, Evie and Kylie let out a whoop of excitement. As long as the last ax sticks, we'll win.

I take a deep breath and step up to the line. I glance over my shoulder at my friends and give them a saucy smile. Rhys catches my eye and mouths, "You've got this."

That heat from earlier is back, coursing through my veins, making me question whether there's more to what's going on between us than I'm ready to admit to myself. I shake off the feeling, focusing instead on using the same throwing technique that scored my previous points.

The ax flies through the air, the handle spinning over the blade multiple times. I close my eyes as the ax nears the target, afraid I've thrown it wrong and that it will bounce. But the sound of a blade sticking in the wood, and the eruption of cheers from my friends makes me open my eyes. The blade is halfway between the inner circle and the middle circle, more than enough points for the women to win our competition.

Evie and Kylie rush forward and high-five me as they cheer. Andrew and Sebastian hang back, raising their glasses in concession. In the midst of Evie and Kylie's celebration, I see Rhys making his way toward me. My friends make room for him, and as he approaches, he slides his hands around my waist, pulling me to him. His lips find mine in a congratulatory kiss, and it feels so natural, it makes me want to forget that none of this is real.

CHAPTER 13

Rhys

The energy in the car on the drive back from the ax throwing place to my house is loud and buoyant. Jaclyn turns on the radio and sings along with the songs on the classic rock station at the top of her lungs. We pull into the parking area for my townhouse, and I turn off the car. The radio keeps playing for a moment, but I press the button to silence it as Jaclyn belts out the chorus of The Doors' "Light My Fire."

The sound of her voice reverberates through the car, and her eyes shine as she grins at me. There's something in her expression, like she's daring me to do what the lyrics say—to set tonight on fire—and for once I'm hopeful that the feelings I have for this woman aren't one-sided. Because I'm ready to move past pretending.

After her decisive final throw, the one that clinched the win for the women in our group, I marched right up to her and kissed her, and there was no hesitation on her part in kissing me back. It's a gamble I'm willing to take, to hope that was a signal that she wants to move our relationship from this half-truth to something more.

"Want to come in?" I ask, willing my voice not to shake with nerves.

"Sure." There's a bit of a question to her response, but it's not enough to make me lose my confidence.

As we walk toward the door, we fall into step with each other. My hand finds hers, and she doesn't pull away. I squeeze her hand twice, the way we've been doing lately, and she stops abruptly. When I turn to look at her, she doesn't say anything but blinks back at me with her mouth slightly open. She takes a deep breath, and I wonder if she feels it—the shift in the way we are with each other.

She doesn't drop my hand as she resumes walking, and in fact, she moves closer to me, tucking herself into my side with our arms twining around each other. I'm certain she can feel my pulse, the way it's galloping through my veins.

The walk to the front door is too short. I want to stay like this forever, with Jaclyn clinging to me like we're a real couple. But before I can savor the moment, we're at the front door, and our hands untangle so I can unlock my flat and turn on the entryway light.

We step inside, and she slips off her shoes and puts them on the mat I keep by the entrance while I close the door behind us. It shouldn't make my heart rate kick up the way it does—she's been here many times before—but it means she plans to stay a while.

I deposit my shoes on the mat next to hers, and it looks right for both pairs to sit there together. Like they belong with one another.

We make our way into the living room, neither of us saying anything. For my part, I don't want to screw this up by breaking the silence too soon. I can only imagine what's preventing Jaclyn from speaking, but I hope it's because she feels it, too. The possibility and anticipation that what we're doing tonight is the right move.

"I had fun tonight," she says, turning toward me.

We're standing close together, as though we have a tacit agreement that we need to be within touching distance of each other. I want to reach out my hand and touch her cheek, to tuck a strand of her hair behind her ear.

"I had fun, too." I avert my eyes from hers, afraid that even that small admission will reveal more than I'm ready to tell her.

"You looked amazing every time you threw an ax tonight," she says suddenly. "It kind of...turned me on."

At that my gaze shoots back up to hers, unsure if I'm imagining things. I open my mouth to say something, but nothing comes out. No matter. Jaclyn is speaking again, and I make myself listen so that I'm sure this time I'm hearing her correctly.

"You've been doing that a lot lately. Turning me on, and I..." She trails off, but I don't dare interrupt her.

She steps away from me, as though standing too close

will make it easier to say whatever it is she needs to say. With her back toward me, she starts again.

"I haven't...had sex in a while. Months, really. And every time we've kissed, it's seemed like you're as into it as I am. So what if..."

I'm certain she can hear the deep thumping of my heart as I wait for her to finish her sentence. She surprises me by turning around and facing me again, looking me in the eyes as though making sure I understand what it is she's saying.

"What if we dealt with that? With the fact that it seems like maybe we'd both benefit from a night where we weren't pretending we're not into whatever this is." She gestures between us.

I stare at her, not daring to breathe. Because I can't believe my ears. Jaclyn Beckett just invited me to unleash the desire I've had for her for the past four years. I would be a fool to say no.

She shakes her head suddenly. "Forget I said that."

She's embarrassed. I let too many seconds tick by, and she must think I don't want this. I rush to correct that assumption.

"No, I won't forget. Because I don't want to pretend either."

"Oh. That's...that's good."

"It's also been a while for me, and to be totally honest, you've been turning me on, too." I step closer to her, sliding my hands around her waist. Her breathing shallows, and she sinks her teeth into her lower lip in a move so sensual I have to hold back a groan of desire. I bend my head toward her, ready to take her mouth with mine.

"It doesn't mean we're a real couple," she says, and it stops me in my tracks. At the confusion on my face, she adds, "I mean, I assume we're both sexually frustrated right now, so this will be good for us. Get it out of our systems."

"Right. Of course."

"It doesn't have to mean forever. It can be just for tonight."

Just for tonight.

I'm sure she thinks she's giving me an out, but I don't want one night. I want them all. But I can't tell her that. Not now. Because I don't want her to shut this down. Maybe that's selfish. Or maybe it's practical. I don't know.

What I do know is that the possibility of kissing Jaclyn tonight, without the pressure of pretending I don't want her, is slipping away the longer I wait to respond to her invitation. It's not the way I hoped this evening would go, but she's right that sexual frustration is a constant state for me, especially since the kiss at the wedding.

Before she can change her mind, I slide my fingers into her hair and gently guide her face to mine.

"Is this what you want?" I ask.

"Yes, please." Her lips brush mine as she speaks, and then she's kissing me.

It's tentative at first, as though we're unsure how this works when it's not for the purpose of feeding the lie of our relationship. But it quickly morphs into something more deliberate.

Heat and passion course through me, and I have the

urge to cover her body with mine. I guide her toward the sofa, and when the backs of her legs hit the cushion, she grabs my collar and pulls me down with her.

Then it's a matter of finding our rhythm, which doesn't take long because every time we've kissed, I've cataloged the things she likes. My lips on the spot below her ear. A firm squeeze of her ass. A gentle bite on her shoulder.

What's different this time is the way I feel free to explore the rest of her. This time, I collect the sounds she makes when my hand glides over her breast or tangles in her hair or tilts her head back to expose the place where her neck and shoulder meet—every moan and sigh and whimper of pleasure.

I finally take the opportunity to slide my finger over that freckle of hers, and I am not disappointed at the result. Her skin pebbles beneath my touch, and the resulting shiver has her body arching against mine.

She explores me, too—hands sliding under my shirt, kneading my back muscles. When she grips my ass, pulling my hips closer to hers, I can't help the contented groan that escapes me. She smiles against my lips.

"You like that?" Her voice is a husky whisper, and my only response is another groan of assent. She laughs wickedly and tugs on my hips again.

I slide against her in response, and the gasp she lets out at the friction between us sends another wave of heat through me.

"I would kiss you like this every night if I could," I say against her collarbone.

As soon as the words are out, the air around us shifts, and Jaclyn pulls back slightly. I push myself up, searching her face.

"What's wrong?" I ask, as though I don't already know that I've ruined the moment.

"It's nothing," she says. But she pushes herself up on her elbows, forcing me to move off her to the other end of the sofa.

"Do you want to stop?"

"Yes. No. I don't know." Her eyes have a panicked look to them. As much as I want to reach for her and soothe her fears about my accidental admission that I want more than one night, I don't want to make it worse.

"It's alright. We don't have to keep going," I say. Now I'm the one trying to give us a way out of this mess.

"I know, and I don't want you to think I wasn't enjoying this..."

"Until you needed to stop," I say, filling in the silence when she trails off. "So we'll stop."

"But what about..." She tilts her head toward my lap, where my reaction to everything we've been doing is painfully obvious.

"I'll be fine." I laugh wryly, rubbing my hands on my thighs. If she only knew how many times she had put me in this state with no chance of true relief.

"I'm sorry. I shouldn't have suggested this. Sleeping together would be..."

I can guess what she was going to say. That we were about to make a huge mistake.

"You're right." I can't deny that taking tonight any further would have irreversible repercussions for our friendship. For me if not for her.

Jaclyn yawns, and I glance at the clock on the wall behind her. She turns to look at it, too.

"It's late. I should probably get home." She gives me a timid smile as she stands. "This was nice, even if it wasn't the right thing for us."

Her words split my heart in two.

Absurdly, my gut reaction is to tell her. About how I went out tonight with this amazing woman, and we made out on my sofa but then she told me it "wasn't the right thing for us." About how she broke my heart. About how I want to start the night over. To tell her that I'm in this for real.

Because telling each other our deepest wants and thoughts is what we've always done. Except the one want that I've kept from her for four years.

"What if it was the right thing?" At her intake of breath, I stand and face her.

"What are you saying?" Her voice is breathy, and I can't decide if that's a good thing or a bad thing.

"Come to bed with me." I reach toward her, offering my hand.

But she doesn't take it. Instead, she stares at it as though it's a snake that might bite her.

"Why?"

"Because I want this, and I think you do, too." I swallow. "Just for tonight, right?"

"I'm sorry. I need to go," she says as she turns toward the front entry.

I start after her, but she grabs her shoes and slams the door behind her before I reach her. By the time I'm out the door, she's already in her car, and I'm left standing in the entryway watching her speed away.

CHAPTER 14

Rhys

The only thing worse than being rejected by the woman whose idea it was to give in to our growing physical relationship is having plans with that woman the following night that you can't get out of. But that is exactly the situation I find myself in the evening after Jaclyn sped away from my house because I couldn't keep my mouth shut about how much I wanted her.

Sunday nights are free general admission at the Sapling Grove Stingers baseball games, and Jaclyn insisted we needed to attend at least one game during our pretend relationship.

"When I was growing up, if you wanted to announce you were with someone, you went to a football game in the fall or a Stingers game in the summer," she told me. "Half the town will be there, and my mom will expect it."

So I agreed. But that was before she suggested we try getting our attraction out of our systems and left me frustrated in my living room.

This weekend wasn't the first time I've almost told Jaclyn how I feel about her, but it was certainly the most disastrous.

The first time was three years ago at Aiden's New Year's Eve party. Jaclyn and I hadn't been friends long, but we'd hung out a few times just the two of us. She hadn't been on any dates with other men in a few months, and I thought it was a sign that she felt the same way about us as I did. I'm a sucker for a romantic comedy. I grew up watching them with my Nan, and they've always held a certain fascination for me. I had grand plans about how I was going to have my "When Harry Met Sally" moment and pour my heart out to Jaclyn at midnight.

Like her mum, Jaclyn loves a good bit of gossip, so we made a game of finding the juiciest morsels of intel throughout the night and meeting up by Aiden's Christmas tree to swap stories. We spent the evening whispering secrets and jokes to each other.

As we approached midnight, I made my way to the tree, ready to share something better than the silly pieces of gossip that we'd been trading all night. I planned to kiss her when the clock struck twelve and tell her everything I loved about her.

But Jaclyn wasn't at the tree. As the countdown began, I searched the crowd for her, but there were so many people and the lights were so dim that it was hard to find her. To my dismay, I finally caught sight of her as the final seconds of the year ticked by. She was across the room, arms draped around a man who looked like he spent most of his free time at the gym.

It crushed me to watch her kiss that man, but the blow to my ego back then has nothing on the devastation of watching Jaclyn practically run from my house after I hinted at my true feelings for her.

Because back then, all I had was a gut feeling and an over-inflated sense of romanticism. But now? Now I'm certain there's something there, because Jaclyn only runs away when she feels vulnerable.

I arrive at the baseball field a few minutes before we planned to meet. With the way we left things last night, I'm not even sure she'll show up. I linger outside the entry gate while I wait for her.

She was right about half the town being here. The game doesn't start for another thirty minutes, but the parking area is already full. As new cars arrive, people are parking in the grass and along the sidewalk in ways that I'm certain can't be legal.

I watch as a car the same make and model as Jaclyn's whips around the corner and jerks to a halt on a narrow patch of grass. When the door opens and Jaclyn steps out, I shake my head even as an amused smile threatens to break across my lips.

"There's a reason I always insist on driving," I say as she approaches.

"I have no idea what you're talking about. I'm an excellent driver," she says.

"More like you drive like an extra in an action film," I tease.

Her laugh is sparkling, and it's nice for a moment to fall into a conversation that feels like our normal, friendly pattern. But thinking about our friendship makes my mind snap back to the way we left things last night. I stop, suddenly needing to make sure that everything between us is alright. That we'll be able to enjoy ourselves this evening instead of sitting in an awkward silence in the midst of the very people we're trying to convince that we're dating.

Jaclyn is two steps ahead of me, and she gives me a questioning look as she turns around.

"You coming?"

"Yes, sorry," I say, closing the distance between us.

She slides her hand into mine as though nothing is different than it was before we went ax throwing. I stop again, this time gently tugging on her hand so she stops, too.

"Actually, before we go in, could we talk for a second?"

She furrows her eyebrows, and I have the sense she knows what's coming but would rather avoid it. Even so, she nods, and I continue.

"Is everything alright? Between us?"

"Of course! Why wouldn't it be?" She has that cheery tone she gets when she's lying.

"You seemed..." I search for the right word. "Upset. By what happened last night."

"Rhys, come on. It was late, and I was tired. That's all."

"Don't do that. I was there. I remember what happened." I give her a pointed look, and she playfully rolls her eyes.

"You're acting like this is a much bigger deal than it was. So we didn't...you know. No big." She says it with a shrug, and my gut twists with dejection.

"You don't think it was a big deal that we almost..." I glance around us and lower my voice so that no one will overhear. "That we almost made love?"

"Well, if you're going to call it that, I'm glad we stopped when we did." Her tone is teasing, and it pisses me off.

"Forget it," I say and start toward the entrance.

"No. Rhys, wait." She grabs my arm. I want to shake off her grip and keep walking, but the remorseful sound of her voice stops me. "I'm sorry. You know I don't handle emotional stuff well. Last night just felt a little too real."

"I know," I say with a sigh. My exasperation evaporates as I survey her face. As much as I want to talk this out with her, now is not the time. Not only because we're standing in an ever-increasing crowd of people queued for the baseball game. But because she's not ready. If I push this too fast, I'm afraid she'll run again.

"Ready to watch watered-down cricket?" I ask, deliberately trying to make her laugh.

"You don't even like cricket." Her smile is genuine. She grabs my hand, and we join the throng of people making their way into the game.

In fact, I rather enjoy baseball. Aiden likes to organize group outings to the games, so Jaclyn and I have been to our fair share over the years. Aiden's dad is the grounds manager, so he gets discounted tickets. In fact, I wouldn't be surprised if Aiden is here tonight.

The stadium is no state-of-the-art sports complex. The three sections of stands are mismatched. Along the first base line is a tall section of concrete stands with a dubious-looking fence at the top, I assume to keep people from falling over the back of the stands. Behind home plate is a small reserved section with individual stadium seating. It is by far the nicest of the sections. The third base line hosts a set of metal bleachers that look like a strong wind could knock them over. Fortunately, Jaclyn's mum has season passes and offered us her seats in the reserved section.

We weave our way through the crowd, passing by the concession stand where a long queue is waiting for snacks and drinks. Next to the concession stand is a red and yellow striped food cart with the words "Hanson's Wieners" emblazoned across the front. The cart isn't usually here, but the restaurant must be sponsoring tonight's free general admission.

In fact, as I look around, I realize it's not the only local business with a setup in the concourse—although concourse is too strong a word for the concrete area on the back side of the first base stands.

"Did you know that all these businesses would be here?" I ask as we round the corner to the reserved seating.

"Yeah, that's why I wanted to come tonight specifically," Jaclyn says. "It's local business night. I have people I need to talk to about the community center."

If we were a real couple, I might be offended that she

decided to use our date to work, but all I feel right now is admiration. Jaclyn is the kind of woman who sees what she wants and finds a way to make it happen, and I love that about her. I wish I had the same confidence. If I did, maybe I would be here as her actual boyfriend instead of her fake one.

Thinking about this ruse we're in reminds me that part of why we are here is to convince as many people as possible that we're actually a couple. With that thought, I shift our hands so that our fingers tangle together.

As we're about to ascend the steps to the reserved seating, someone behind us says our names. We turn in tandem at the sound. Aiden is walking toward us, a ridiculous grin spread across his face. Jaclyn quickly drops my hand, and I don't blame her. Aiden will gloat if he thinks he had anything to do with setting us up. Even if what we're doing isn't real. But we can't tell him the truth about our "relationship." Aiden is the worst secret keeper I've ever met. I've never told him about my true feelings for Jaclyn because of it.

"I thought that was you," he says as he joins us. "What are you doing here tonight?"

"Hi, Aiden!" Jaclyn says. "It's been a while."

"How have you all been?" he asks with a knowing lift of his voice. It probably means he's already heard about us.

"Oh, you know. Same as always," Jaclyn says, and I'm grateful she's the one taking the lead.

"That's not what I hear." Aiden wiggles his eyebrows suggestively, and any hope I had that he might not know about our supposed relationship status is dashed.

Jaclyn grimaces in a way that suggests we've been caught.

"I knew it! I knew from day one that the two of you would end up together," Aiden says.

"You were right," I say. "I guess it took us both a while to see it."

Jaclyn glances at me, but I can't read her expression.

"I'm so happy for you both. I can't think of a couple who fits together more perfectly."

We chat with Aiden for a few more minutes, but then the public address announcer's voice comes through the speaker above us with the starting lineup.

"I'd better get back to my group," Aiden says, gesturing toward one of the tables in the concourse. There are so many people here, I didn't see the sign for Bowers, Bowers, and Carter, Aiden's law firm, as we were making our way toward the stands.

"We'll catch up soon," he says before disappearing into the crowd. No doubt the next time we see him, he'll want all the details of how we finally admitted our feelings for each other.

"Well, that was awkward," Jaclyn says as we make our way up the steps to find our seats.

"Undoubtedly," I agree.

Most of the seats in the reserved area are full tonight. Unsurprising, given the special event this evening. But the seats next to ours are empty for now. We settle in, and I reach my arm along the back of Jaclyn's seat, resting my hand lightly against her shoulder. I tell myself it's for the appearance of dating, but the truth is I wanted to touch her.

Jaclyn is fully committed to making connections with people tonight. Within minutes of sitting down, she strikes up a conversation with the couple in front of us. I recognize them as the owners of one of the antique stores in the downtown area.

She's just managed to get the antique store owners to pledge their support for the community center when a shadow crosses the space next to her.

"Fancy seeing you here," a familiar voice says. I look up into the face of my boss, and an uneasy feeling settles over me.

"Larry," I say in greeting.

Jaclyn excuses herself from the conversation with the people in front of us and turns to say hello.

"I forgot your seats were next to my mom's," she says, although from her tone I doubt that's true.

"I've had the same seats for the past ten years." Larry sounds like he doesn't believe her.

"Oh, silly me!"

I don't know why she's acting like she had no idea that Larry might be here, but then it hits me. She didn't only plan this evening to network with business owners. No, her agenda goes deeper than that. She's going to try convincing Larry to support the community center. There's nothing I can do to stop her from trying, even though I know he'll shut it down as soon as he finds out she's after the Elm Street property. With the way he all but threatened my job over that house, I have to play this cool.

Larry takes his seat, and I brace myself for the inevitable train wreck that's about to happen. But Jaclyn is smart. She doesn't immediately launch into her spiel about the community center. In fact, she engages him for the first two innings in a conversation about some of the finer points of baseball as a game. I do my best to follow the conversation, but I've never picked up on all the nuances of the great American pastime, most likely because unlike Jaclyn, I didn't grow up watching the sport.

"Larry, you're someone who cares about the things that make Sapling Grove a good place to live," Jaclyn says casually as the first batter of the third inning steps up to the plate.

"That I am," Larry says. There's a hint of warning to his voice that I'm fairly sure is directed at me.

"That's what I thought. Which is why I'm hoping you'll agree to sponsor a project I've been working on."

"Always happy to help with local projects."

"Glad to hear it," Jaclyn says, then gives Larry her standard pitch.

He listens attentively and asks questions as she talks. For a moment, I relax because from the way he reacts to her description of the need for a new community center, I wonder if I misjudged what his response would be.

"And where would this new community center be located?" he asks.

"We haven't finalized a location, but we're looking very seriously at the house on Elm Street. The one that recently went on the market," Jaclyn says with full sincerity.

"I see," is all Larry says. His gaze flits toward me, and all I can do is give him a half-hearted smile. I'm certain he's figured out that I knew all along what was special about that property, and I suspect I'm going to pay for it.

"What do you say, Larry? Does the community center have your support?" Jaclyn asks, oblivious to the silent communication my boss and I are engaged in.

"I'll think about it," he says, but in a way that implies he won't.

"That's all I ask," Jaclyn says. She has no idea what she's just unleashed.

Somewhere in the middle of the game—the fifth or sixth inning, maybe, I've lost track—Jaclyn leaves to find snacks. As soon as she's out of earshot, Larry moves into her vacated seat so that he's next to me. He leans over so that his eyes are still on the game as he speaks out of the side of his mouth.

"Blackwell, you lied to me. You knew, and you didn't tell me."

When I don't respond, he tries a different tactic.

"No matter," he says. "It's actually better this way. Because now you can convince your girlfriend to let that place go."

I almost laugh at his absurd request, but I stop myself at the last second. For a man who has known the Becketts for as long as he has, he should know that convincing them to do something they don't want to do is next to impossible. With the way Jaclyn loves that house on Elm Street, there's no chance that I could persuade her to give up trying to buy it for the community center.

I'm about to tell Larry to fuck off with this ridiculous notion, but he turns fully toward me, a hard look lining his features.

"Let me be totally clear, Blackwell. This isn't optional. I want that property, and in this town, I get what I want."

"And if I don't help you?"

"Maybe I forget to turn in the final paperwork for that Green Card of yours."

A chill snakes its way down my spine. "Is that a threat?"

"It's a promise."

"You wouldn't."

Larry laughs, but it's a mirthless sound. "Are you sure you want to test that theory?"

Jaclyn reappears at the bottom of the stands before I have time to answer. Larry moves back into his own seat, and Jaclyn hands me a bag of popcorn and a bottle of water.

"Did I miss anything exciting?" she asks.

"A strike out and a walk," Larry says, as though he wasn't just threatening not only my job but also my ability to stay in Sapling Grove.

CHAPTER 15

Jaclyn

Grade statistics reporting is boring enough on its own, but when your mind won't stop replaying your mistakes from the weekend, it's hard to concentrate on even the most interesting task. Those mistakes already made the baseball game torturous to get through. I was barely able to focus on talking Larry into supporting the community center plan because I spent the whole night worrying that Rhys and I would end up back at his place again.

The problem is, I don't know which was the worse mistake. Suggesting that Rhys and I have a one night stand or putting the breaks on when the reality of the situation crashed into me. It's only that when he said he would kiss me like that every night if he could, I freaked out.

I know it was the kind of thing you say in the heat of the moment, but it was too close to sounding like a confession of real feelings. And with the way that almost-confession made my stomach swoop, if we had gone any further, Saturday night would have been a one-way ticket to tangling sex up with emotions.

It doesn't help that when he asked if I thought it was the right thing for us, for a second I wanted to say yes. Not only to the sex but to all of it. But I'm not about to screw up a four-year friendship by going all moon-eyed over Rhys.

With a sigh, I turn back to the reporting software on my screen and continue entering my data. Because it's summer, things are quieter than usual on campus. No students stop by to inquire about ways they could receive extra credit on the next test. No other faculty members wander down the hall past my office. I haven't even seen our building housekeeper today. She normally stops by mid-morning to chat with me about her son who recently graduated high school and will start classes here at Cooke in the fall. In other words, I've had ample time today to let my mind wander over the new pathways of sexual frustration and confusion that this weekend carved out in me.

So when someone knocks on the door frame a little after lunch time, it's all I can do to keep from visibly startling. My lips turn down for a second when I look up to see my boss, Ron, standing in the doorway, and I over-correct with what I'm sure looks like a fake smile.

"What's up?"

"Just dropping in to say hello," he says.

I stop myself from raising a doubtful eyebrow. Whenever Ron "drops in," it's usually the preamble to him assigning me some task that he should be doing for himself. He's got that look in his eye like he's about to ask me—no, tell me—to do something he doesn't want to do, which means it's probably something especially onerous.

"Actually, since I'm here, there's something I wanted to talk about with you."

I brace myself for whatever hours-long task he's about to slide off on me as he sits down in the chair across from my desk. It's never a good sign when he sits down for one of these talks.

The thing about Ron is that I can never decide if it's that he loves the sound of his own voice or if he's sincerely convinced that everyone is in need of the "wisdom" he likes to impart. I've sat through more programmatic development meetings where he's waxed poetic about the demographic cliff—the idea that people didn't have enough babies in the early 2000s and beyond so hundreds of colleges and universities will fall short of their enrollment needs within the next five years—than I care to count. Once Ron gets going, it's hard to stop him, too. He once kept me in a two-hour meeting, just the two of us, to talk about the best way to define credit hours for laboratory requirements. The Social Sciences department doesn't even have classes with laboratory requirements.

The chair he's sitting in has high arms, and the first thing he does is lean his elbows on them and steeple his fingers, resting his chin on his joined index fingers. This is a classic Ron move and usually portends a monologue, the quality of which will be somehow both fascinating and mind-numbing. He takes a dramatically deep breath and says, "I had a conversation with Dr. Dobson about you earlier."

My stomach lurches. Dr. Dobson is the provost, so he's Ron's boss. I'm not actually worried about whatever it is that Ron and Dobson have discussed about me because Dobson and I get along fine. It's the way Ron says it that has my stomach in knots because maybe this is the conversation I've been waiting for. The one where Ron tells me he's finally decided to retire and has suggested to Dobson that I be promoted to the Dean position.

My hopes are dashed pretty quickly, though, because the next thing Ron says is, "Have you given any more thought to the yearbook committee?"

"I haven't really had time," I say.

Ron waves a hand and says, "Don't worry about it. Dobson and I decided it wasn't the right fit for you anyway."

He sounds so purposefully sincere that I almost think he's joking, but Ron never jokes.

"Thank you?" I manage to say, but I know it sounds like a question. I should have expected that he'd drop the idea eventually. He does this kind of thing all the time. Asks me to join some committee or do some research project for him, and then a few weeks later decides he'd rather have me work on something else. That's part of why I never say no to him on this kind of thing, because I know that most of the time, if I wait him out, I won't have to do whatever asinine task he thinks will help me advance my career.

"Instead, he'd like you to sit in on the contract non-renewal meetings for the department."

I blink at him. This is the one dean-level thing that Ron has always done himself. I am weirdly excited about being asked to take this on—well, not excited, exactly. Telling people their contracts haven't been renewed isn't the thing I'm most looking forward to about maybe being dean one day. In fact, it ranks pretty low on my list. But that eager hope from the beginning of this conversation is back. If he's asking me to help with this, it could be a test for how I'll handle the position when he retires.

I bite down on a real smile that threatens to burst out on my face and fix my expression to one of casual aloofness.

"I would be glad to help with that." I wince internally at the hyper-professional robotic sound of my voice.

"Sounds great. There are only two, but you'll need to prep for them. I'll send you the files with the performance reviews. The first meeting is Wednesday. Thanks for doing this, Jaclyn."

Then, in what may be the most shocking moment of this interaction, Ron stands up from the chair and leaves. I'm sure it's the shortest conversation I've ever had with the man, but it's somehow left me more rattled than even the longest monologues I've had to endure from him over the years.

Once the door closes, and the sound of his footsteps fades down the hallway, I let out a squeal of delight. For the first time in months, it feels like things are looking up with this Associate Dean position.

When I took on the role, I had the naive hope that I'd be able to make some real changes with the way the department was run. But it quickly became apparent that the problems with the department—faculty getting double booked for classes at the same meeting time, a high rate of students transferring to a different university, general administrative incompetence—weren't the fault of the previous Associate Dean. No, the real problem is that this university tries to solve 1980s problems with 1950s processes.

I was able to fix the scheduling issue, but the rest of it has been a constant pain in my ass for the past three years. This meeting with Ron might be the start of something good, though. With the dean position comes the ability to implement policies that don't feel like they belong in *Back to the Future*. The third one where Marty is in the 1880s.

I spend the rest of the afternoon attempting to focus on the grade report but mostly daydreaming about what the Social Sciences department would be like under my deanship. It's a better distraction than fixating on everything that happened with Rhys after we went ax throwing. The thoughts of productive departmental meetings and a program to identify students in danger of transferring are still on my mind as I pack up my things at the end of the day.

My phone chimes seconds after I stash it in my work bag, and I take it back out to read the message. My pulse picks up when I see that the text is from Dr. Dobson.

DOBSON: Ron told me you were filling in for him on the contract non-renewal meetings next week. Thanks for doing that. Scheduling them has been a trial with his vacation. Appreciate your willingness to pick up the extra work.

I frown at the phone. Ron didn't mention anything about vacation when he was here earlier. In fact, he made it seem like I'd be sitting in so I could see how these meetings go. As an *observer*. Not as the person representing the department on his behalf.

I reply to Dobson's text with a quick "You're welcome," then almost storm into Ron's office to ask him what the hell is actually going on with this request, but his lights are off. Because of course they are. He probably left hours ago. I don't think he works more than about twenty-five hours a week, because I'm doing more than half the work he should be doing. And yet, he pulls in a full-time paycheck.

My excitement from earlier is nothing but a memory now that I've found out the real reason Ron was so eager to give me the kind of work I've wanted to do for so long. In fact, as I drive home, my annoyance simmers into something more like rage.

It shouldn't shock me that Ron would do something like this. It's exactly the kind of bait and switch he's pulled before. But this is what I get for holding on to the hope that things will ever change with him.

I'm still raging by the time I get home, so much so that I don't notice the person standing by the mailboxes at the end of my driveway until I park in the garage and get out of my car. The person waves to me, and I lift my hand to return the gesture but pause when I realize that I recognize him. None other than Landon Cunningham is standing in the driveway immediately parallel to mine.

I have no idea why my ex-boyfriend is here or how he knows where I live, but he has picked the wrong time to randomly show up. For a second, I debate closing the garage door without even acknowledging him, but he jogs toward me before I can hit the control button.

"What the hell are you doing here?" I cross my arms and anchor my feet a shoulder's width apart.

"I just moved in." He motions toward the condo next to mine, and I suppress a scream of frustration. Because of course my cheating asshole of an ex is going to be my immediate next door neighbor.

"What? When?" I don't want to prolong the conversation any more than I have to, but I'm annoyed with myself for missing the fact that Landon somehow managed to buy the unit next to mine without my knowledge.

"Closed on it last week. You didn't notice that the 'for sale' sign was gone?"

Honestly, there have been so many sales of units in this neighborhood lately that it had escaped my notice entirely, but I don't want to tell him that. With the shifting housing market in Sapling Grove, I've given up paying attention to who is buying what. Well, with one notable exception. The Elm Street house flashes in my mind, but I don't dwell on it because right now I need to figure out how to end this conversation and put this shitty day behind me.

"Is your boyfriend around?" The word feels strange coming from him in reference to someone else.

"Why do you want to know?"

"Just trying to meet all my neighbors. Figure out who I can ask for a cup of sugar if I run out."

I eye him suspiciously, trying to decide if he means that as an innuendo. But he should know I would never consider cheating on Rhys. Even if Rhys isn't my *real* boyfriend.

"He's not here right now. But he will be. We're having dinner soon." I make a mental note to text Rhys as soon as I'm inside and ask him to dinner. With everything that happened this weekend, I can only hope things will feel somewhat normal between us.

"Do you do that often? Eat dinner here together?" Landon asks, raising an eyebrow.

"Yes, of course. All the time," I bite out. When he doesn't lower his eyebrow, I add, "He's moving in with me, in fact."

Oh fuck. What did I just say?

The color drains from my face, but Landon either doesn't notice or isn't interested in calling my bluff. Instead, we stand and stare at each other, an uncomfortable tension wrapping around us. I need to end this conversation, but apparently tonight is for rash decisions.

"Is there something else you wanted?" I ask against my better judgment.

"Actually, now that you mention it. If you have a free evening some time, I'd like to take you to dinner."

"Are you actually hitting on me right now? What the hell, Landon?"

He holds his hands up in an apologetic gesture. "No funny business. I only want to talk."

I narrow my eyes at him, because he sounds sincere. But there's something familiar in the look he gives me, and I'm instantly transported back to the night when everything between us fell apart.

"What could you possibly have to say to me that you think I want to hear, Landon?"

"You're right. I don't have any right to assume you do."

That gives me pause. Landon Cunningham has never been the kind of person who cared about how his words and actions affect others. When we were in high school, I thought it made him cool and edgy, but that was when his devil-may-care attitude didn't impact me. After everything that happened at the end of our relationship, I realized he was actually just an asshole.

"Just...don't say no immediately. Please."

I don't know what to do with the tangle of emotions his "please" elicits, because it sounds genuine. But that can't be possible, because Landon Cunningham never says please. If for no other reason than satisfying my curiosity, I should find out what more he has to say, but Landon has picked the absolute worst time to spring something like this on me, and I react badly.

"Get out of my driveway."

"Alright. If you change your mind, let me know." He inhales deeply and walks toward his condo, a defeated slump to his shoulders.

I watch as he climbs the steps of the front porch and

disappears into his condo.

I remain fixed on the spot in my driveway, my mind running over our conversation, especially the part where I said that Rhys was going to move in. Given the way we left things on Saturday, I don't know how he'll react to the suggestion that he spend the next few weeks living in my guest room.

I jump when my phone dings alerting me to an incoming message. I dig my phone out of my bag to check who it's from as I finally make my way inside.

RHYS: What are you doing tonight? Want to have dinner?

It's like he knew we needed to talk, and I'm at once grateful and filled with trepidation at the prospect of dinner with Rhys. I text him back and ask how he feels about burgers. When he responds positively to my suggestion, some of the tension in my shoulders releases. Dinner together on a random Tuesday is something we've done many times before, and it feels like maybe we'll be alright despite the strangeness between us lately.

Besides, this is Rhys. My best friend. Surely he won't mind if we have to live together for a few weeks.

CHAPTER 16

Rhys

I avoid Larry at work in the days following the baseball game. When he first approached me about the Elm Street house, I dismissed his directive as some kind of divorce-related anxiety. But outright threatening to sabotage my Green Card is a new low.

I text Aiden about the situation. I don't have enough hubris to think this is something I can deal with on my own. He texts me back with a list of resources and an assurance that he'll do what he can to help.

But I don't tell Jaclyn. I still don't want to worry her. Besides, when it comes to Jaclyn, I have other problems. Like helping her feel less vulnerable about the possibility of a real relationship. Figuring out a way to move things forward with Jaclyn is also a welcome distraction from my conversation with Larry at the baseball game.

I'm certain that the events of Saturday night are still on her mind, because she messaged me Monday and said she needed some time to herself instead of our planned dinner at the Indian restaurant run by one of Helen's friends.

I haven't received a similar text today, and I hope that's a sign that she's ready to see me again. I message Jaclyn as I'm leaving the clinic and ask if she'd like to have dinner together. I don't want to rush things with her, but I'm hopeful that she'll agree to a romantic dinner at that new bistro downtown.

But when she texts me back, my heart sinks.

JACLYN: Dinner would be great. I had a shitty day. Bud's?

Bud's is a strange little east Tennessee institution. They have restaurants all over this area, with drive-through locations everywhere from the biggest cities to the smallest hamlets. They're easy to find, too, because they're all constructed with bright blue bricks and are decorated with giant fiberglass versions of their main menu items: a hamburger, a hot dog, a red drink cup with a yellow and red striped straw, and fast food bag of what they call "Friendly fries."

In other words, it's not the vibe I was looking for with my romantic dinner plan. But it's better than nothing, so I respond in the affirmative.

ME: Sounds great. I'll pick up food and meet at your place. What do you want?

JACLYN: Bless you. My usual, please.

ME: A tea and a double junior burger with cheese, no mayo or onion?

JACLYN: Yes, exactly. And some Friendly fries

I send her a thumbs-up emoji and find my wallet and keys. As I get in my car, another notification chimes on my phone.

JACLYN: And a chocolate milkshake.

That's not a good sign. I'm usually the one pushing us to order dessert. Jaclyn likes sweets, but she very rarely gets them for herself. If she's asking for a milkshake, something has gone very wrong.

It doesn't take long to pick up the food. Bud's advertises "Swift Service," and it's probably the most accurate fast food slogan I've ever seen.

When I arrive at her condominium, I'm careful not to practice what I'll say out loud like I did the day after the wedding. If she's already upset, I don't want to make things worse by springing my feelings on her until I've had a chance to assess how bad a day she's had.

I let myself in the front door and call her name so she knows I'm here.

"In the kitchen," she shouts back.

I walk down the hallway and cautiously step into the great room. Jaclyn's condominium doesn't have the characteristic charm of many of the older houses in Sapling Grove. This neighborhood was constructed five years ago, and the layout and finishes are sleek and modern, with one exception. While the cabinets are home-improvement channel generic white, she's added a deep blue backsplash and bright lemon-yellow accents throughout the kitchen. Even in the fading light of the evening, it feels homey and inviting.

It reminds me of Jaclyn, in a way. This woman is so sharp and prickly on the outside but has a penchant for making people feel like part of her community. Once you're past her outside walls, it's easy to see that she's all bright light and warmth. But most people never get that close.

Jaclyn is standing in the kitchen furiously chopping a pile of what looks like it used to be spinach. There is something terrifyingly beautiful about the intensity of her movements and the disarray of the kitchen. It makes me want to take the knife from her hand and kiss her hard on the mouth until she relaxes.

She looks up at me, and I swallow, certain that my thoughts are visible on my face. If they are, she doesn't acknowledge them. Her shoulders fall slightly, and some of the sharpness of her expression melts away as I hold out the bag of greasy food and the drink tray with her tea and milkshake.

"Oh, thank god. I'm starving."

She takes the drink tray from me and dislodges both cups from it. She puts the tea in the refrigerator then takes a seat at the dining table.

"You're not drinking the tea?"

"Saving it for later."

"But the ice will melt."

She shrugs. "I like it better that way."

I do my best not to react to that revelation. I'll never

understand Americans' obsession with iced tea, especially here in Tennessee where the norm is to sweeten it to within an inch of its life. To me, it tastes like overly sweet watery brown nothingness. Ironic, perhaps, given my love of desserts, but I like my sugar to have some substance to it.

"What were you making?" I ask as I join her at the table.

"Mini frittatas. I'll freeze them so I can reheat them for breakfast on the go." Jaclyn only cooks when she's stressed, which isn't a good sign for the way I hoped this evening would go.

"Sounds great."

We slip into silence as we eat. I don't know whether to ask about what made her day so bad or to dive right in to confessing my feelings for her. Fortunately, I don't have to decide where to take the conversation because she breaks the silence a few minutes later.

"Ron pulled another bait and switch on me today."

I pause with my burger halfway to my mouth and raise my eyebrows. "What busywork did he dump on you this time?"

She laughs wryly. "That's the worst part. It's not busywork. It's something with actual responsibility."

She exhales and closes her eyes, like she's expelling all her frustration. When she opens her eyes, a tinge of sadness has bloomed in its place, and I have the urge to scoop her into my arms and hold her until Ron either retires or drops dead.

"He tricked me into handling the contract non-renewal meetings. He's making me fire people."

I nearly crush the sandwich in my hands. "He's doing WHAT?"

"I don't need you to fix it. I just need you to listen." Weariness lines her voice, and I take a long breath in through my nose then incline my head toward her, ready to listen.

"I haven't decided what to do about it yet. But I think Dobson knows that Ron pulled a shitty move this time."

"What makes you say that?"

"He texted me. Thanked me for filling in. I'm not sure he always knows when I'm the one doing the work because Ron usually takes credit for it."

At that, my fury from before threatens to reignite, but I keep myself in check. If Jaclyn needs me to hear her out without coming up with a solution for her, I'll do it.

"I'm going to ask Dobson if we can talk briefly tomorrow. Use the excuse of having some questions about how the meetings will go then feel things out to see how much of this crap he's aware of." She tears small pieces from the burger wrapper, a telltale sign that she's stressed.

"I think that sounds like a good idea." I try to keep my tone casual, even though my thoughts are anything but casual. I hate that she's having to deal with a boss who can't see how good he has it by having Jaclyn on his team.

"Thanks," she says, the corner of her mouth tipping up in a tentative smile.

I survey the remains of our dinner as she sips the last bit of her milkshake. I've lost my appetite for the now-cold burger and the overly salted Friendly fries. I stand and reach for the pile of paper bits from her burger wrapper, sweeping them into the takeaway bag.

"Want some help finishing the frittatas?"

"That would be great." She gives me a real smile this time, and it plants a shoot of warmth in my chest.

There's something achingly domestic about the way we move around the kitchen. Almost like she's inviting me past those carefully constructed walls that she usually keeps in place, even with me.

She finishes chopping the spinach and some shallots—with much less force than before—while I crack eggs into a mixing bowl.

"Not too much salt," she cautions as she hands me the salt cellar.

"Yes, ma'am," I say teasingly. She shoots me an annoyed look, but there's playfulness behind it.

By the time we get the frittatas in the oven, she seems to have relaxed enough from her earlier anger that I could bring up the direction of our relationship without further contributing to her bad mood. But now that the opportunity to talk about it is here, I find myself unable to say anything.

We stand at the sink, silently cleaning up from Jaclyn's stress baking. I wash dishes while she dries things and puts them away. The air around us feels charged, and I wonder if she's thinking about this weekend, too.

Before I can figure out a way to casually bring it up, she breaks the silence.

"Rhys? I have something to ask you."

I'm caught off guard by the timidity in her voice. It's not

an emotion I've heard much from her, if ever. Whatever it is she wants to ask must be something heavy. I don't dare to hope that it's the same thing I came here to discuss. But my heart doesn't get the memo, and it thunders in my chest.

"Yes?" I keep my tone as neutral as possible.

"Landon moved in next door."

It's not what I expected—or hoped—she was going to say. In fact, it's so far from my expectation that it takes me a moment to fully wrap my mind around what she's said. I have to recalibrate quickly, because she keeps talking.

"He cornered me in the driveway when I got home. I was so frustrated at Ron that I wasn't thinking. I didn't mean to say it, but I did."

"Didn't mean to say what?"

Jaclyn takes a step away from me, wringing her hands.

"I think he's on to us, Rhys. I think he knows that the kiss at the wedding was the first time we'd done that." She swallows, and for the second time tonight, I want to scoop her into my arms and hold her until whatever it is that's causing her distress is over. But I stay where I am, letting her take the lead.

She turns back toward me, a wrinkle of concern between her brows. "I'm worried we haven't been convincing enough, because I think Landon was trying to see if there was any chance we could get back together."

A cocktail of emotions hits me at once. Jealousy and a touch of trepidation swirl in my stomach, but they don't prepare me for the next thing Jaclyn says.

"How would you feel about moving in together?"

CHAPTER 17

Jaclyn

"How would you feel about moving in together?" My stomach churns as I say the words out loud, and my dinner threatens to come back up. I mentally kick myself for choosing greasy food when I knew I'd have to ask Rhys to take our fake relationship to a level he never bargained for.

He doesn't respond immediately, which isn't helping my nausea. Instead, he stares at me with his mouth slightly ajar and a panicked lift to his brow. He's more speechless than usual, and I have the uncontrollable urge to fill the silence.

"Just for a few weeks. I mean, it might mean extending the faking it past the end of the month. But I promise, it wouldn't go more than an extra week or two."

I move toward him, hoping that closer proximity will

make this conversation somehow easier. It's irrational, but nothing that I've said or done in the past few minutes has been rational.

I reach for his hand, and he doesn't pull away. That's got to be a good sign.

"Please. I know it's unusual. But I told Landon you're moving in, and it will only look suspicious if you don't."

He closes his mouth and swallows, but I can't parse the exact emotions in his expression. He exhales slowly, then looks me in the eye.

"Let me get this straight. Landon, who you dated in high school, is your neighbor?"

I nod but don't say anything because he continues.

"And you told him that we were moving in together because you think he bought the place next to you so he could get back together with you?"

I open my mouth to respond, but nothing comes out. I snap it shut because when he says it like that, it sounds ridiculous.

Rhys turns and takes two steps away from me, muttering something under his breath that sounds like, "This woman is going to kill me."

With his eyes off me, I find my voice again. "I know it seems nonsensical. I'm sorry. I'll tell him the truth, and you won't have to deal with my—"

"I'll move in with you."

I suck in a sharp breath and blink at him as he retraces his steps back to me. There's a glint of something fiery in his eyes that has my heart rate picking up.

"I'll bring my things by this weekend," he says as he walks toward the hallway. "I'll see you later."

I'm left staring after him, not completely sure what just happened. Because it sounded a lot like Rhys agreed to move in with me with zero hesitation. Almost like he's excited for the chance to move in together. Which, given what happened between us last weekend, might be the case.

But he doesn't know that I feel it. This pull we have toward each other, that for me is more than physical attraction. One thing is for sure. I'll need to keep my increasing feelings for this man buried deep down while he's living here.

"Are you sure this is a good idea?" Evie asks with a tilt of her head. When I texted to say I needed input from her and Kylie, I expected Evie to be on my side. Instead, my friends stare at me across our usual table at our favorite bar with twin looks of disbelief at the news that Rhys and I are moving in together.

I knew Kylie would be opposed, of course. She's not one to go for this type of scheme. But Evie? The woman whose life could literally be the plot of a romance novel? Her reaction has me questioning whether I should try locating a time machine so I can go back and stop myself from ever kissing Rhys in the first place.

"I mean, no. But I don't really know what choice I have. Besides, it will make my alleged heartbreak more believable when we 'break up' in a few weeks." That's one small blessing I hadn't thought of until after Rhys left yesterday evening. It's a surefire way to keep Mom from pushing any new suitors my direction for a long time.

"Put aside the fake dating part of this for a second." Kylie pauses and takes a sip of her margarita. "You haven't lived with a man since, when? College?"

I mumble my reply, hoping she won't press for a clear answer.

"What was that?"

Dammit.

I knock back the rest of my drink, bracing for the judgment I'm about to receive. "Never. I've never lived with a man."

That, at least, leaves both my friends speechless. But the silence only lasts a few seconds, and then the cacophony of questions begins.

"What do you mean you've never lived with a man?" collides with "Are you freaking serious?" and I wish that I had saved some of my drink to savor while Kylie and Evie's minds reel and they barrage me with their disbelief. I close my eyes and take a few deep breaths. When I open my eyes, both my friends fall silent.

"As you know, my preference is one and done." I keep my tone calm, but for some reason, something unpleasant hitches in my chest as I speak. Unbidden, the look on Rhys's face above me on his couch flashes through my thoughts. I ignore the sensation and continue. "I've kept things that way for as long as I've dated. With one exception."

"Landon." Kylie is the one who says it; a statement, not a question.

I tilt my head toward her. "Precisely."

"But why?" This comes from Evie.

Because Landon broke my heart, and I decided never to let that happen to me again.

The thought is immediate, but I don't dare voice it out loud. It's too raw. Too emotional.

Kylie must pick up on what I've left unsaid, because she jumps in and saves me from answering.

"In other words, you're about to make the huge life decision of moving in with someone for the first time—someone who you're not actually dating—in order to deceive your mother and your ex?"

"Well, when you put it like that..."

She holds up her hands in surrender. "Just trying to make sure I understand the situation."

I let out a huff of annoyance, but I don't snip at her again. Most of the time, I like Kylie. She just has this... attitude sometimes that gets under my skin and makes me prickle. It's probably because we're both eldest daughters. I don't like to admit it, but we're a lot alike in some ways. Both proud, independent women who like to get our way. Of course, when her way and my way don't align, things can get dicey.

Luckily, Evie grounds both of us. She is ever the mediating force between us, including tonight.

"I think what Kylie is trying to say is that we don't want you to get hurt."

"How would I get hurt?" I already know the answer. But there's no way I'd let on that Evie's meaning is totally clear to me.

Evie looks at Kylie, and the two of them seem to have some kind of silent conversation. They exchange looks and shrugs for a moment, and I'm about to ask what they're doing when Evie says, "We think you have feelings for Rhys."

"What?"

"Evie! You weren't supposed to tell her that!"

"I know, but you both helped me see that I was in love with Andrew, and I thought..." She turns to look at me, but I just stare, blinking at my friends.

"I have no idea what you're talking about," I finally say. It's another lie to add to my pile of lies.

"I mean, the fact that you keep kissing him makes it pretty obvious that something's happening between you," Kylie says.

"We keep kissing for the believability. Not because of anything else." My words ring hollow, even to my ears.

Evie raises a skeptical eyebrow but doesn't say anything. Kylie, on the other hand, barrels through instead of politely ignoring my obvious lie.

"We all saw you together at ax throwing. The possessive way you stepped between him and the instructor? The kiss when you threw the last ax? You mean to tell us that wasn't evidence of real feelings between you two?"

"I..." I don't have a good answer for her. At least, nothing that won't sound defensive and false. I haven't told them about what happened after we got back to Rhys's house after ax throwing, and I'm worried they'll be able to tell I'm keeping something from them if I say anything more. I deflect my discomfort back at Kylie. "You're one to talk. What about that weird tension between you and Sebastian? What's that all about?"

Kylie's eyes go wide with something like panic and guilt.

"I don't know what you're talking about," she says, mirroring my own words back at me.

"Sure you don't." My tone is sharp, a little meaner than it should be. But this conversation has teetered on the edge of emotional reflection for too long, and I'm in defense mode.

"I think what Kylie was trying to say is that the line between pretending and having real feelings is starting to look a little fuzzy," Evie chimes in. I note that she ignores my accusations toward Kylie, and I wonder if she knows more about whatever is happening with Sebastian than she's letting on.

"No it isn't." I sound like a petulant child.

Evie and Kylie exchange looks again, but they let the subject drop. Instead, they ask me about another sore subject. My meeting with Dobson about Ron's contract renewal subterfuge. Somewhere between running into my ex in my driveway and asking Rhys to move in, I texted them to get their take on how to approach my meeting with Dobson.

"It was about what I expected," I say. "Dobson started the meeting by telling me how grateful he is that I'm filling in for Ron. He was so effusive, I didn't feel like I could be angry about it."

"I hate when he does that. It feels so manipulative," Kylie says. She and Dobson don't always get along, and she's usually the first among us to criticize the provost.

"Did he give any indication that he knows Ron tricked you into being part of the meetings?" Evie asks.

"Not really. You know how he is once he gets going."

Evie and Kylie both make sounds of understanding. Dobson is famous among the Cooke faculty for side-stepping the hard conversations. He's a people pleaser at heart, which can be good, but sometimes means he doesn't deal with problems among faculty in a timely manner.

We spend the rest of our evening gossiping about work. Evie tells us about a new grant she's recently secured for the Center for Teaching and Learning. Last fall she started a new role at the university where she splits her time between the library and the CTL. Most of her work now involves funding projects related to advancing teaching practice.

I don't bring up Sebastian again, even though I'm dying to know what's going on with him and Kylie. But doing so would likely turn my friends' attention back on me and my rash decision to move in with Rhys. Unfortunately for me, when we finally part ways for the night, I'm no less unsettled than I was before I asked my friends for advice.

CHAPTER 18

Jaclyn

The unsettled feeling doesn't go away. In fact, it's still there on Saturday afternoon when, true to his word, Rhys shows up with a car load of housewares and clothes.

Landon is on his front porch when I let Rhys into the condo, and I suppose that's one good thing about this bizarre turn of events. At least we will definitely convince my ex that Rhys and I are a real couple.

What's less clear to me is how I'm going to tell my mother that Rhys and I have moved in together. Because I don't want her to get her hopes up about what this means for the longevity of our "relationship."

I help Rhys carry his things into the guest room, which is down the hall from my room. Thankfully, there's a separate bathroom for guests, so we don't have to figure out the awkwardness of sharing.

"Do you want help unpacking?" I ask as we set down the last of the boxes. I'm a little surprised by how much he's brought, but I suppose it's all in the service of authenticity for our deception.

"I can handle it on my own."

I don't push him to let me help, in part because it's awkward to have him on the upper floor of my condo. Even though we've spent a lot of time hanging out at my place, I can probably count the number of times he's been upstairs on one hand. Usually he comes over for dinner or drinks after work, and we sit on the back porch or in the living room when it's too cold. In fact, the only time I recall him being up here was when he helped me put together a bookshelf in my home office, which is exactly where I go once I leave him to finish unpacking.

The office is down the hall, adjacent to my room, and I can hear him as he puts away his things. There's part of me that wonders if I should have insisted on helping him, if I should have been a better host. But the idea of going back and offering now would be awkward.

I try to focus on my laptop screen, where the browser with information about the schedule for the Give Back event blinks at me, instead of on the sounds of the man who's been haunting my sexual fantasies lately moving about my house. I received the invitation to present my proposal a few days ago, and between Ron's shenanigans at work and orchestrating Rhys's move-in, I haven't done much to prepare. It seems like I won't make much progress today, either, if my current level of distraction holds.

I don't know how long I sit staring at the screen, not really doing anything. I finally force myself to click on my presentation draft, when a knock startles me.

"Sorry, didn't mean to frighten you."

Rhys stands in the doorway, one arm leaning against the frame right above his head. His t-shirt is slightly damp, and a bead of sweat lines his brow. The contours of his stomach muscles are visible through the dampness of his shirt. It's a warm day, so it shouldn't surprise me to see him like this, but it does. I swallow back a sound of desire that threatens to escape me.

"I'm finished putting things away. Going to take a shower if that's alright." He motions toward the guest bathroom with his thumb.

I nod and let out a sound that's meant to be a "yes" but comes out more like a squeak. I don't know why he felt like he needed permission to take a shower, but I suppose a warning is helpful since the guest bathroom door is next to my office door. He turns toward the bathroom, and it's not until he's closed the door behind him that I let out the breath I've been holding.

Get yourself together, Jaclyn.

If the sound of him organizing the guest room was distracting, it has nothing on the disruption to my concentration that knowing Rhys is currently naked in my house does.

I give up trying to work on the presentation and instead

busy myself tidying my office. Not that it needs to be tidied, but picking up objects and moving them takes less brain power than explaining why the bank should support the community center's bid for financial backing.

The water shuts off, and the sound of the shower curtain hooks scraping along the curtain rod catches my attention. I can't help imagining what's happening in the guest bathroom.

Rhys, climbing out of the shower, grabbing a towel, wiping his face, then wrapping the towel around his waist.

At the thought of Rhys in a towel, I suck in a breath. Not because of the lusty image but because I remember that the guest bathroom doesn't have any full-sized towels at the moment.

I wrench the office door open and nearly collide with Rhys as I step into the hallway. I stop short, barely managing to keep my footing. He reaches a hand to stop my forward momentum. When my equilibrium is steady, I look up at Rhys. My brain doesn't immediately register what I'm seeing. When it clicks, I gasp.

Rhys is almost completely naked except for a hand towel that he's holding in front of his unmentionables. A cloud of steam swirls around him, and he's all toned chest and arms, glistening with condensation from the shower.

I have no idea where to look. Instinctively, I look down to avoid his eyes, but that means my focus is on his muscular thighs. I glance toward his mid-section instead and realize too late that I should not, under any circumstances, look anywhere near the place where his waist tapers into his pelvis. The jut of his hip bone and the trail of hair leading below the very small towel is an image that is now forever burned into my brain.

I'm frantically trying to find a place to look that won't make me think about the way his body feels against mine, but it's too late. My mouth goes dry at the thought, and I'm pretty sure I let out a breathy, "Oh my god."

Rhys clears his throat, and my entire face is on fire. I close my mouth, which has been hanging slightly open, and swallow.

"This was the only towel I could find."

I finally look him straight in the eyes, but my brain can't form sentences.

"Do you have any bigger towels?"

He doesn't sound nearly as affected as I am by the fact that he is standing in my hallway all but naked, but there is a strained look in his eyes, like he's trying not to let on how he actually feels about the situation.

He releases my arm and takes a slight step back like he's retreating into the bathroom. He keeps his front toward me, towel still awkwardly in place. A rapid movement would render the towel moot, and I try not to think about the fact that I kind of want that to happen. To see the whole picture instead of filling in the gaps with my rampant imagination.

I slap a hand over my eyes and shout, "Laundry. I washed everything this morning. The big towels are downstairs in the laundry room. I'll get one for you."

I start toward the stairs but have to remove my hand from my eyes so that I don't tumble to the first floor. I move past him, careful not to brush his skin with any part of me. Once I'm at the top of the stairs, I look over my shoulder, in time to see him turn to go back into the bathroom. I bite down on a strangled sound at the sight of his shapely ass and the ripple of his thigh muscles as he moves. I recover myself as quickly as I can, but time has slowed to the flow of honey, and it takes longer than it should for me to make my way down the stairs to the laundry room.

When I return to the second floor, the door to the bathroom is closed, which is a relief.

I set the towel on the floor then knock and let him know I'm going into my room. With the bedroom door closed firmly behind me, I lean against it, close my eyes, and take a deep breath. I should not be having the kinds of thoughts that my mind seems hellbent on having. I swore to myself that I would not go down that road with Rhys. Because that road only leads to heartbreak.

I let out a string of expletives, mad at myself for the way I ogled my best friend. My self-berating is interrupted by a knock on my bedroom door.

"Who is it?" I call out, knowing full well there's no one it could be except the one person I don't need to see right now. I need to sort myself out before I can face him again.

"It's Rhys," he says, and damn him for playing along. "Can we talk?"

I should not open that door. I should talk to him through the door like any self-respecting woman in my situation would do. Except apparently I've lost all sense. I open the door, and there's Rhys in a pair of gray sweatpants and a well-worn t-shirt. Somehow this outfit is as arousing as the towel-only version of him.

"I'm sorry this is so awkward!" I blurt at him. I'm not usually the kind of person who says things in a rush, but I'm so confused by this emotional pull he seems to have on me that I am not acting like myself.

Rhys reaches out a hand and places it on my arm. "It's ok. I should have taken my bathrobe with me to the shower."

I shake my head, forcing myself to calm down.

"Why can't we be the way we were before?" The question comes out unbidden.

Rhys's eyes widen, and for a second I think he's going to deny that anything between us has changed. But I watch as he loses whatever internal battle he's having with himself, and he casts his eyes down, defeated.

"It's my fault. I don't know how to act around you after..."

He trails off, but he doesn't have to finish the sentence. I know exactly what he means.

"Have you been thinking about it, too?" The intimacy of his question is only enhanced by the softness of his voice.

My heart stutters, and the memory of that night pops into my mind. The way kissing him felt like the most natural thing in the world. The way he seemed to know exactly what I liked.

Other memories join the mental movie playing in my brain. The way he looked in that suit at the wedding. The smooth slide of his thumb against my lips as he wiped ice cream from them. The growl of pleasure that he lets out every time our lips meet. I try to tamp down the memory of his mouth on mine, the taste of his tongue, the fact that I've never felt anything so perfect as the way his hands fit in my curves. Like they were made to go together.

I know why I've been replaying those moments every night before bed. Because there's no use denying that I am into Rhys. But his question implies that I'm not the only one haunted by this thing that's happening between us, and I don't know what to do with that knowledge.

I open my mouth to say "No, of course not," but instead what comes out is, "I can't *stop* thinking about it!"

Shit shit shit.

"I want to do it again."

I'm confused for a second because it sounded like Rhys said those words, but that's impossible because they were the words in my head. Or did *I* say them out loud?

I stare at him, trying to make sense of how Rhys could have possibly known my thoughts.

"Is that...Is it something you want, too?" I've never heard Rhys sound so unsure before. But there's no mistaking what he's asking.

Rhys Blackwell wants to take me to bed. Even after I ran from his house.

"I..." Of all the times for my voice to stop working. My heart thunders, and somewhere in my mind I'm screaming through the rumbles to say, "Yes, of course I do!"

But I can't make anything more than a squeak move past my lips.

"Fuck. I shouldn't have told you." Rhys hangs his head. "I've made this living together situation a mess already, and it's only been a few hours. I'll stay out of your way while I'm here."

He turns toward the guest room, hanging his head. The resignation in his posture pierces through my stalled out brain, and I shout, "Wait!"

It's a little too loud for the distance between us, but I don't care. All I care about is the fact that Rhys wants me, and I almost let the opportunity walk right out the door. He swings back around, and there's something raw in his gaze, like what I say next will decide the course of our relationship for the rest of the time we know each other.

"Yes. I want that."

I don't know what's happening in his head right now, but he steps toward me and takes both my arms in his hands. He searches my face, and I don't know what he sees there, but whatever it is turns the light in his eyes dark with desire.

He leans closer to me and says into my ear, "What, exactly, do you think about when you think about us together?"

It's not at all what I expected him to say. It's better.

My breathing goes shallow, and my heart pounds in my chest. My mouth is suddenly dry, so I lick my lips. He tracks the movement with his eyes, and his gaze sears me to my core.

"Tell me," he whispers. The sound sends a shock through my system, like I've touched a live wire.

"Bourbon and lemonade." My voice is barely above a murmur.

"From my drink at the wedding?"

I nod shakily. "Yes. Your lips tasted like it."

"And did you like it?" He practically purrs the question.

"Yes."

"What else do you think about?"

Alarm bells are going off in my mind. This conversation is dangerous, and I need a way out. But Rhys's hands are still on my arms, and I'm pretty sure we've moved closer together. I glance up into his eyes, and everything I see in them is heat and desire.

"The way you bit my lip. And the way you kept your hands on me all night afterward."

His chest rises and falls, and I don't know which one of us leans toward the other—maybe both of us do—but the next thing I know, his lips are brushing against mine.

"Like this?" he asks before nipping at my lower lip.

I let out a sound that I don't recognize. Something between a "yes" and a moan.

His hands slide around me, pulling me closer. My chest grazes his, sending delicious heat through me at the contact.

"Jaclyn."

I have never been so turned on by the sound of my name on someone's lips as I am at the way Rhys says it. Like my name is the oxygen he needs to breathe. I hook my finger into the waist of his sweatpants and tug him to me as I crash my mouth into his.

There's no moment of hesitation from him. No pause

before he fully commits to kissing the hell out of me.

He shifts us so that my back is against the wall, and his lips make a trail down my neck, past my collarbone. He stops at the neckline of my shirt, and I let out a little whimper at the loss of his mouth on me.

He looks up at me, and my breath catches at the fire in his eyes.

"May I?" he asks, as his fingers play along the fabric at the hem, lightly grazing my sensitive skin.

I don't even know what, specifically, he's asking to do. I only know that whatever it is, I want it. I nod shakily, and the sound he makes in response is so raw that I'm no longer sure we're faking things anymore.

He finds the bottom of my shirt and drags it slowly up over my head. The sudden blast of cool air from the vent above us makes my skin prickle, but the sensation doesn't last long because Rhys's hands are on me, rubbing warmth back into my skin and sending sparks through my bloodstream.

He doesn't immediately move to kiss me again. Instead, he stares at my bare skin, a half drunk look in his eyes.

"God, you're beautiful," he breathes out.

The low rumble of his voice sets my body to trembling again, but this time it's not with nerves. It's with anticipation.

He's back on me in seconds, resuming his kisses along my neck, then lower. He slides a leg between my thighs, and the friction is so, so good.

"I have condoms in the nightstand," I croak out.

He looks up at me from where he's been kissing my chest, and his grin is delightfully wicked.

He straightens and guides me to the bed. He kisses me again, and the force of it makes me lose my footing. We tumble onto the mattress entwined around each other, and I am utterly lost to anything but the sound of my name on his lips and the feel of his skin against mine and the growing certainty that a one night stand isn't going be enough this time.

I wake from a deep sleep to the sound of my phone buzzing, not with a text but the long, insistent vibrations of an actual phone call. At first, I try to ignore it. I'm too cozy under the covers, and I'm not awake enough to use words. The phone stops after a few moments, and I breathe deeply, hoping to fall back to sleep. It's Sunday morning, after all, and sleeping in is the only thing on my agenda.

But as I start to drift off, the phone rings again. If someone is calling twice in quick succession, I probably ought to answer. I grope for the phone on the bedside table, but it's not in its usual spot. I peek one eye open and see it lying on the floor next to my pants, so I lean out of bed and pick it up. I barely look at it as I swipe to answer. I must be less awake than I thought, because the phone feels strange in my hands. Like the bumps and ridges of the phone case aren't in the right spots.

"Hello?" My voice is craggy with sleep.

"Jaclyn?" The voice on the other end sounds surprised, which doesn't make sense. They called me.

"Yes?" I dimly recognize the bright British accent, but in my half-asleep haze, I can't figure out why.

"Is Rhys there?"

At the mention of Rhys, I jolt to total awareness, realizing that I am not alone in bed, and this is not my phone.

As though he's heard his name, Rhys rolls over with a hum of pleasure and wraps his arms around my waist.

"Rupert?" I ask tentatively.

I can hear the smile in his voice as he replies, "The one and only. Can you put my brother on the line? I have some questions for him."

I don't like the way he says "questions," like a pleased cat with a trophy kill. I can guess what kind of questions he has. *Why did Jaclyn answer your phone this early in the morning? Are you in the same bed? Did you sleep together last night?*

I disentangle myself from Rhys's grasp and try to wake him so that he can talk to Rupert, but Rhys is a heavy sleeper. I poke him in the side and try coaxing him awake by saying his name. After a couple pretty hard jabs in the ribs, he finally opens one eye and looks at me.

"What are you doing?" He asks, but it sounds more like "Wha 're you doin'."

"Trying to wake you up. Your brother called." I hold the phone out to him and try to keep my face neutral.

Rhys suddenly snaps to attention, eyes widening. He

mutters the word "fuck" under his breath. I suspect he knows that his brother is about to tease him for getting caught in bed with someone he shouldn't be getting caught in bed with.

He moves the covers aside and takes the phone from me, and I try not to stare at him as he grabs his sweatpants and tugs them on over his naked ass. He leaves the room, closing the door behind him, and any hope I had of eavesdropping on their conversation is gone. I flop back on the bed and throw my arm over my eyes.

My thoughts immediately turn to last night and what it means for the status of our fake relationship. More importantly, what it means for our friendship, especially after this fake dating thing is over.

Last night should get him out of my system, right? I needed to scratch the itch I've had since that kiss at the wedding, and now we can move on. But the problem with scratching an itch is that you have to keep scratching to maintain the relief.

That thought gives me an idea, one that hopefully Rhys will go for. I spend the minutes he's out of the room thinking through how to ask my best friend to become my best friend with benefits. If he's amenable, it could mean that I suddenly have Sunday plans after all. If that's the case, my first order of business is dealing with the terrible morning breath that I can only hope he didn't notice.

CHAPTER 19

Rhys

"Care to explain why Jaclyn answered your phone at eight o'clock your time?" Rupert asks as I step into the hallway. There's a teasing quality to his tone that I don't like.

"I do not."

Rupert's laugh is so loud, I have to pull the phone away from my ear. I make my way to Jaclyn's guest room and close the door behind me.

"Here's my theory. You finally told her how you feel, and she reciprocated. One thing led to another, and you woke up in the same bed. Do I have all that right?"

"No."

It's not a lie. Because I didn't tell her how I feel. I only told her I wanted to take her to bed, which was true. Just not the full truth.

"Then what were you doing in bed together?"

"Sleeping."

"Rhys, come on. I need more than one-word answers. Did you talk to her? What did she say when you told her?"

I pace the room, my thoughts a tangle. Because I don't want to admit to my brother that instead of finally clearing the air between us, I complicated things more. I let my hunger for something physical get in the way of the actual relationship I want with Jaclyn.

"Rhys. You did tell her, right?"

I hesitate too long, my silence an answer. Rupert picks up on it and chides me.

"Rhys, you have to tell her. I don't know what happened last night, but whatever it was, I'm worried about you. That you're setting yourself up for heartbreak."

What happened was that I let my lust get the best of me. Knowing that the desire I've felt for years was reciprocated —I couldn't think straight. The way her eyes slid over my body, the hunger in them. I couldn't ignore it. But I'm not about to tell my brother about that.

"You're right. I'll tell her. I promise."

"Good. Don't wait too long. The longer you wait, the harder it will be."

He's right, and I know it. But I don't want to rush her. Because the thing about Jaclyn is that emotions scare her. It's taken us four years to get to this point, and the only reason we're here is because she needed to take action to get her mum off her back. I don't want to push her away by being too needy.

I let out a long breath, thankful that he's not pushing me for more details.

"How's Colin?"

"Eh, he's alright. Hit a roadblock on the manuscript, and he's been in a mood the past few days. But he'll get through it."

We chat for a few more minutes, and I set aside all thoughts of Jaclyn for the moment. But once we say goodbye, there's no escaping the rush of memories that flood my brain.

Jaclyn's eyes on mine. The breathy sound she made when I lifted her shirt over her head. The warmth of her breasts against me.

God, the sounds she made last night.

But Rupert is right. Before this goes any further, we need to talk about what exactly it is we're doing here. I'm not ready to barge into her room and confess that I'm in love with her, but I can at least feel out what she's thinking.

With that conviction, I tap lightly on the door to her bedroom before opening it and stepping into what I hope is the start of something new between us.

Jaclyn is standing in the frame of the door to the bathroom, and I stop short at the sight of her. She's put on a robe, and it's a surprising piece of clothing. I think of her as someone who wears dark greens and blues or black with subtle red accents. But this robe is pale pink and shimmers like silk. It makes me wonder what other treasures she's been hiding in her wardrobe that I've never had the opportunity to see.

"How was Rupert?" Jaclyn's voice draws me back from imagining her in a rainbow of pastel undergarments. She sounds like she's trying for nonchalance but there's something slightly stilted to her speech.

"Nosy, as always."

An awkward tension hangs in the air, like we don't know what to do with ourselves now that we've seen each other naked. Neither of us moves from our respective thresholds, and I give myself an internal shake at the trite metaphor.

"I have a proposal for you," she says at the same moment that I say, "About last night."

"You go first," she says in a way that is more demure than her usual tone.

"I was going to say that last night was..." I pause and closes my eyes. I take a sharp breath before continuing, "It was fucking amazing."

"I was going to say the same thing." Her voice is quiet, more timid than usual.

"But I don't think we should do it again."

"Oh." There's a flash of hurt in her eyes.

"Not until we talk about things first," I add quickly.

I find myself losing my nerve now that I'm standing in front of her. It's something about the way she's standing there in that robe. That little freckle I like so much is peeking out from the neckline. Instead of talking to her, I want to cross the room and scoop her in my arms. I want to toss her in the bed and keep her there for the entire day, not letting her leave until she's had her fill of pleasure.

"What things did you want to talk about?" she asks when I don't continue, and I force myself to look away from that spot so I can focus.

"I know you usually only sleep with someone once, so I understand if you want this to be a one-time thing. We don't have to keep—"

"I want to!" She clamps her hands over her mouth as though she didn't mean to let that out. She slowly lowers her hands, and I wait while she takes a deep breath.

"What I mean to say is, at least for the rest of our pretend relationship, I'd like to keep doing this." She gestures between us. "Friends with benefits, you know?"

"Oh," is all I can manage.

"Unless you don't want to," she says, and there's a hint of apology in her tone.

I don't want her to apologize for wanting to sleep together. I want her to say that she's in this as much as I am. But I will take what she offers, even if it's only half of what I want.

"Alright," I say before she can rescind her offer.

She looks relieved, and I suppose that's something.

"That's good." She clears her throat, and an uncertain silence covers us.

It seems like there should be more to it than her asking to be friends with benefits and me agreeing. Parameters or rules or something.

We've never really talked about our sex lives in detail. Our likes and dislikes. I know there are friends who tell each other those kinds of things, but it's never made sense for our friendship, even though we're open about most other areas of our lives. Besides, it would have been torture for me, knowing specifics of what she likes and not being able to give that to her.

It feels like each of us is waiting for the other to say something. Or do something. It's still unclear to me what this means for the long term, but I don't want to scare Jaclyn off with talk of commitment. But that conversation can wait, because right now, there's something else I want to do.

"Does this mean I can kiss you any time I want?" My question comes out in a low register, and I relish the way her mouth falls open slightly at the sound. I take deliberate steps toward her, finally crossing that threshold.

"Yes." Her response is quiet, like if she says it too loud the air around us will shatter.

"Does this mean I can kiss you now?" I'm within an arm's length of her now.

"Yes," she says again, although this time it's barely a word.

I run my fingers through her bed-tousled hair.

"Good. Because I want to kiss you now." I lean forward to meet her mouth with mine, and I tell myself that this is enough.

After taking advantage of the newly arranged "benefits" of our friendship, I expect that we'll spend a lazy morning together, maybe cuddling and watching a movie, but Jaclyn practically jumps out of bed the moment we're finished and closes herself in the bathroom. When she comes back, she's tying the belt of her bathrobe. There's a strange finality to it, as though she's done with intimacy for the day.

"This was fun, but I have things to do," she announces.

There's a slight lift to her voice, and I wonder if she feels as business-like about this as she's trying to sound. But the terseness of her words is so Jaclyn-like that I can't be offended by her kicking me out of her room.

"Alright. I was planning to go for a run anyway."

I gather my clothes and make my way down the hall to the guest room. Jaclyn's neighborhood is on the outskirts of town, but there's a convenience store about a mile away that has good breakfast sandwiches. I'll stop there on my way back and bring her something delicious for breakfast.

As I step into the hallway, I glance toward Jaclyn's room. Her door is still closed, but I'm tempted to burst through and kiss her again before I leave. I don't, because I have a feeling that would lead to more of what we did last night. As much as I would like to spend the rest of the day in her bed, it was clear she needed some time to herself.

Downstairs, I shove my feet into my shoes and start toward the door. I'm looking at my phone, texting Jaclyn to let her know where I'm going. As I reach for the handle, the doorbell rings, startling me. I drop my phone and mutter a curse. When I pick it up from the floor, there's a crack in the case. Annoyed, I jerk the door open with more force than I mean to.

"What the fuck do you want?" I growl at the person standing on the step, then curse under my breath.

Helen Beckett is standing in front of me, a takeaway bag in hand, staring at me wide-eyed and open-mouthed. It doesn't take her long to recover the power of speech, though.

"Is that any way to greet the mother of your girlfriend?"

"No, Ma'am. I'm sorry." I feel like a schoolboy caught breaking the rules and getting reprimanded by the teacher.

"Where is that daughter of mine, anyway? I have her favorite." She holds the bag a little higher. It's from this little donut shop downtown called Hole-In-One. The donuts are good. Freshly made each morning and practically melt in your mouth. But all the decor is golf-themed, and I've never figured out why. The nearest golf course is half an hour away.

"Upstairs." I turn and point toward the staircase as though she doesn't know where it is. A creak on the top step lets me know that Jaclyn's heard at least part of this exchange and is making her way down to the foyer.

"You're here awfully early. If I'd known, I would have brought you a donut." Helen's eyes narrow—not with disapproval necessarily. More like an attempt at appearing disapproving but with a hint of a smile.

"Mom, leave him alone," Jaclyn says as she joins us. She's standing next to me, our arms brushing, and I have to force myself not to take her hand in mine.

"Rhys and I were just chatting." Helen gives Jaclyn an innocent look.

Jaclyn starts to speak at the exact moment that I burst out, "We've moved in together!"

Jaclyn's nostrils flare. I don't dare look her in the eyes, unsure of what I'll see there, because clearly she has neglected to tell her mother about this latest development in our alleged relationship.

Helen, on the other hand, can barely contain the joy that blooms on her face. Now I know what emotion she was trying to keep hidden. There's no way Helen Beckett, queen of trying to matchmake her daughter, would be upset to find a boyfriend at Jaclyn's house in the morning. No, that emotion from earlier? It was hopefulness.

"Well, this is certainly unexpected, but I'm not surprised. For as long as you've been friends, I've always thought there was something more between you. I'm so happy for you both!" Helen beams at us, but Jaclyn tenses beside me.

"Mom, why are you here this early?" Jaclyn asks.

"Oh, I just wanted to bring my daughter some breakfast. Is that so wrong?"

Jaclyn eyes her suspiciously. "You never bring me breakfast."

"Well, I did today." Helen pauses. "And I also wanted to tell you that Larry Montgomery made an offer on the Elm Street property."

Jaclyn goes rigid. "What? I thought you had talked him out of that one."

"I thought so, too, but he was insistent."

A sick feeling settles in my stomach as I watch the anger

that settles across Jaclyn's face.

"How much is he offering?" There's a tightness to Jaclyn's mouth as she asks the question.

Helen replies with the figure, and Jaclyn curses.

"I'm sorry, sweetie. I know how much you wanted that house for the community center."

Jaclyn takes a deep breath, like she's steeling herself against a foe. "I'll figure something out. I've got the presentation next weekend, after all."

Helen frowns and shakes her head. "I'm afraid that will be too late. The sellers are reviewing the offer this week and are supposed to let Larry know if they'll accept by Friday."

Jaclyn closes her eyes, and her chin trembles slightly. I've never seen her look defeated like this before. It makes me wish that we were a real couple. I would take her in my arms and hold her while she let out whatever emotions she's been keeping inside. But we're not a real couple.

"I'll figure something out," she says, a sharp edge to her voice.

"I'm sure you will," Helen says. She reaches for her daughter and gives her a squeeze on the arm.

Helen leaves the donut, but Jaclyn puts the bag on the hall table. I doubt she'll eat it later. We stand in the foyer, and I debate pulling her into my arms after all.

"There are other houses," I say in an attempt to ease the blow of the bomb Helen just dropped on Jaclyn. "Other properties that might be better suited to what you want to do with the center."

"What? Why would you say that? I can figure out a way

around this."

"I'm not so sure. Larry told me a couple weeks ago that he wanted to buy that house. I think he's determined to have it."

She tilts her head at me in a question. "You let me go on and on at the baseball game about all the plans for how that house would be perfect for the community center while Larry was sitting there already planning to buy it?"

"I'm sorry. I should have told you sooner."

"Damn right, you should have." She turns to me, a glint of steel in her eyes. "We need to find out who owns that property and convince them to decline Larry's offer."

My mind flashes to Larry's not-so-subtle threats about my job, and I hesitate. If I try to prevent Larry from buying that property, I'll be flying back to London before the ink is dry on his new mortgage.

"What is it?"

"I..." That sick feeling is back, and I hate myself a little for what I'm about to say. For what it will mean for the tenuousness of everything between Jaclyn and me. "Does it have to be the Elm Street house?"

Jaclyn looks at me like I've slapped her, eyes widening in shock and disbelief.

"Why would you say that?"

"I'm worried you're hung up on that house to the point it's getting in the way of your other plans."

"Are you fucking serious right now?" The pitch of her voice goes up in indignation. "You know I love that house, and I won't see Larry Montgomery snatch it away from the community center."

She crosses her arms and stares at me. There's a wild, angry look in her eyes, and her jaw is clenched. I close my eyes and breathe deeply, bracing myself for her continued wrath at what I'm about to say next.

"I'm not sure it's worth it to keep fighting for this one."

Instead of raging, Jaclyn replies softly, "I'm not sure you need to be here right now."

It's so much worse than if she had yelled at me. I've hurt her, and what's worse is that I didn't want to do it. But as long as Larry holds the power over my sponsorship, I don't have a choice but to do what he asks.

I don't say anything as I turn to leave, afraid if I do, I'll only make things worse. Instead of going for a run, I get in my car and return to my lonely flat.

CHAPTER 20

Jaclyn

After Rhys leaves, I spend a long time staring at the empty spot in the foyer where he stood. I shouldn't be irritated that he listened when I told him to go, but I am. The second he walked out the front door, I wanted him to come back. To listen to me rage and cry, then kiss me and tell me we'd figure something out.

It's just like him to do that, though. To listen and do what I ask of him, even when it's a ridiculous request like pretending to be my boyfriend or moving in together temporarily. He's always so steady and patient and...there. I never have to worry that he'll bail on me when we have plans or, better yet, push me to make plans that he knows I'd rather cancel. It's why I value his friendship so much. I can be myself around him without feeling like I have to perform sociability.

When it's clear he's not coming back for a while, I force myself up the stairs to my office to get my laptop. It's a pleasant morning, so I take the computer and a cup of coffee with me to the back porch to work on the presentation for the Give Back event. There are only a few days until the event, and the presentation is nowhere near ready. I've tried to make it my main focus in the evenings, but between doing Ron's dirty work for him with the non-renewal meetings and going out with Rhys, my concentration has been shot by the time I'm home.

As I settle onto the porch swing, I'm reminded of Rhys. Of the way he's started sitting next to me on the swing instead of across from me. Of the feel of his thigh against mine as we gently rock back and forth and listen to the sounds of birds and insects in the copse of trees behind my condo. Of the way his eyes brighten when he looks at me.

It's that last thought that threatens to destroy my attention span this morning. Because the way he's been looking at me lately reflects the way I feel when I look at him. Which is bad, because it's getting harder to deny that something like feelings have crept in where Rhys is concerned. But I don't want to admit it, not even to myself. Because I don't believe in feelings. Feelings only lead to heartbreak.

I set my laptop aside, annoyed that Rhys has ruined my concentration yet again, and he's not even here. I check my phone, hoping that he's messaged to say when he's coming back, but there are no notifications, not even from Evie or Kylie.

I finally give up trying to work on the presentation and take my coffee cup back to the kitchen. As much as Rhys filled my head outside, it's worse in here. I see him everywhere I look. At the dining table with a greasy burger and fries, listening while I complain about Ron. Helping me make frittatas, moving around the kitchen as though he belongs.

Even if I left the house, he'd still be everywhere. The restaurants downtown, the ice cream place, the walk along the river.

I spend the entire day moving from room to room, not really accomplishing anything. Progress on my presentation is a bust, and I can't find the energy to do any housework. I try to read the book I've been meaning to, but I keep reading the same paragraph over and over again. The salad I throw together with random things from the refrigerator ends up tasting disgusting, and I pick at my lunch.

I keep checking my phone, picking it up and putting it down an alarming number of times throughout the day. But Rhys never texts or calls.

By evening, I am annoyed at myself for spending the day wallowing over a man who I'm not even really dating, and I decide to get out of the house in the hopes that it will get me out of this funk. I get in my car and drive toward downtown Sapling Grove as though I'm on autopilot.

My stomach growls as I drive, the salad from earlier failing to keep me satiated. Few restaurants are open on

Sunday evenings downtown, but there's a fast food taco place on my way. Tacos in hand, I find a place to park near the river.

I eat the tacos as I wander the mostly empty downtown blocks. It's not only that it's Sunday night in small town Appalachia that has this place feeling abandoned. It's the fact that so many storefronts have "for lease" signs in their windows that have been there for years. I remember when this area was thriving, when nearly every shop was open. It hasn't been that way since I was a kid.

That's why I want the community center so badly. I want this place to regain some of its old sparkle. To feel like the home I had before the countryside was marred by strip malls and Dollar Generals.

A lightning bolt of inspiration hits me as I walk, and the outline of my presentation for the Give Back event is suddenly clear. I open the Notes app on my phone and type furiously as everything clicks into place. The judges for the competition are sure to be people who will remember downtown in its heyday, and I need to appeal to their sense of nostalgia if I want to win the funding.

By the time I'm back at my car, I have nearly the entire presentation written, and I'm so excited I want to call Rhys and celebrate. But thinking about Rhys right now feels like biting down on a sore tooth. A sharp, sudden pang.

At home, I head straight for my office, ignoring the impulse to look into the guest room and wish Rhys was here. I wonder again if I pushed too hard this morning. I shake my head to clear the thought. Right now I need to focus on the presentation.

It's late when I finish putting everything from my phone into the presentation software and writing up my notes in a more coherent outline. So late, in fact, that my phone has put itself in "sleep" mode. I swipe past the locked screen and check to see if I've missed any messages. There are a few from Evie and Kylie that I can answer in the morning, but there's also one from Rhys.

RHYS: I'm going to stay at my place tonight. Have some things I need to do over here. But I'll see you tomorrow.

I can't read the emotion in his message. Is he upset that I kicked him out this morning? Does he really have things to do, or is it an excuse to avoid me? But he also said he would see me tomorrow, so there's at least a little hope that I haven't completely fucked things up.

I respond to his message, even though I doubt he'll see it until tomorrow.

ME: Thanks for letting me know. I'm sorry I kicked you out this morning.

I stare at the phone, unsure if I want him to reply immediately or not at all. Three dots appear, indicating that he's typing. But they disappear after a moment. I toss my phone on the bed, not bothering to darken the screen, then go about the business of getting ready for bed.

I'm surprised to hear what sounds like my phone vibrating as I'm brushing my teeth. Toothbrush still in hand, I don't so much walk as sprint back to the bed, tapping the darkening screen before it locks.

RHYS: I understand why you did it. I'm sorry for suggesting you give up on the Elm Street house.

An odd sensation prickles behind my eyes, and my throat goes tight with emotion.

I don't know what to do with the feeling of warmth in my chest at his apology. Men never apologize to me. It seems like a really low bar—that a simple apology would elicit such a strong reaction in me—but I haven't always had good examples of men doing the right thing in my life.

I send him another message, typing with shaky fingers. It's not a deep or emotional message, at least on the surface, but there's a hopefulness and a wanting to it that I don't usually feel. I take a deep breath as I hit the send button.

ME: Thank you. I'll see you tomorrow.

CHAPTER 21

Rhys

I don't know what to expect when I arrive at Jaclyn's house after work the next day. Some awkwardness, perhaps. Maybe an oblique acknowledgment of our argument before we move on and try to act normally. Certainly not for Jaclyn to kiss me when I walk through the door.

But when she opens the door to let me in, she grabs the lapels of my jacket and pulls me to her. My hands slide around her waist as our mouths meet, and I let out a hungry sigh at the feel of her lips on mine.

As the kiss ends, she looks up at me, her expression vulnerable.

"I'm sorry for yesterday," she says. She wraps her arms

around my back and leans into me, resting her head on my chest.

"It's alright." I hold her close, not daring to question the unguarded intimacy of the moment. Jaclyn never seeks out comfort like this, and I want to savor the way she feels against me, hearts beating in time together.

Part of me wonders if this would be a good time to tell her about Larry's threats. But I don't know what she could do about it. It's not like she could take over as my sponsor. Not without taking this fake relationship to a level that's a hell of a lot harder to undo. Even if our relationship were real, I doubt our sudden marriage would pass muster with the United States government's Green Card process. I'll deal with Larry's bullshit on my own.

Neither of us moves for the longest time, and when we do, it's because Jaclyn looks back up at me with heat in her eyes.

"Take me upstairs?" There's a hint of a question, as though she's not sure I'll agree to her request.

In truth, I probably shouldn't. We should talk first. But the uncertainty in her voice and the sensation of her in my arms has me acting against my better judgment.

The corners of my mouth slide into a grin, and she bites her lip. I bend to pick her up, tucking one arm under her knees and wrapping the other around her back. She squeaks as I lift her off the ground.

"Rhys! Oh my god! Put me..." She trails off as I steady us, and she hooks her arms around my neck.

"I've got you."

"I didn't mean literally take me upstairs."

"I know." I chuckle, and she shivers as I take the first step. "But you like it."

I know from the sound she lets out that I've hit the mark.

Upstairs I set her on the bed, and if I wasn't already breathless from carrying another person up a flight of stairs, the look she gives me would steal my breath away. Need and heat and a bit of moxie that is pure Jaclyn.

I dispense with my shoes before joining her on the bed. She reaches for me, shoving my jacket off, then tugging at my shirt before crashing her mouth into mine. A small voice at the back of my mind calls out in warning, reminding me that I should stop and finally talk to her about what I want from her, but I ignore it. Instead I lose myself in the oblivion of Jaclyn's hands and mouth and the crush of her body against mine.

Light filters into the room from the French doors that open onto a private balcony on the back of Jaclyn's townhouse. Like the kitchen downstairs, Jaclyn's room is surprisingly homey, considering the modern design of the condominium. Pale green walls and cream colored curtains lend an unexpected brightness to the space. From the energy Jaclyn projects, it seems like she'd be the kind of woman to paint bold, severe colors throughout her house. But there's a lightness to the way she decorates that hints at her secretly whimsical side. Like that pink robe I've come to appreciate so much these past few days.

Not that I would ever dare to verbally accuse her of whimsy. Not if I want to wake up in her bed ever again. Which is something I most definitely want to do.

We've spent every moment we could over the past several days learning each other's bodies in ways I never imagined possible. Not only that, but we've found a rhythm of life together that feels real and natural. If it weren't for the fact that she keeps referring to our "benefits situation," I would almost believe she shared my feelings about us.

A few times, I almost tell her. But like all the other times I've resolved to finally say something to her, the words won't come when I need them to. I don't know how long I can keep up with the half-truths of what we're doing, but for now, it's enough.

I haven't slept in the guest room once since moving my things into Jaclyn's condominium. Last night was no exception. In fact, the only time I left her bed last night was to accept a pizza delivery that Jaclyn insisted we needed. She hadn't wasted any time pulling me upstairs when I came in from work, and we were both hungry by the time we were finished with the first round of our regular evening activity.

"Eating pizza naked with you might be my new favorite pastime," Jaclyn had said last night as we sat against pillows with the pizza box between us.

"Really? Not any other naked activity?" I had said teasingly.

"Definitely not." If it hadn't been for the mischievous

quirk of her mouth, I almost would have believed her.

This morning, I've been content to watch her sleep, marveling at the fact that I get to wake up in her bed every morning, even if it's only temporary.

As though she can sense my eyes on her, Jaclyn shifts beside me, curling herself into my side with a sigh. I wrap my arm around her, tucking her close. Her eyes flutter open, and she looks at me confusedly.

"Rhys?" Her voice is still thick with sleep.

"I'm here, love." I kiss her temple and silently rejoice when she doesn't push me away for either the kiss or the endearment.

"What time is it?" she asks through a yawn.

"A little after six."

If we didn't both have work today, I'd suggest we stay here. But rescheduling patients so that I can have a lazy day in bed with my not-girlfriend isn't my style, although the temptation is high.

Jaclyn stretches, and I'd be lying if I said I didn't enjoy the way her breasts lift as she reaches her arms above her head. She catches me staring and gives me a playful wink.

"I'm going to take a shower," she says as she stands. She walks toward the bathroom and pauses halfway there, looking over her shoulder. "Aren't you coming with me?"

I don't say anything but make quick work of disentangling myself from the sheets. Her mouth slides into a sultry grin.

Once we're dressed and breakfasted, we go outside to drive to our respective workplaces. Before I open my car door, Jaclyn tells me to wait. She moves toward me, wrapping her arms around my neck and pulling me into a kiss. My hands find their new favorite place on her hips. As the kiss ends, she glances over my shoulder. I turn to look behind me, but she stops me.

"Landon is watching," she whispers.

I will my face not to betray the disappointment that engulfs me at her words. From the way this week has gone, I thought things had changed for her. For us.

"Right. Have to keep up appearances." My words sound bitter, and Jaclyn draws back, settling her mouth into a concerned line.

"What's wrong?"

"It's nothing." I move toward my car, but she follows on my heels.

"That didn't sound like nothing, Rhys." She grabs my arm and tugs, making me stop.

"I don't want to talk about it right now."

"Don't want to talk about what? Rhys, I don't understand what's going on." Her hand slides into mine, and she does a double squeeze. It's the same gesture that she used that night we ran into the bloke from the bank. The one that felt like the beginning of something real between us. But none of this is real, and I've been fooling myself into thinking it was.

"I have to go to work."

I jerk my hand out of hers and stomp toward my car. I drive away without glancing back toward her, even though I want to.

My mood does not improve when I arrive at work. It's one of those days with back-to-back patients and barely a moment to breathe between them. Around two o'clock, I shovel a sandwich into my mouth in a sad semblance of lunch. By six-thirty, my head throbs with dehydration and the sense that whatever brief bliss I had with Jaclyn is over. Hell, our friendship might be over.

I debate whether to go back to Jaclyn's place or hide myself away at home. It would be easier, avoiding her. No less painful, but easier.

But there's the fucking rub. As much as I want this to be easy, I know that one of these days I'm going to have to do the hard thing and actually tell her how I feel. No more excuses. Because I want her to come to the same conclusion that I have, and it's clear that won't happen unless I do something about it.

CHAPTER 22

Jaclyn

Instead of working on the syllabus template update I was supposed to finish last week, I spend the first few hours of my day playing this morning over and over in my head, trying to pinpoint the moment everything went sideways. Everything seemed fine until Rhys and I kissed in the driveway. I can't decide if it was the kiss itself or the fact that Landon was there that made Rhys react the way he did.

Around mid-morning, I wander over to the library to refill my travel coffee mug. The library always has fresh coffee available for anyone who stops by, and it's a frequent stop when I need to get out of my office.

Kylie is in the lobby when I arrive, and after I fill my mug, I walk over to chat with her. I hate to admit it, but she's probably the best person to talk to about my interaction with Rhys this morning. Not because I prefer to go to her for dating advice, but because she will give the problem her signature straightforward analysis. Sometimes you need the person who isn't going to overthink things.

We exchange pleasantries, and I decide to take a page from her book and come right out with what's troubling me.

"I screwed up with Rhys, but I can't figure out what I did," I say almost before she's finished saying hello.

She lifts an eyebrow. "What makes you say that?"

I fill her in on the details, including the fact that Rhys and I agreed that we would reap the benefits of living in the same space for the next few weeks. She listens impassively, only interrupting to ask clarifying questions. When I'm finished, she tilts her head slightly, her expression bemused.

"You really don't know what upset him?"

"I am completely in the dark."

"Seriously, Jay? Your entire career is based on observing people and their behaviors." She pauses and studies me for a moment.

"What?"

"Wow, you really don't have a clue, do you?"

"No, that's why I asked you for help." I scrunch my face in annoyance. This is not going the way I expected. Kylie was supposed to listen to what happened and tell me what I did wrong. It's her superpower. But for some bizarre reason, she's refusing to use it.

"Look, I can tell you what I think, or you can go talk to him. Because I think there's probably something you're not telling me. That you're maybe not even telling yourself." She gives me a pointed look, and I bristle under her gaze.

She's hit too close to the mark, and I don't like it.

"Whatever," I say. I know I sound far more immature than a woman in her mid-thirties has any right to sound.

I'm walking through the door when she calls out, "Talk to him."

The door closes behind me, and I try to ignore her words.

Rhys doesn't show up at my place until late in the evening. He's usually off work by five, but tonight it's almost seven before I hear his car pull into the driveway. Something about his late arrival puts me on edge.

Is it because he was upset this morning? Is he still upset?

I shake the thoughts away, but they threaten to stay, peering around the corners of my mind.

I try to look busy as he comes into the living room. I fluff a pillow from the recliner as though I've been tidying. I'm sure he knows it's an act, because this room is always tidy.

He stops when he sees me, and the air in the room shifts. His mouth settles into a firm line, and I get the sense he's still angry about this morning.

"How was your day?" I ask, keeping my tone light even though the question feels strangely heavy.

He cuts me a look, and I know from the weariness around his eyes and the hard set of his jaw that he hasn't had a good day.

"My day was...illuminating," he says after a pause.

I tilt my head to the side, unsure of his meaning.

"What I mean is, I figured something out."

He takes a determined step toward me. I have the instinct to back away, but I stay rooted to my spot by the couch.

"What did you figure out?"

He takes another step, putting us within an arm's length of each other.

"That I need to say some things to you. About this morning...and about the future."

"I'm not sure I want to talk about it right now," I say. The thought of discussing our future is somewhere between thrilling and terrifying.

"That's too bad, because I'm in a talking mood." There's a decisiveness to his tone, and I am hit with a mixture of emotions. Concern for what he's about to say but also a touch of arousal.

"I'm tired of what we've been doing."

I suck in a surprised breath. Because I thought he was happy with our friends with benefits deal, but I must have misjudged things.

"Is that why you got so mad this morning? Because you didn't want me to kiss you?"

He gapes at me, and I don't know what to make of his expression.

"That's not why."

"Then why?" I practically yell it. "Because you may have hand an epiphany today, but I've spent the day trying to figure out what I did wrong."

"You looked at him instead of me." His volume matches mine.

I stare at him, unsure what he means. He takes a step toward me, and there's something electric in his movement.

"You kissed me as we were leaving for work, and I thought it was because you were kissing *me*, but it was just for show." Rhys's voice crackles with raw emotion.

"I don't under—"

Rhys lets out a humorless laugh, and there's an untamed look in his eyes.

"I love you, Jaclyn."

You know that sound effect in movies right after an explosion where everything is extremely loud and then goes quiet for a moment? Then all that's left is a shrill buzzing and muffled voices. That is exactly the sound my brain is making as I process Rhys's words.

I shake my head—whether to clear the buzzing or to deny there's any way Rhys could love me, I'm not sure.

"I love you," he says again. "I know none of what we've shared these past few weeks has been real to you, but it has to me."

I blink at him, completely lost for words. When I find my voice, it's shaky with confusion.

"No, that's not...You're not serious, are you?"

"I am totally fucking serious, and I can't take keeping it from you anymore."

"For how long?" My voice is barely above a whisper, but

except for our breathing, there's no other sound to drown it out.

"I..."

"How long, Rhys?"

He swallows, then looks me in the eye, and I can tell that what he's about to say is going to tilt my understanding of reality.

"The day we met. I knew from the first sarcastic barb you threw in my direction."

Moments from the four years we've known each other play across my memory. Rhys's revelation puts so many things in a new light. The way he's always available to hang out at a moment's notice. The fact that he hasn't really dated anyone in the time we've been friends. The way his eyes searched mine after our first kiss.

"But we didn't know each other."

"I know. I wish I could explain it, but I just...knew."

The idea of *just knowing* that he was in love with me doesn't compute. How could he possibly know that after barely a moment of meeting me? That's not how love is supposed to work. It must have been lust. Desire. Anything but love.

But if it wasn't more than simple attraction, he wouldn't have waited this long for something to happen between us. He would have kissed me first. Right?

"You never made a move."

"I wanted to. So many fucking times." I hear the ache in his voice. The yearning.

"Then why didn't you?" My question is little better than

a whisper between us, but he hears it, and his voice cracks with emotion as he replies with his own question.

"Even if I had, do you think we would have lasted?"

I consider telling him it would have. I want to believe it because I care about our friendship, about Rhys. But we have lied enough lately. "No. It wouldn't have lasted."

"I didn't think so."

My breath catches as he takes a step toward me. Bizarrely, I think he's going to kiss me, but he drops his voice to a low rumble.

"But I'm done pretending. If you don't want this to go further, I need to know."

My chest rises and falls, and I want to reach out and touch him. But something holds me back, and my hands remain at my sides.

"You don't have to decide right now. All I ask is that you consider what this could be." He gestures between us. "That we could be something that lasts forever."

"I don't want forever." The words are immediate, but they sound wrong to my ears. Because I've never wanted forever with anyone, but something about this thing with Rhys is different.

Rhys takes a step backward and stumbles a little. When he rights himself, I see the naked vulnerability in his expression, and I have the sense that I've hurt him deeply.

"Figure out what you do want, then." He doesn't yell or rage or exhibit any emotion, really. His words are calm, coolly indifferent. It's worse that way, knocking the wind out of me, and I want to turn back time. Just enough to stop myself from saying the shittiest thing I've ever said to him.

"I think I'm going to stay at my place for a few days." Rhys turns to leave, and my heart splits in two. I want to run to him and soothe the creases from his brow. To reverse the defeated slump of his shoulders.

My thoughts swirl with more questions I want to ask before he walks out the door—about where we go from here, about what our friendship looks like now that I know he has feelings for me—but the only one that comes out is awkward and selfish.

"What does this mean for the Give Back event?"

Rhys stiffens, and I feel even more like an ass than I already did. The man tells me he loves me, and all I can think about is making sure our town believes that he and I are together? Really earning the title of Complete Asshole™ tonight.

"I'll still go to the event with you, if that's what you want. I'll pretend in front of your mum and Landon and the whole fucking town if I have to. It's what I've been doing for years, after all."

I stand stock still, watching as he disappears down the hallway. It's only when I hear the sound of the door slamming behind him that I allow myself to crumple onto the couch and curl into a ball. Something tickles my cheek, and when I reach up to wipe it away, I realize my fingers are wet with tears.

CHAPTER 23

Jaclyn

The lights are off when I arrive home from work the next day. I wander through my dark townhouse, and the quiet is overwhelming. There's nothing on the TV. No sounds of Rhys's deep chuckle as something funny happens in whatever show he's watching. No pots and pans clanging as he makes dinner.

Instead, there's an eerie silence, and I wonder how I lived like this before he moved in.

I throw my work bag on the table in the hallway, then go upstairs to change into lounge pants. While I'm in the bathroom, a notification chimes on my phone. I force myself not to rush to check it, half hoping it's Rhys, knowing it's probably not.

I don't want forever.

My words from last night echo in my mind, not for the first time today. I spent large portions of the day staring blankly at my computer screen, playing the scene of last night over and over in my head, instead of working on the stack of paperwork I have to turn in following those contract meetings that Ron tricked me into doing.

In a cruel twist of fate, the hours I was at work dragged by, and yet the end of the day arrived too soon. Like waiting for a root canal.

I pull on a sweatshirt, then glance at my phone. As I suspected, it's not a message from Rhys.

KYLIE: You seemed off today. Everything ok?

Evie, Kylie, and I had our weekly summer lunch date today, and even though I felt like shit, I made myself go. I tried to act normal, but I guess Kylie picked up on things.

ME: Rhys moved back to his place for a few days.

KYLIE: Oh.

I toss my phone on the bed, not wanting to get in to the details with Kylie, of all people. We've been getting along alright these days, but I don't need her relationship advice.

I flop on the bed, fully prepared to lose myself in a murder mystery series I've been meaning to watch. But then my phone buzzes twice in quick succession, and I give in to the temptation to look at my messages.

KYLIE: I'm coming over with margarita mix.

KYLIE: Want me to invite Evie?

I laugh at her older sister tendencies, but the truth is, it's exactly the kind of thing I would do if my sister was having a shitty day because of man. I text Kylie back, because there's no use trying to keep her from coming over here and distracting me from my troubles.

ME: Not this time.

She sends me a thumbs-up emoji, and I burrow back into my pillows.

A little while later, I hear the front door open, and Kylie's voice calling my name. I should probably stop giving keys to all my friends.

"Up here," I shout.

"I'll meet you in the kitchen," she calls back.

I pull myself out of the bed and make my way downstairs. The scent of limes hits my nose as I step into the kitchen. Kylie hands me a glass with a perfect salt rim and a lime wedge. I shuffle to the couch in the living room and put my feet up on the coffee table. Kylie joins me moments later, following suit.

"Do you want to talk about it?" she asks, taking a sip of her drink.

I shake my head.

We enjoy our drinks in silence, slowly savoring the citrus and tequila. I know the alcohol is working its magic, because the tightness in my jaw loosens as the liquid in my glass diminishes. When I swallow the last drop, Kylie reaches for the glass.

"Want another one?"

"Yes, please."

I follow her to the kitchen. While she mixes up a second round, I find a jar of salsa in the fridge and pour us each a small cup, then grab a bag of tortilla chips from the pantry. I haven't had dinner yet, and two margaritas on an empty stomach seems like a bad idea.

We return to the couch with our fresh drinks and our snack.

"Let me drink some more of this first," I say.

Kylie raises an eyebrow. "I didn't say anything."

"I know what you're thinking."

She shrugs, but I can see the curiosity in her eyes.

I eat some of my chips and salsa, then take two big drinks of my margarita before I'm ready to talk.

"He's in love with me."

I expect her to gasp in shock or stare at me wide-eyed, but the expression on her face is one that says "Yeah, I knew that."

"And you're not in love with him?" she asks casually.

"I..." I search for the right way to phrase the conclusion I came to last night after he left. After I picked myself up off the floor and dried my tears. "I think I'm in lust with him."

"Oh."

"But..."

"But?"

I take another swig of my drink, delaying saying the words out loud. Because once I say them, they'll be real, and I'm not sure I'm ready for that. I cut my eyes toward Kylie, who's sitting forward now, anticipation in her posture.

"I think I could fall in love with him." It's barely a whisper, but it feels like standing inside a ringing bell, the vibrations thrumming through my skin and into the core of my being.

Kylie doesn't move. Not even so much as a facial twitch or a raised eyebrow.

"It's ok. You can say something."

"I'm proud of you," she says at last.

Now it's my turn to freeze. I stare at her, unsure how to respond.

"The Jaclyn I met five years ago would never admit that she's capable of love."

My instinct is to argue, but she's right. Hell, even two months ago, I wouldn't have been able to say something like that.

"That's great and all, but Rhys thinks I don't want him."

"So tell him."

"It's not that simple."

I don't want forever.

Then figure out what you do want.

"Anyway, grand gestures are Evie's department. Tonight, can we just get drunk and not worry about me and Rhys?"

"If that's what you need."

An hour later, we've eaten all the chips and salsa and each downed another margarita. Kylie is beyond tipsy at this point, and I am learning fascinating things about my friend.

"What the hell is up with Sebastian Thacker, anyway?" she asks after margarita number...actually I've lost count at this point.

"You mean besides the fact that he wears the tightest pants known to humans?" I ask with a laugh.

Kylie gestures wildly, both hands spread wide. "Yesssss. You get it. He's always walking around campus with those annoying tigh' pants and those annoying sexy li'l glasses." Her speech is slightly slurred, and I wonder if I should take her half-finished drink away from her before she spills it all over my couch.

"Oh yes, very annoying that he wears sexy little glasses." I smirk at my friend.

"I know, right? And I'm ninety-nine point nine-nine-nine percent sure that he's the one who keeps sending me those meeting requests." She holds her thumb and index finger a fraction of an inch apart, and I laugh.

"You mean the ones from the fake students?" A few months ago, the librarians started getting appointment requests from "students" with names like Jacques Strap and Ricky T. Bridge. No one has any idea where they're coming from, and Kylie gets more of them than anyone else.

"Yes! A new one every week, clogging up my clalendal... calendar." She takes another sip of her drink, then looks at me with wide eyes. "And how *dare* he move here? He *knew* what he was doing. But nooooo. Had to jus' show up and ruin everything."

Now that's interesting, I think. Almost like Kylie and Sebastian have some kind of history. But that can't be, because when he started, she acted like she'd never seen him before. I want to ask for more details, but she's closed her eyes. A small snore escapes her, and I chuckle to myself.

I ease the glass out of her hand so my couch won't smell like tequila and regret in the morning. I find a blanket and throw it over her, then make my way to the stairs. When the steps start moving, I realize I'm as drunk as Kylie is. Instead of attempting to scale the wobbly staircase, I grab another blanket and a pillow and curl up in the recliner across from her.

The sound of a groan startles me awake, and I'm immediately aware of a pounding in my brain and the too-bright light of the sun creeping through the curtains. I force my eyes open and squint across the room.

"Oh god. I haven't drunk that much since college," Kylie says as she stretches slowly.

My bones feel like they're all in the wrong places as I unwind myself from the recliner. I'm in worse shape this morning than I was after Andrew and Evie's wedding, and that's saying something.

"I'll make some coffee."

In the kitchen, I fill up the coffee pot and start the grinder. The noise is excruciating. Pushing past the clanging in my head, I find a couple glasses and fill them with water. I hand one to Kylie as she shuffles to the kitchen island.

"Thanks," she says as she downs most of the water in a single gulp. "Sorry I passed out on your couch."

"It's ok. I needed this."

Kylie gives me a smile that more closely resembles a grimace—from the look on her face, she feels as bad as I do—then her brows knit together.

"Did I...say...anything last night?"

I snort. "You mean something specific?"

"I mean about...never mind." She looks away from me, and for a moment I consider pushing her to say more, but the coffee maker chimes indicating that it's ready. Coffee mugs in hand, I join Kylie at the kitchen island. I take a tentative sip of the scalding hot coffee, the chocolaty aroma of perfectly roasted beans reviving my senses.

I wonder if she's unsure what she said about Sebastian, and while my curiosity is most definitely piqued, I know better than to prod Kylie for more information if she doesn't want to give it.

"So, what are you going to do?" she asks, and for a moment, I have no idea what she's talking about.

"About Rhys," she continues, sensing my confusion.

"I don't know," I say with a sigh.

"Listen, I know you're an oldest daughter, too, so taking advice from your older and wiser friend makes your skin crawl."

I open my mouth to protest, but she gives me a pointed look, and I snap my mouth shut. I hate that she has my number like that.

"Trust me when I say that with relationships, nothing good ever comes from not talking to the other person. Even when you think talking is going to make the problem worse." She pauses, then grabs my arm and looks me dead in the eye. "Especially when you think it will make the problem worse."

I resist the urge to ask if her statement has something to

do with Sebastian.

I know in my gut that she's right. I only hope I haven't screwed things up so completely that Rhys is lost to me forever.

CHAPTER 24

Jaclyn

I find the dress at the back of my closet. I've only worn it once for a dinner with the Sapling Grove Business Association that Mom invited me to as her plus-one. That event was black-tie, and I wasn't bold enough to wear a tux, even though I would have looked hot in a tux.

The dress is a deep emerald green with a halter top that hugs my curves and leaves the skin on my upper back exposed. It zips on the side, which is great, because part of what I hate about dresses is the impossibility of zipping and unzipping them. Without a partner to take care of the zipper for me, I end up bouncing around my bedroom contorting my arms in weird positions just to get the damn things on and off.

But this dress spoke to me when I was looking for

something to wear to Mom's dinner, and I bought it without much consideration for the fact that I rarely have occasion for such a garment. Plus it looks amazing on me.

I flush at that thought, because who am I kidding. I don't have any reason to dress like this—sexy and like I'm hoping someone will notice. Because the only person I want to notice is barely talking to me right now.

But I don't have much else in my wardrobe that screams "fancy community gala."

A knock at my door startles me out of my thoughts.

"You ready?" Rhys asks, his voice muffled through the wood.

We haven't seen each other much since he told me he loved me, but we agreed—via text—that it would look odd if we showed up to the Give Back Event separately.

"Yes, just a minute," I call. I slide the dress on, checking to make sure my breasts are adequately covered, then pull the zipper up. It snags a little about halfway up, but I'm able to get it past the problem spot. I check my hair and make up one last time, and open the door to find Rhys standing in the hallway.

Something in the way he holds himself makes me wonder if he's trying to keep his eyes trained on my face, refusing to let them scan over the way this dress cascades around my curves. Or maybe it's that I'm the one trying desperately not to check him out. He's in the same suit that he wore to the wedding, and I'm reminded of the jolt of desire I felt when our lips met for the first time.

We smile tightly at each other, and I consider canceling

our plans. Giving up on the hope that the community center will ever be funded and crawling in a hole until I can forget the fact that I've schemed to the point that I'm in danger of losing my best friend.

But Rhys clears his throat and nods at me, as though to say we're in this together so we might as well make the best of it. I take a deep breath, ready to face whatever happens at the Give Back event.

The microphone squeals with feedback as Jason Whitehead, former football golden boy and the closest thing to a local celebrity that Sapling Grove has, steps to the podium on the makeshift stage in the high school gymnasium. Jason led the Sapling Grove Fighting Sapsuckers to two state championships when we were in high school, and he had the potential to go pro if it hadn't been for an injury he sustained playing college football at the University of Tennessee. Now he sells insurance and does appearances for local events like the annual Christmas tree lighting and the Fourth of July parade.

Tonight he's using his status as the most famous person in Sapling Grove to act as the emcee for the evening's competition. He's wearing a tuxedo that looks like it's from the 1980s. I'm sure he rented it from Susan's Tux and Gown Emporium, where every teen in Sapling Grove has gone for decades to rent formal wear.

Jason clears his throat, then turns on his golden boy

charm and speaks into the microphone. "Good evening, ladies and gents! Are you ready to make a difference in our town?"

The crowd cheers, although I suspect it has less to do with their philanthropic tendencies and more to do with the fact that Jason has this way of pumping up a crowd that is infectious.

"Since this is the inaugural Give Back event, allow me to go over the rules for tonight's competition."

I glance around the room, curious to see who else is here. I lift my chin in greeting when I see Katie Price sitting a few seats down from Rhys and me. Katie teaches biology at Cooke and is involved in the local Naturalists Club. They do monthly river clean up projects and maintain the trails at the local state park. If the community center project is going to lose the competition to anyone, I wouldn't begrudge her the win.

Katie looks about as comfortable in a dress as I feel. I suspect if this event hadn't specified formal attire, she would have showed up in a pair of jeans and her farm boots. She returns my greeting with a slight roll of her eyes toward her black dress, and we both turn back to pay attention to what Jason is saying about the rules.

"Each presenter will have five minutes to present their proposal to our panel of judges, followed by the question and answer round, where the judges will ask for clarification on any unclear aspects of the proposal. Once all the proposals have been presented, the judges will deliberate. Winners will be announced at the end of the night. Throughout the evening, Hanson's Wieners will have their food truck set up outside. We'd like to thank Hanson's for sponsoring tonight's event."

Only in Sapling Grove could you find a black-tie gala sponsored by the local hot dog stand. The absurdity is almost too good to be true.

On the stage, Jason finishes his spiel about the competition. "And thank you to all our sponsors, especially the Sapling Grove Federal Savings Bank, Montgomery Therapy, and the Sapling Grove Women's League for their generous donations to the SGFSB Foundation."

I suck in a breath. I didn't know that Montgomery Therapy was one of the big donors. A sense of foreboding crashes through me. I'm not usually given to bouts of anxiety, but if Larry is involved in tonight's competition, I might as well abandon all hope of ever getting the community center fully funded.

Rhys must sense my sudden nervousness, because he reaches for my hand and gives it two squeezes. It reminds me of the night that we ran into Daniel Sutton at the pizza place, when I took his hand and squeezed out a "thank you." My breathing instantly steadies at the gesture.

The sound of applause fills the gym, and when it dies down, Jason resumes his address. "Now, who's ready to meet our judges?"

Another round of applause erupts, and Jason has to raise his hands to quiet everyone. The Give Back organizers have kept the names of the judges secret—I suspect it's to prevent any attempts at trying to canvas for votes ahead of the competition. But the not knowing adds an extra layer of anxiety to the evening, and I flex my hands tight with the concern over who is about to walk out onto the stage. Unfortunately for Rhys, I forget that he's holding one of my hands, and I hear him mutter, "Fuck, that hurts."

I slide my eyes over to him, making sure to release his hand from my death grip.

"Sorry," I mouth.

He reaches his arm around my shoulders and pulls me closer to him.

"It's alright. I'm here," he whispers. Then he does something that almost cracks the walls around my heart in two with how tender it is. He brushes his lips ever-so-lightly against my temple. I swallow back a new wave of emotion. One that I'm not used to. One that's making my vision blur with dampness.

The problem with knowing that Rhys is in love with me is that now I don't know how to act around him. Maybe if I hadn't come up with the ridiculous idea to pretend to date him, it wouldn't be so bad, because then I wouldn't feel like we needed to touch each other in public.

I shift away from him. Away from the pesky emotions that are threatening to disrupt everything that I've been working toward for the community center. Instead, I focus on the stage, where Jason is reading out short biographies of each of the judges.

So far, there are no surprises. It's a panel of five judges, and he's announced three of the five so far: Bob Greenlee, the president of the bank; Diane Whitehead, Jason's mother and owner of the insurance firm he works for; and Coach George, who coaches basketball at the high school. I've never been sure if George was his first name or last name, but in Sapling Grove, it doesn't matter. Once you're a coach, "Coach" *is* your first name.

It's not a perfect lineup for the community center's chances, but it could be a lot worse. Bob and Diane aren't likely to be openly antagonistic and might even be open to the idea. Coach George is one of the most affable people in town, but he's also the kind of person who will go along with whatever the others decide. He's never been one to want to rock the boat. I get a boost of encouragement when the fourth person is announced.

"Joining this fine group of judges, we have a woman who's known for her philanthropy as much as her musical talent. Please welcome Barbara Kensington to the stage!"

The crowd cheers as Barbara walks out from behind the curtain waving both hands. Barbara is the choir director at the local Baptist Church and the woman responsible for countless Sapling Grove kids' music lessons growing up. I even took piano from her for a year when I was in elementary school. Not only is Barbara well-loved in town, she's also a formidable figure in Sapling Grove politics as the longest serving member of the City Council and the president of the Sapling Grove Women's League. She looks like a sweet grandma, with her graying box braids pulled into a bun and the laugh lines around her dark eyes. Like the kind of woman who would bake you cookies and give you a glass of lemonade when you scraped your knee—and she would—but under that soft outer appearance is a force to be reckoned with.

I don't know where she'll land on the community center proposal, but if she decides that it's worth it, I doubt the others will be able to overrule her. Precious little happens in this town without the backing of Barbara Kensington.

As she takes her seat, I smile confidently at Rhys who squeezes my shoulder in encouragement. I hold my breath as Jason introduces the last judge.

"Our final judge for the evening is someone you all know and love," Jason says with an admiration that gives me pause. "The owner of the ten-time recipient of 'Business of the Year' award from the Sapling Grove *Sentinel*, the man responsible for bringing more revenue to the Sapling Grove Business Association than any previous president, the one and only Larry Montgomery!"

If the crowd was loud for Barbara Kensington's announcement, it's nothing compared to the absolute wall of sound that erupts at Jason's words now. Larry's entrance only increases the crowd's fervor. He points toward the back of the room where members of the high school cheerleading squad have t-shirts at the ready to toss to people in the crowd. If I had to guess, they're shirts branded with the high school mascot on the front and "Montgomery Therapy" in big letters on the back. In other words, exactly the kind of free t-shirt that people in this town go bananas for.

My unease from earlier is back with a vengeance. With Larry on the judging panel, my proposal is probably sunk.

There's no way he'll vote in favor of funding that could potentially take the Elm Street house from him, and he has enough influence that turning a majority of the judges against the proposal will be a breeze.

"Rhys, what do I do?" I ask while the throng around us continues to excitedly wave their hands, hoping for one of the free t-shirts. I expect him to say something encouraging, but when our eyes meet, I see my own worries reflected back at me.

"I don't know."

It's not the response I wanted.

"Listen, there's something I need to tell you about the Elm Street house," Rhys says. The urgency in his voice isn't helping my concern about Larry being the deciding vote on my proposal.

I gesture for him to go on, but he glances at the stage. Larry's eyes scan the crowd, but they stop when they land on Rhys and me. The smile he gives us, like he's just moved his queen into the checkmate position, makes my blood turn to ice. He knows he's won and that there's nothing I can do about it.

Rhys's jaw clenches, but I don't know what to make of the fact that he looks like he wants to throttle his boss.

"What do I need to know about the Elm Street house?" I ask, drawing his attention back to me.

"Fuck it." He nods once, like he's decided something.

"Excuse me?"

"You are Jaclyn Fucking Beckett, and you're going to get that money, no matter what happens up there. What you've done for the community center already is amazing. I know that the next phase is going to be even better."

I don't think it's what he was planning to say, but it doesn't matter. Because he's right. I *am* Jaclyn Fucking Beckett, and I'm not afraid of Larry Montgomery.

When Jason calls my name to take the stage for my presentation, I turn to Rhys, a smile on my face. He leans his forehead against mine.

"You've got this."

"I know."

He kisses me softly, and even though I know he's only doing it for the show of it all, it doesn't feel fake. I stand and roll my shoulders back, imagining myself taller than everyone else in the room.

Standing behind the podium isn't that much different from standing in front of a classroom of undergraduates. Even the level of attentiveness is about the same with about half the crowd not-so-subtly looking at their laps where their phones are hidden. But my focus is on the judges and convincing them that the community center is the best use of the funds available.

Before I begin, Barbara tilts her head to the side and asks into her microphone, "Aren't you Helen Beckett's girl?"

"Yes, ma'am."

"The one who used to stage one-woman protests in the middle of downtown?"

I fight a flush of embarrassment. Back in high school, I was an activist in search of a problem. I blame it on listening to the *Hair* soundtrack a few too many times early in my Classic Rock discovery phase and my adolescent fascination with the Vietnam War protests in the late 1960s.

"Yes, ma'am."

"Proceed." I catch the quirk of a smile as she picks up a pen and makes a note on the pad of paper in front of her. At least, I hope she's taking notes and not just doodling while I speak.

"Thank you." I take a deep breath before I launch in to what I came here to say.

As I lay out my proposal, my eyes scan the crowd. People are nodding and smiling, and one person even lets out a whoop of excitement when I mention that the new community center would offer free weekly classes in fiber arts, yoga, and basic home repair.

When I finish, the applause is deafening, almost to the same degree it was when Larry came out on stage. I take my seat and try to relax as I listen to the remaining presentations.

CHAPTER 25

Rhys

Telling Jaclyn I love her went about as well as I expected, which is to say not well at all. I've been on edge ever since, and being at this competition has been torture tonight. Not least because I've spent the whole night trying not to look at Jaclyn in that dress.

As soon as the host dismissed the crowd so the judges could deliberate, I made my way to the bar. I could tell Jaclyn was in need of a strong drink, and I needed a little distance from her and the dress that's going to be the star of my dreams about her for the foreseeable future. Unfortunately, half of Sapling Grove beat me into the line, so I've been standing here for ten minutes waiting my turn.

But the good news is, that's ten minutes I've had away from Jaclyn and the temptation to ask her if we could get out of here and do something about the dress. When she opened the bedroom door back at her place, it took everything in me not to flick my eyes down the length of her body. If I had, there is a high likelihood we would have missed the Give Back event because I would not have been able to resist the urge to tell her we should forget everything I told her on Wednesday so that we could go back to the partial peace of being friends with benefits.

In the four years we've known each other, I don't think I've seen Jaclyn in a dress once, but I seriously hope this is not the last time I do. Because this woman can wear the hell out of one. It clings to her figure in a way that is so sexy, I can't look at her for more than a few seconds or I'll need to go somewhere private until things calm down. Which is a problem.

Drinks finally in hand, I turn to make my way back to Jaclyn and am surprised to find Helen standing behind me.

"I thought Jaclyn did a wonderful job on her proposal," I say.

"She did. I'm really proud of her." Helen smiles.

"Me, too." I pause, unsure. Right before Jaclyn went up on the stage, I realized there's something I can do to put an end to the dispute over the Elm Street house. But I'm going to need Helen's help to pull it off. "Helen, did the sellers accept Larry's offer on that house?"

"They're...negotiating. Why do you ask?"

"Because I'd like to put in an offer on it. I've been thinking about buying for a while." My plan had been to buy a house and move out of my flat. Make a more permanent home here. But watching Jaclyn work so hard to get the community center going makes me want to be part of something here. More involved in the community than I have been.

"But you can't tell Jaclyn," I add. "Not yet. I want it to be a surprise."

"Oh, I like a bit of intrigue," Helen says with a sly grin. There's a gleam of mischief in her eyes that makes me wonder if Larry has any idea what he's up against when it comes to the Beckett women. "But before I agree to keep a secret from my daughter, I need to know one thing."

She fixes me with a serious look. "Why?"

"What do you mean?"

"I mean, why are you doing this? Is it because you hate Larry?"

I don't have to think about my answer, but I don't want Helen to get the wrong idea about where things are with Jaclyn and me.

She waits, and I can see she won't take my offer seriously until she's satisfied I'm doing this for the right reasons. My heart pounds in my chest, but I keep my voice steady as I speak.

"Because I love her. I always have."

"That's what I thought." She sighs before continuing, "Do you have any idea how long I've been waiting for you and Jaclyn to stop pretending you're dating and actually tell each other how you feel?"

I'm midway through taking a drink, and I nearly choke on it, coughing as some tickles the back of my throat. Helen pats my back as if that will clear the liquid from my throat.

"I don't know what you're talking about," I say once I've recovered from the coughing fit.

"I'm not as oblivious as Jaclyn likes to think. I know you had never kissed her before the wedding."

I start to protest, but Helen lifts an eyebrow in a knowing look. There's no use arguing when a Beckett looks at you like that.

"Please don't tell her you know. Things between us are... complicated."

Her expression softens, and she reaches out to pat my hand reassuringly.

"Your secret is safe with me."

"Thank you." There's an odd relief to Helen knowing the truth about Jaclyn and me.

We chat for a few more minutes, and Helen enters a note in her phone with the details of my offer.

"I'll message the sellers right now," she says. "I think they will be glad to have an alternative to Larry's offer."

She wishes me well and walks toward the bar, and I resume navigating my way through the crowd to find Jaclyn.

I reach her as the emcee steps back up to the microphone and announces that the judges have finished their deliberation.

Once the crowd settles back in their seats, the emcee cedes the stage to Bill Greenlee to hand out the prizes for the evening. There are three prizes and only five proposals, so Jaclyn's chances are good.

"Our third place winner tonight is the Sapling Grove Naturalists Club with their proposal to expand their river clean up radius."

The crowd applauds as the woman from the Naturalists Club accepts the prize. Jaclyn whistles and claps her hands loudly, and the woman on the stage tips her head in acknowledgment.

"In second place, we have the Parks and Recreation Department's proposal for the purchase of a heater for the community pool."

I almost contracted hypothermia the one time I swam in that pool, and it seems that most of the people here have, too, based on the chatter around us.

I glance toward Jaclyn. Her applause is less enthusiastic this time, and I can feel the nervous anticipation radiating from her.

"And now, the moment you've all been waiting for," Bill says, and the audience quiets.

"No matter what happens, I'm proud of you," I whisper to Jaclyn.

She takes my hand and gives it two squeezes.

"Our inaugural grand prize winner is Sapling Grove High School's own Coach Phipps. The Fighting Sapsuckers will have a resurfaced football field for next fall's season!"

Around us, people stand and cheer, and the sound is deafening. But Jaclyn remains rigid in her seat.

"Are you alright?" I ask. When she doesn't respond, I wonder if she heard me over the noise of the still-celebrating crowd.

"Jaclyn—"

"Can we just go?" She looks at me finally, and the hurt in her eyes makes me want to storm the stage and give Larry a piece of my mind. But that would certainly have dire consequences for my employment status. Besides, I get the sense it wouldn't help Jaclyn, either.

"Of course," I say.

We weave our way through the crowd, our hands clasped so we don't get separated.

"Unsurprising, given who was on the judging panel," Jaclyn says when we're almost at the door. There's a defeated sound to her voice.

"You think the judges were unfair?" someone asks behind us.

We both tense because there's no mistaking that voice. Sure enough, Larry stands behind us with a smug look on his face.

"I think the judges did exactly what everyone expected," Jaclyn says coolly. "Which is to say that you awarded your pet project the grand prize."

Larry's nostrils flare, and I wonder if he expected something else from her. Fawning and apologizing perhaps. If so, he clearly doesn't know shit about her.

"We awarded the project with the most potential for positively impacting the town," he says, recovering himself.

Jaclyn scoffs. "You chose the football field over the community center. The football field that only a handful of Sapling Grove kids will be able to use."

Larry's eyes narrow, and he takes a step closer to Jaclyn.

I would intervene, but Jaclyn seems to have everything under control. She rolls her shoulders back, and there's a flash of anger in her eyes that I wouldn't mess with if I were Larry.

"Listen here, missy. In this town, we do what's best for everyone, and what's best for everyone is what I say it is."

"I fail to see how the football field is best for everyone when the community center will impact a broader slice of the population," Jaclyn says.

Larry grinds his teeth, and his mouth settles into a frown. Jaclyn has managed to render him speechless, and I couldn't be prouder.

She smiles at him in a smug way that I shouldn't find as attractive as I do.

"That's what I thought," she says, clearly satisfied with displaying greater town pride than Larry. She turns to me and tilts her head toward the door in a "let's get out of here" gesture. We make haste to leave Larry stewing in his defeat.

We've almost made it to the door when he shouts, "Ms. Beckett!"

Jaclyn and I turn in tandem toward him.

"Ask your boyfriend what happens if I don't get the Elm Street property," he says.

"What does he mean by that?" Jaclyn frowns.

"It's nothing."

"Rhys, that didn't sound like nothing. It sounded like a threat." There's an edge to her voice, like she's ready to fight me. But her fight isn't with me. It's with the man holding my livelihood in his hand and getting in the way of her dreams.

"He threatened to withhold my final paperwork for my Green Card if I didn't help him convince you to give up the Elm Street house."

"What the hell?" Jaclyn takes a step toward the place where Larry has disappeared into the crowd, but I put my hand on her arm, stopping her from whatever it was she was about to do. Punch him in the face, would be my guess, based on the way she's clenching her fists.

"You don't need to worry about it," I say. "I'll take care of it."

At that, she raises an eyebrow. "How, exactly, are you going to care of the fact that your boss said he'd fuck up your immigration status over a property dispute that you're not even involved in?"

"I have a plan. But I need a little more time before I tell you about it."

She looks like she wants to press for details, but instead she closes her eyes and lets out a breath. When she opens them, she looks tired, and I'm sure the stress of preparing for tonight and not winning the money is weighing on her.

If I were to guess, I'd say she wants nothing more than to get back to her place and shut out the world for the rest of the weekend. If it weren't for the fact we're still ostensibly pretending to live together, I would drop her off and let her do exactly that. I don't know where we stand after I told her I love her, and I still want to give her space.

As we make our way to the car, we clasp hands, and the pain of the past few days renews in my heart.

CHAPTER 26

Jaclyn

The ride home from the Give Back event is too quiet, but I don't dare break the silence. I have the sensation that if I say anything, an avalanche of emotions will tumble out of me. Not only did I not win the competition, but now Rhys is keeping secrets from me. His feelings for me, yes, but also whatever this mess is with Larry and whatever plan he's come up with to get out of it.

I don't know what to make of this latest revelation, but it seems the night isn't finished dropping little surprises. A few minutes into our drive, a text notification pops up on the screen in the center console of Rhys's car.

"Why is my mom texting you?"

"No idea," he says.

"Want me to play it?" I reach toward the screen to tap

the message icon.

"No!"

"Rhys, what the hell is going on? First the thing with Larry, and now my mom is involved?"

We come to a stop at a red light, and Rhys turns to look at me. He seems to debate with himself before letting out a long breath.

"I was going to wait to tell you until things were finalized, but I'm tired of keeping things from you."

"Until what's finalized?" I ask when he's quiet for too long.

"I put in an offer on the Elm Street house. Larry's offer is still in negotiations, and it seemed like the right thing to do."

I gasp, and the light changes. He turns to pay attention to the road, but he keeps talking.

"If the sellers accept the offer, it's yours. For whatever you want to do with it." He rubs a hand on the back of his neck, as though he's suddenly embarrassed by his over-the-top gift. "I didn't want Larry to ruin a place you love so much."

"Thank you," I manage, but I don't know what else to say.

I spend the rest of the time in the car processing what Rhys said. Because he bought me *an entire fucking house.*

Who does that?

Annoyingly, I know the answer. A man in love, that's who.

I can't hold back that emotional avalanche any longer. I have to sit with the warmth and a side of ache and that damn pricking feeling behind my eyes that keeps popping up at inconvenient times. If this is what being loved feels like, I don't want it.

But the reverse? I don't want that, either.

No, the thought of losing whatever this is with Rhys puts my stomach in knots.

It's not only that he's buying me the house I've dreamed of owning since I was a kid. It's all the little things, too, that threaten to crack my heart open and let him settle there. The encouragement to stand up for myself with my boss. The way he notices things about me and anticipates my needs.

The fact that he came to the event tonight even though I told him I didn't want forever with him.

He shows up for me when I don't deserve it, and I don't know what to do with that.

When we arrive at my house, I don't have any more clarity about the feelings that have crept into my heart. What's worse is that I want to talk to Rhys about it, but I can't because these feelings are about him.

I have the sense he doesn't want to come in when we get to my place, but of course Landon is sitting on his front porch when we pull into my driveway. I look at Rhys but don't have to ask the question that I'm sure is evident on my face.

"Right. I'll come in," he says.

As soon as we are inside, I make my way up the stairs. I want nothing more than to get out of this absurd dress and into something more comfortable. I know that sounds like an innuendo, but I mean it literally. A pair of formless sweatpants and a t-shirt are exactly what I need right now. Except for some reason I don't want to acknowledge, I linger in the hallway until he follows me up.

"You looked lovely this evening," he says in a rush. He's clearly surprised to see me still out here.

I cannot help the tinge of pink that blooms on my face.

"You, too," I say. There's a beat of awkwardness, and then I add, "Well, goodnight."

He looks like he's about to say something more, but I panic and quickly step into my room, clicking the door closed behind me. I turn on the bedside lamp instead of the overhead light. It's irrational, but I can't deal with the emotional fallout of tonight's revelations in the full light of my bedroom.

I take a few deep breaths to calm my nerves, then start on the work of changing clothes. I reach for the zipper on the side of the dress, but in my haste, I tug too hard. There's a snap, and the zipper pull flies from my fingers and bounces on the floor.

"Shit."

I try to wrench the zipper down with my fingernails, but I can't get traction on the tiny piece of metal that's keeping me trapped in this constricting garment.

"Fuck. Dammit. Shit. Farts." I stomp my foot in frustration each time I attempt to pinch the slider and it slips out of my grip.

A knock at my bedroom door makes me still.

"Are you alright in there?" Rhys's voice carries through

the closed door.

"I'm fine," I lie. I'm anything but fine, but he doesn't need to know that. "My zipper is stuck."

"Do you want help?"

I know it's a bad idea, because being in the same space as Rhys increases the risk that I'll say something I'm likely to regret. Something like, "I changed my mind, and I do want forever."

But I want to get out of this damn dress.

"Yes," I call. My voice even sounds mostly normal.

The door opens slowly, and I turn to see Rhys standing in the frame with his hand over his eyes. He's discarded his suit jacket and removed his tie. The top few buttons of his deep black button-up shirt are undone. In this lighting he looks like one of those cologne models, shades of black and gray highlighting the angles of his face.

"You can look."

He lowers his hand, then steps toward me slowly, cautiously. I know the action is meant to be respectful, but all it does is make a flash of heat and desire slide through me. I take a fortifying breath and gesture to the gap in my dress where the zipper is halfway down. It's caught on the place it snagged when I was getting dressed.

"The pull broke," I explain.

He grunts an acknowledgment then leaves the room momentarily. When he returns, he's carrying his suit jacket and fumbling for something inside it. He tosses the jacket on the bed and holds up a tiny safety pin.

"This should work," he says, half to himself. "May I?"

I nod, then try not to let my skin break out in goosebumps as he reaches for the offending rift in the fabric. He threads the safety pin through the tiny hole in the zipper slider and gently pulls on it. It's still stuck, so he zips it back up slightly, then drags it down again. As he does, his fingers graze my skin, and I fight to suppress the shiver that threatens to expose my invasive thoughts. The thoughts that are telling me that the next thing he should do is push the fabric aside and run his hand along my side, skin against skin.

The air goes still because I've either spoken my thought out loud, or he's had the same one. His fingers are splayed on my side, lightly gripping my skin. Too late, I realize I've involuntarily stepped backward into his touch, my ass pressed against him.

"Jaclyn." His voice is rough, like sand tumbling through an hourglass.

"We shouldn't..." I trail off as Rhys nips a little bite on my collarbone then soothes it with his tongue.

He presses closer, his other hand finding my hip, our bodies touching in the most delicious ways. I gasp as I feel the effect of our contact through his dress pants.

"Oh god." I don't know if I say it because I'm aroused or because I'm flustered.

He must take my words as an invitation because he spins me around so we're facing each other. I take him in, from his perfect lips to the rise and fall of his chest to the flames of desire in his eyes, and that's when I know I have no choice but to tell him that the Jaclyn of a few nights ago was monumentally wrong.

I don't know how to go from the heat and pull of what we've been doing to having a conversation about how I made a mistake when I said I wasn't in this for real, but I don't have time to ponder it because the next thing I know, he's stepping back, shaking his head.

"I'm sorry. I shouldn't have done that." He hangs his head as if in defeat, and something in my heart finally cracks. Because it's my fault he thinks this is all one-sided.

Rhys tries to make a hasty retreat, and I know that even if I let him walk out that door right now, we'll have another chance to make things right between us. But I don't want another chance. I want to make things right this instant.

And so before he can pass over the threshold back into the hallway, I reach for him and ask him to do the one thing he's been doing since the day we met.

"Wait."

CHAPTER 27

Rhys

Jaclyn's hand rests on my arm, and the sound of her asking—no demanding—that I wait still echoes in my ears. I stand completely still, knowing that if I move toward her I won't be able to walk away from kissing her again.

In the pause between when I stopped moving and her continuing to speak, I allow myself to drink her in—every disheveled inch of her. From her hair that's lightly mussed by my hands to the way she now holds the front of her dress up to cover her breasts. It would be so easy to slide my hand back in between the gap in the fabric and let the dress tumble to the floor. To guide her to the bed and make love to her until morning. To forget that with Jaclyn the best I can hope for is a half relationship, one that's only physical.

But then she's speaking again, and I make damn sure to pay attention.

"Senior year of high school." She takes a deep breath, and I can tell that whatever it is she's about to say is hard for her. "That's when we found out about Dad's affair. It all blew up around the same time as..."

Another pause. Another breath.

I take a cautious step toward her. When she doesn't back away, I reach for her. She steps into my arms, and I can feel the tension leaving her body.

"It made me so angry. Especially because Mom just seemed to let it happen. She didn't fight with him. Just let him leave."

A tear threatens to fall down her cheek, and I wipe it away with a gentle sweep of my thumb.

"I shouldn't have been surprised when the same thing happened to me. When Landon cheated on me exactly like my dad cheated on my mom." She laughs, but there's no mirth to it. "Like mother, like daughter."

"Jaclyn—"

"Don't. I don't want pity." Her words are sharp, defensive. She wrenches herself out of my embrace and steps away from me. She turns so her back is to me, and I feel it in my gut.

"That's not..." I sigh. I'm not surprised by her confession —if one can even call it a confession when she and her mum are the ones who were wronged. "Neither your dad nor your boyfriend should have done those things. I don't pity you. I'm angry on your behalf. And your mum's behalf.

You're both amazing women."

That draws a wry smile from her.

"You've always seen the best in me," she says, dropping her eyes and looking at the floor. "Even when I'm at my worst."

Her eyes flick up to mine, and in them I see all the hurt and vulnerability she carries because of those two assholes. She inhales deeply before continuing.

"I promised myself I wouldn't let that happen to me again. That I wouldn't ever let myself fall for someone who might hurt me."

She looks away from me, as though facing this conversation head-on would be too much.

"Do you remember the day we met?" she asks.

"Do you even have to ask? You know I do."

"I've never connected with anyone so quickly before. Or since. It made me wonder if there could ever be something more than friendship between us. Not at first. Later, around that first winter we were friends. I almost said something at Aiden's New Year's Eve party."

Her words slam into me, knocking my breath away. It takes me a moment to recover my power of speech, and when I do my voice is raw, all the pain and regret of the past four years at last expressed.

"But you went home with someone else that night."

Now it's her turn to look stricken. Another two steps, and she's completely out of my reach. Only then does she slowly spin back around to face me. Her eyes glisten with unshed tears, and I barely keep myself from rushing to her side and folding her in my arms.

"I know, and I'm sorry. I was scared. I haven't been serious about anyone since Landon. Because the only close long-term relationships I had ever seen ended in pieces." She pauses long enough to take a deep breath. When she speaks again, her voice is so soft I can hardly hear it over the pounding of my heart. "I told myself I was only physically attracted to you. But I never acted on it because I valued our friendship."

Time freezes as her revelation sinks in. My mind is both somehow blank and full of so many chaotic thoughts that I don't know where the thread of one ends and another begins. But somewhere in that frozen moment, Jaclyn moves toward me again, and it's all the permission I need to close the distance between us. In half a second, she's in my arms.

She leans into me, burying her face in my chest as I run my hand up and down her back. She still won't look at me, though, so I hook a finger under her chin and tilt her face upward. There's a hint of fear in her eyes, and my heart splits in two at the thought that she could possibly still think she's about to lose me.

"I'm scared, too," I say. "Scared that this is a dream, and that I'll wake up like I've woken up so many times since I met you. Alone and frustrated."

She frames my face with her hands, holding my gaze like it's the only thing keeping her anchored to the earth.

"When I said I didn't want forever with you, I was lying. To you and to myself." She swallows hard. "I love you,

Rhys."

I stare at her, stunned and elated and feeling like my heart will burst.

"I'm sorry it took me so long to realize it."

"I don't care how long it took," I say, and I mean it. I would wait an entire lifetime for this woman.

"It shouldn't have taken me this long to see it. To see that what we had was more than friendship and more than attraction."

"I told you, it doesn't matter." Before she can protest further, I brush my lips across hers and take her mouth in a searing kiss. It catches her by surprise, and she doesn't return it at first. But then she recovers, and kisses me back with all the fervor and heat of a raging fire.

I don't know how long we stand like this—limbs tangled, lips and tongues caressing—but I know it won't be the last time or even the next to last time that I get to kiss the woman I love. Because I want forever. And so does she.

CHAPTER 28

Jaclyn

I didn't know that intimacy with someone you are actively choosing to love would be so different from the type of intimacy you get with a one night stand. Or maybe I did, but I was too afraid to let myself experience it.

In truth, what I had with Landon was only a shadow of what Rhys and I have, and I am done keeping my feelings hidden in the shadows behind lies to everyone I know.

Rhys and I while away our Sunday in bed. It is some of the best sex of my life, but that's not all we do—although there is an element of making up for lost time to the vigor and frequency. Around mid-morning, Rhys gets a message from my Mom letting him know that the owners accepted his offer on the Elm Street house, and that ignites another round of celebratory love-making.

We also spend a generous portion of the day just being ourselves. Talking, laughing, eating a meal together. But with hand holding and kisses and lazy circles drawn on each other's backs with our fingers.

When Rhys's brother calls and we tell him the news, his only response is, "About goddamn time."

I can tell Rhys is relieved once our conversation with Rupert is over, and I want that for myself when I tell Mom the truth about us. But Rupert knew the whole time what we were doing, and my mom...she has no clue that I've been lying to her.

When I tell Rhys that I'm nervous to talk to her, he says, "It will be alright. Probably not as bad as you expect."

I wish I had his confidence.

I text my mom and ask her to meet me for coffee first thing Monday morning.

When I arrive at the donut shop, Mom is already waiting at a table with two coffees and a giant donut for each of us. The thing about the donuts at Hole-in-One is that they're huge. Like as big as your face huge. Always freshly made each morning, they're like eating a cloud of sugar and yeasty dough. They're one of Rhys's favorite sweet treats, and I decide to buy one for him before I leave. They're not as good when they aren't fresh out of the fryer, but even a not as good donut from Hole-in-One is better than most donuts you can get anywhere else.

I take the seat across from my mother and picture Rhys standing beside me and squeezing my hand twice as though to say "You've got this."

Mom launches into talking about potential properties for the community center, but I interrupt her.

"I need to say something before you go any further."

She stops mid-sentence and blinks at me. "Is everything alright, honey?"

"I need to confess something. It's related to Rhys."

She leans forward, clasping her hands in front of her.

"Rhys and I haven't really been dating. Or at least, not as long as we've led you to believe."

I wait for the shocked look or a gasp or something to indicate that my mother has heard me and understands what I'm saying. That I've been lying to her for the past month and a half. But instead, she pats my hand and says, "I know, dear."

I am the one to gasp, to look at her in shock.

"What? But...you...and we...What?"

She gives me a placating smile. "Jackie, did you really think that kiss at Andy's wedding was convincing? Poor Rhys looked so stunned when you finally laid one on him that I'm amazed he didn't spontaneously combust."

"I thought it was pretty convincing," I mutter under my breath. Not quietly enough, though, because my mother laughs at me. Actually laughs.

"Oh, sweetheart. I'm sure it convinced *you* of something. That Rhys was worth pursuing romantically."

I sputter. "That's not...I mean...Mom. What is going on?"

"I knew you needed a little nudge, so I gave you one." She shrugs like she doesn't see the big deal.

My eyes narrow to slits as I stare at her. "What exactly

does that mean?"

"It means that I was tired of watching poor Rhys moon over you while you continued to live your life oblivious to him."

"Oblivious?"

"Yes, dear. Oblivious. Ask your friends. They noticed it, too."

I want to ask if Evie and Kylie had anything to do with whatever machinations Mom cooked up, but their retribution can wait. "I don't understand. You kept setting me up with weirdos who were clearly not right for me. But you wanted me to date...Rhys?"

"Exactly. But you're so stubborn sometimes. So I manufactured a little...push."

I stare at her dumbfounded, the words "conniving" and "deceitful" and "cunning" all pinging around in my head. I knew my mother was a force to be reckoned with in the realty game, but I had no idea she was actually a criminal mastermind.

"But what about Landon? You kept going on about how sweet he was and wouldn't it be great if we could get the spark back?"

"Give me more credit than that, please." Her look is incredulous, and it makes me want to scream. If anyone has a right to be incredulous right now, it's me.

"What's that supposed to mean?"

"It means I knew the day you came home from school and told me you were dating Landon Cunningham that it wouldn't last. You're smarter than him, and he's the kind of man who hates that in a woman.”

My mouth drops open as I rearrange everything I ever thought about how my mom saw my dating life. Because I could have sworn Landon was her favorite of my boyfriends.

“Landon aside, did you ever think about what would have happened if I’d actually hit it off with one of those blind dates? Or about the fallout of Rhys and me not working out?”

There’s a twinge of guilt in Mom’s eyes, and I’m glad to see she has at least some scruples.

“I’m sorry. But it sounds like you worked it out, so no harm done!”

“No harm done? Mom, I nearly broke his heart!”

She dismisses that with a wave of her hand. “The important thing is that you didn’t.”

I’m getting nowhere trying to convince my mother that she shouldn’t have meddled, so I give a defeated huff and take a gigantic bite of my donut. I wash it down with a swig of coffee—thankfully it’s cooled to the perfect temperature so I don’t burn my mouth on the hot liquid. My mother sips at her coffee, her expression nonchalant as she waits for me to finish aggressively chewing my donut.

“Rhys told me about the Elm Street house. He said the sellers accepted his offer this morning,” I say after another swallow of coffee. All my frustration and bluster from before melts away as I think about the fact that my boyfriend—my actual, not pretend boyfriend—is buying me an entire house because he knew it would make me sad if it was destroyed. I can't even stay mad at Mom knowing that he couldn't have done it without her.

"Thank you for helping him with that," I add.

She takes my hand and gives it a loving squeeze. "Of course, honey. I knew how much it meant to you."

"I'm just glad it means we don't have to keep looking for a place for the community center."

Mom's brow furrows at that. "Didn't he tell you? When Larry first made an offer on the place, and I started doing the paperwork, I realized that place is zoned as solely residential. You can't use it for the community center."

"What? But that means Larry couldn't use it for his clinic, either."

"I know, and I told Larry that. Multiple times. It's why he and the sellers hadn't finalized their negotiations. That man is more stubborn than a toddler at bedtime. He was convinced he could get the zoning commission to rezone the place. But Phoebe Brandt sits on that commission, and she would have been a pain in his ass until he gave up."

For the second time this morning, I stare at my mother in disbelief. I'm so stunned, I barely register that fact that she's just used one of the words on her list of language not fit for public use.

If Rhys knew the house wasn't zoned for commercial or public use, that means he bought it entirely for me. If I wasn't already in love with the man, this would tip me over the edge.

It doesn't solve the location issue for the community center, but there are other properties.

"More coffee?" I ask, noticing that both Mom's cup and mine are empty.

"None for me, but you should get more if you want it."

I grab my coffee cup and weave through the tables to the bar. While I wait for the server to refill my cup, the bell over the door chimes as someone comes in. I turn to see none other than Barbara Kensington, one of the judges from the Give Back competition, standing in line behind me.

"Ms. Beckett, it's nice to see you," she says, giving me a warm smile.

"You, as well." The server hands me my refilled coffee cup, and I start toward the table where Mom is waiting for me.

"Actually, it's fortuitous I ran into you," she says, stopping me in my tracks. When I spin to face her again, she continues, "I've been thinking about your proposal all weekend. I'm sorry you didn't win the prize money."

Her tone is sincere without being pitying, and I appreciate it.

"I might have a solution for you, if you're still looking for investors."

At that my eyebrows shoot up. "Yes, of course! I'd love to talk with you about it."

Her face lights up with a wide grin, and I match her expression.

"Wonderful. What are you doing this evening at six?"

"Whatever you need me to do," I say.

She laughs. "Meet me at the public library."

"I'll be there," I say. "Oh, and it's Dr. Beckett, actually."

"Noted," she says with a dip of her chin.

As I make my way back to our table, my gaze catches on something through the window. Across the street is one of those empty storefronts that looks so forlorn on the main road through downtown. There's another one a few doors down from this very coffee shop. The Elm Street house may not be zoned for hosting a community center, but these places certainly are.

With my refilled coffee cup in hand, I join my mother again, this time grinning at her in a way that probably looks a little unhinged.

"I have an idea for where we can put the community center."

The sharp thwack of a gavel against a block reverberates around the wood paneled walls of the public library meeting room. At the front of the room, Barbara and another woman sit at a table facing the audience. I arrived as everyone was settling into their seats and slid into a folding chair in the back row.

"The June meeting of the Sapling Grove Women's League is now in session," Barbara says. "Madam Secretary, what is our first order of business?"

"A vote on the proposed budget for the upcoming fiscal year," the woman next to her says.

"Ah yes, and we have some changes to make before we vote," Barbara says. Her eyes scan the crowd, and when her gaze locks on mine, she smiles. "Dr. Beckett, would you care to address the assembly and tell us about your community center project?"

I wasn't expecting to present to the Women's League tonight, but the presentation from the Give Back event is still fresh on my mind.

"Certainly," I say. I make my way to the front of the room and take my place behind the podium that faces Barbara and the secretary.

Although I can't see most of the people in the room, I can hear the murmurs of approval as I describe the way the community center will offer classes and after school programming. I talk about my own experience at the old community center and how it was a place that felt like a home away from home for Heather and me when we were kids.

I lay out the financial plan for sustaining the center—a combination of individual donations, corporate sponsorships, and, eventually, support from the City Council.

A hush falls over the room as I finish speaking, and I hold my breath as Barbara scribbles on her notepad. When she finally looks up, I exhale slowly. Her expression is pensive but open.

"Have you found a location for the center yet?"

I smile broadly before I answer. "Yes. In fact, just this afternoon, I secured a rental agreement with the owner of the building on the four hundred block on East Main Street. The community center will officially have its home at four-twenty-three East Main Street."

It made so much sense to rent one of the empty store fronts downtown that I don't know why I didn't think of it before. But when I saw the "For Rent" sign in the building across the street from the coffee shop this morning, it hit me. Putting the community center in the heart of downtown, instead of on the outskirts, would be better not only for the center but also for the town itself. It would mean there was a hub of activity in the middle of downtown. A place for people to gather.

When I told Mom my idea, her eyes lit up, and she tracked down the owner in record time. It turns out, the owner used to go to a quilting class at the old community center, and she missed having that. She cut us a deal as long as we promised to bring back her quilting class.

At the front of the room, Barbara sets her pen down, straightens her papers, and lifts her eyes to gaze across the crowd.

"I would like us to add a line to the budget to provide funding to the new Sapling Grove Community Center. As president, I cannot make a formal motion. However, I invite any of our members who wishes to make a motion to do so."

For a moment, everything is quiet, and I'm worried that no one else feels as strongly about this project as Barbara and I do. But my worry is short-lived, because behind me, someone says, "I'll make a motion."

I turn to see where the voice has come from, and it's a woman who looks like she hasn't updated her style since the

Reagan administration. But she beams at me when we make eye contact.

The Women's League members debate for a few minutes over the exact amount they'll add to their budget, but it's clear from the discussion that the consensus is favorable toward the community center.

When they finally take a vote, it's unanimous.

After the meeting ends, I linger in the back of the room. The woman who made the initial motion finds me and introduces herself.

"This community center is exactly the kind of thing our sad little downtown needs," she says. "I remember when you could hardly find a place to park down there on a Saturday. It's better than it was, but I think this community center will be just the thing."

While we're chatting, Barbara makes her way across the room to us.

"Thank you," I tell her, with all the sincerity I can muster. "This means so much to me."

"I know a good idea when I see one. I tried to talk the other judges into voting for your proposal on Saturday, but Larry had some bee up his bonnet and wouldn't budge."

I knew as much, based on the conversation with Larry as we were leaving the event. As far as I know, he hasn't figured out that Rhys is the one who made a successful offer on the Elm Street house. Rhys called Aiden yesterday to ask what to do if Larry makes good on his threat to withhold Rhys's paperwork. The final documents have to be submitted this week, but the selling agreement won't be public until after the closing next month. Aiden said to let him know if there's any funny business from Larry.

Before I leave, Barbara promises a hefty personal investment, but even better is that she agrees to add continuous funding for the center into the next city budget proposal. Knowing her influence on the City Council, I have every confidence that she'll make sure the budget proposal passes the vote.

When I get home, Rhys is in the kitchen making dinner. I smile to myself, remembering a time when he would have waited in the car until I came home before letting himself in the front door. I guess it just took pretending to date him to make him feel more at home here.

"How was your day?" he asks as I set my work bag down on the dining table. He moves toward me and slides his hands around my waist. I don't have a chance to answer his question, because he kisses me like it's been ages since we've seen each other, even though we saw each other this morning.

When we finally break apart, I've almost forgotten what he asked. But a few moments without Rhys's lips on mine are enough to reorient myself to things outside our embrace.

"You didn't tell me the Elm Street house couldn't be used for commercial purposes," I say with a lift of my eyebrow.

He shrugs. "I didn't want Larry getting it either way."

"I know I've told you already, but thank you."

He moves to kiss me again, but I pull back. At his concerned expression, I hold up a hand.

"Everything's fine. I just have more to tell you."

I fill him in on the details of the meeting this evening, saving the play by play of my conversation with my meddling mother for last. It's the kind of thing I know we'll talk about for hours. He listens intently, but when I tell him about Mom knowing we were faking it, he doesn't seem surprised.

"I thought you'd have more incredulity over this," I say.

"She told me she knew when I talked to her about the house."

"And you didn't tell me?"

"I was still waiting for you to figure out if you wanted anything more than friends with benefits."

His words are a reminder of how shitty I've been to him this past month, and I frown in disappointment at myself.

"I'm sorry it took me so long to realize you wanted more than that."

"It's not your fault. I was too afraid to lose our friendship to take the chance of telling you how I felt." He tugs me against his chest, and I relish the warmth of his arms and the thumping of his heart against my ear.

"I hate that we could have been together for years instead of only getting started," I say, looking up at him.

"I don't."

At my confusion, he smiles and kisses me softly.

"I don't hate any of the time we've had together, whether as friends or what we are to each other now. I've always wanted to be in your life, Jaclyn, and I'm glad we've found our way to this moment."

A knot of emotion obstructs any more words from me, but it doesn't matter because we don't need words right now. I reach up to kiss the man I love, and it is good and perfect and everything a kiss should be.

EPILOGUE

Jaclyn: Three Months Later

I almost miss the sticky note on my office door. It flutters to the ground as the motion of the door swinging open causes the sticky to unstick. When I bend to pick it up, I notice it's in Ron's handwriting.

"Come see me when you get in. -R"

Ominous, except this is Ron, and his notes are always short and to the point.

I set my things in my office and make my way down the hall. Ron sits at his desk, glasses resting on the end of his nose while he peers over them at something on his computer screen.

I tap lightly on the door frame, and he looks up at me.

"You wanted to see me?"

"My favorite sociology professor! Have a seat."

Ron always calls me his favorite, but it's sort of a joke

because Cooke University is so small that I'm the only full time sociology faculty member. I can't teach all the classes, so we use a lot of adjuncts.

"What's up?" I ask as I sink into one of the plush wingback chairs across from his desk. If I'm going to be stuck here for one of Ron's long rants, at least I'll be comfortable.

"We've talked over the years about what your future might look like here at Cooke."

I keep my face neutral. He's started conversations this way before, and they all turn out to be devised to get me to do pieces of his job.

"I wanted you to be the first to know that I'm planning to retire at the end of the academic year. I spoke to Dr. Dobson on Friday."

I suck in a shocked breath. I never expected this day would actually come.

"I'm sorry, could you repeat that?" I ask once I've regained my voice.

"I'm retiring in May. I wanted you to know, because I know you'll do a great job stepping into the role."

"Surely they'll do a search," I say. I'm still not sure I believe this is real.

"They will, but Dr. Dobson asked me to ask you to apply."

"Thank you," I say, and I mean it wholeheartedly. As much as Ron has irritated me over the years, he's given me good guidance from time to time, and without his influence, I doubt I would be as ready to take on the level of responsibility required to be a dean.

We chat for a while longer, although I'm desperate to leave his office. Not because the conversation is boring or because I want to get started on my regular work. But because I can't wait to call Rhys and tell him the good news.

Not that he'll be able to answer, most likely. The past three months have been hectic for him, what with leaving his job at Montgomery Therapy to start a new practice in the space next to the community center. Larry wasn't too happy when he found out that Rhys bought the Elm Street house out from under him, but we were successful in keeping it secret until after Rhys's Green Card came through. Once he knew everything was safe on that front, Rhys put things in motion for his departure before Larry could fire him.

Tabitha Brandt and a couple other therapists left with him. That pissed Larry off even more, but Rhys reminded him that threatening an employee over a personal matter was something the state physical therapy board might like to hear about.

Blackwell-Brandt Therapy Services has found a niche working with older patients in the area. Since most of Montgomery Therapy's clientèle come in with high school sports injuries, there's not a lot of overlap for the two clinics.

Larry and Joan finally made up, so he didn't have to move the Montgomery clinic after all. They're back to their on-again-off-again divorce rumors. Whatever works for them, I suppose.

Amazingly, Rhys answers on the second ring when I call him after I finally escape Ron's office.

"I have something exciting to tell you," I say without preamble. "Ron's finally retiring!"

"About damn time," he mutters. "What does this mean for you?"

I fill him in on what Ron told me, taking care to be clear the deanship isn't a guarantee for me.

"I'm not worried," he says. "You'll do what you need to to prepare for the interview, and I'm sure Dobson will see that you're the right person for the job."

"I hope so," I say. But I know he's right, at least about the things I can control in this process. Plus I know I have good support from the people in my life. Not only Rhys, but Evie, Kylie, and my mom, too.

"Don't forget I'm picking up boxes from Evie and Kylie before I come home tonight, so I'll be a little late," I say before he hangs up.

"Of course. Thanks for the reminder."

As if Rhys changing jobs wasn't enough, we decided a few weeks ago to move into the Elm Street house. Moving at the beginning of the fall semester isn't the best decision I've ever made, but we didn't want to wait. The lease on Rhys's apartment ends soon, and I'm looking forward to living in a place that has such beautiful architectural features. Original hardwood floors, dark cherry trim throughout the house, built-in bookshelves in the living room.

But more than that, I'm excited about this next chapter for Rhys and me. The house is huge, and I'm excited about the possibility of hosting friends for game nights and dinners. Plus, when Rupert and Colin come for an extended visit, we won't all be crammed into a tiny space.

At the end of the work day, I make my way over to the library to pick up boxes from Evie and Kylie. The library does most of their book ordering this time of year, and they've been saving all those sturdy book boxes for me.

As I walk into the library, a text notification buzzes on my phone. It's a message from my sister. I haven't heard from her in a while, but that's not surprising with the way she's in and out of our lives these days.

HEATHER: Mom told me you're moving. Are you selling the condo?

ME: I haven't put it on the market yet, but yeah, probably. Why?

HEATHER: I'm coming to town. Wondered if I could stay at your place instead of Mom's?

A moment later, another text comes through.

HEATHER: I'll pay rent so that you don't have to worry about keeping up with your house payments.

My brow furrows at that. How long is she planning on staying if she's offering to pay rent?

ME: Ok. I'll call you later and work out the details.

HEATHER: Thanks, sis!

She sends me a series of heart emojis, and I smile at the message.

Evie and Kylie help me load boxes into my car and promise to meet me later to help pack.

When I pull up to the condo a little while later, I'm

dismayed to see Landon lingering near our mailbox area.

"Need some help?" he asks, gesturing toward the boxes. There's none of his usual smarmy skepticism in his tone, and there are a lot of boxes shoved into my car. Reluctantly, I accept his offer to help me carry things inside.

It only takes us a few minutes to stash the boxes in the living room, and then I'm walking him out of my house. He pauses on the front step.

"Can I say something?"

My mind flashes back to the day he tried to corner me before. The day I lied and said Rhys was moving in here. Today there's no flash of anger or anxiety over whatever he's about to say.

"I'm sorry. For the way things ended between us."

I suck in a surprised breath. His apology sounds sincere.

"I shouldn't have cheated on you, and I've regretted my actions ever since. I'm not asking you to forgive me. But I wanted to apologize anyway."

I've imagined Landon apologizing over the years, and every time I've thought I'd rage and yell at him and tell him to go to hell. But instead, all I feel is indifference. Maybe it's because it's been fifteen years, or maybe it's because I found real love with Rhys. But whatever the reason, I accept Landon's apology and wish him a good evening, and then I don't think about him again.

Rhys arrives a few minutes later, and when he rounds the corner from the hall into the living room, I wrap him into a tight hug.

"A hug from Jaclyn Beckett? How did I get so lucky?" he

asks teasingly.

Turns out I don't mind getting hugs from Rhys, even if I hate them from other people.

"I just wanted to show you that I love you," I say.

"I love you, too."

Saying it so frequently still feels a little strange, but every time we tell each other, I know it's the truth.

Acknowledgments

Writing can be a very solitary experience, but revision should not be. *The Boyfriend Setup* would not exist without all the friends, family, and readers who made their mark on this book.

First and foremost, thank you to BJ. For getting the kids out of the house on the weekends. For reading and re-reading drafts of this book. For letting me cover the walls in our room with sticky notes so I could figure out the plot. I couldn't do any of this without you.

Thank you to S. and A. for being patient while your mom was writing. You are not allowed to read this book either.

Thank you to Sarah, Alex, Ben, Trey, Adam, Jacob, and Eleanor for playing Dungeons and Dragons with my family. I write so much while you all are defeating goblins and orcs or whatever it is you do at D&D.

Thank you to Hilary, Marisa, Amora, Jenny, and Flick for beta reading! Your input and suggestions made this story better.

Thank you to Amora, Jenny, and Anneliese for the coffee meet-ups to talk about writing.

Thank you to Tisa for the feedback on the story description.

Thank you to Benny for solving the zipper problem, and for the encouragement when you found out I was secretly writing a romance novel.

Thank you to Sierra for the feedback on that one really specific physical therapy exercise.

Thank you to all the independent bookstores and libraries who bought *The Spreadsheet Situation*! Your support has made preparing to release another book less stressful. I love working with you and being part of your community.

Thank you, as always, to Keri-Lynn, Alex, and Jennifer. And to Anna, Ashley, and Shelley. Your friendship means the world to me!

And last, but certainly not least, thank you to my readers! You are amazing, and I'm so glad I can share these stories with you.

About the Author

Dawn Banks is an academic librarian and romance author. When she is not writing, she is reading, although she still hasn't found the pirate romance of her dreams. She believes cats should be named after classic literary characters. Dawn lives in Tennessee with her husband, kids, and two cats (Eowyn and Peaseblossom).

Find out about upcoming books:

Website: www.dawnbankswriter.com
Instagram & Threads: @dawnbankswriter